MW01659623

Dedication

For my family.

Acknowledgement

All my gratitude to my Artistic License sisters: Connie Barrett, June Diehl, Marilyn Heffernan, Julie Jennings, Faye Whyte, and Sharon Moles. You've made me the author I am today.

With special thanks to Milli Thornton, who believed in me before I did.

CHAPTER ONE

Don't kick. Don't move.

Sara Stark dug her fingers into the dirt edge of the chasm. Her flashlight lay shattered somewhere far below her dangling legs. Utter blackness amplified each rasp of breath. Drake should be here, not back in Houston sitting behind a desk. No way would he sweet-talk himself out of this one.

The packet had been waiting for her at the airport. A simple mission: penetrate an abandoned mine and find a stolen medallion. Drake said no guards, said it was an in-and-out operation, an easy job.

Easy my ass.

With a grunt, she pressed one heel against the side of the opposite boot. A blade clicked open from the boot's toe and she buried it in the dirt wall, giving her the leverage needed to boost herself onto solid ground. Grey light filtered forward from the depths of the catacomb passages, carrying with it the echoing shouts of Mexican guards. They shouldn't have had any interest in stopping her, yet they'd almost killed her.

Resting against the wall, her breath still harsh, she evaluated her options. She was too tired to outrun them and without a flashlight, they'd catch her before she fumbled her way to the exit. The Tazer on her belt might help, if they didn't take her down before she could zap them all. She needed an edge, an element of surprise.

Bare earthen walls emerged from the ink around her as the guards closed in. Support beams rose up each side of the passage and abutted a thicker one above. The big beam offered some hope. The shaft was narrow enough, if she worked fast and ignored her weariness, she'd have the edge she needed.

Sara sucked in the dank odor of moldering lumber and leaned forward. Palms pressed against the wall in front of her, legs braced on the wall behind her, she worked her way up spider-style until her back brushed the ceiling. Hidden behind the beam, knees locked, arms burning from the pressure, she waited and tried not to sweat.

They called her awful names in Spanish. With luck, they'd fall into the hole for that alone. But flashlights, jostling in the hands of running men, lit every surface, including the grubby edges of the hole.

Great, if they see me, I'll be nothing but a glorified piñata.

Luck was not on her side. They slowed, their lights illuminating the broken blackness in the floor. Five to one, each armed with made-in-America M2 Brownings.

Just perfect.

Not terrible odds, but it could have been better. A tremor ran through her arms and she silently cursed Drake again. Where the hell was the Intel on this job? Someone better have some damn good answers. This wasn't in her job description.

The guards leaned over the chasm, searching for her. From her vantage point, the pieces of her flashlight were small on the bottom of the wide cavern beneath. Better the light than her, she supposed, and better to act now before her limbs gave out. She released herself.

The rush of air from her descent was their only warning. Twisting in midair, she planted the sole of each boot into the backs of two guards. The pair plunged headfirst into the crater with matching cries of surprised fear. She landed, rolled, and flipped to her feet.

The remaining three whirled on her and Sara drove her fist into the center guard's nose. He windmilled on the precipice for a scant second, then dropped in to join his pals. The shorter, stocky *hombre* on her left reacted faster than the stringbean on her right.

A roundhouse kick to the side of Stocky's head kept him from raising the muzzle of his weapon. Stringbean didn't lift his M2. His thin, incredibly strong arms grabbed her in a bear hug. They plunged against the wall in a cloud of hair oil, gun oil, and rank cologne.

Air exploded from her lungs with a woof. Dirt sifted over them. She went limp, pretending more than her sense of smell had been injured. He grinned, proving the ploy worked.

Just give me an opening.

Playing the frightened female, she slumped further down the wall. He taunted her with a lurid comment and a slimy smile.

Thank you.

She brought her knee up in a hard, quick thrust. His mouth curled into a small 'o' of surprised pain. A gurgling, high-pitched whine whistled from his throat. He fell to his knees, clutching the crotch of his khaki pants.

Satisfied, she yanked the Tazer from the back of her belt and delivered a jolt that would keep him immobile for fifteen minutes. He collapsed, face down.

Stocky howled with blind rage behind her. She turned, sidestepped him easily, and touched the Tazer to his back. His momentum propelled him headfirst into the wall. He landed on the outstretched arm of his partner.

She exhaled a relieved breath. Smiling, she said, "You two make such a cute couple."

Unable to move, they only stared at her with anguished eyes. The Tazer nestled back in her belt, she patted the drawstring bag tied over one hip. The medallion hadn't appeared to be worth much–neither for the effort it had taken to steal and hide it here, nor the expense of hiring her to find it.

Despite the perplexing interference of the guards, she'd succeeded and the client would be pleased. On the other hand,

Drake would not be happy to see her. Boss's son or not, he had a lot to answer for.

From the bottom of the cavern, the three guards yelled for help. She plucked a flashlight from the floor and shined the beam into the hole. In Spanish she explained their *compadres* would recover soon and rescue them. She wriggled her fingers in a cheerful wave. They raised their M2's and uselessly fired as she moved out of range.

In the following quiet, she chuckled and called, "It's been a slice, gentlemen."

Sara left the mine with the treasure and a grin.

Drake flipped through the long list of repairs. The east wing needed new paint, patching, and a thorough refurnishing after their live-round exercise last week. The upper floors of the sprawling estate were in dire need of rewiring and two guest cottages had suffered flooding during the late summer rains. None of which was of great concern, he just hated the boring duty of hiring men and signing checks.

Starlight Estate, as his mother had named the old family home, had expanded like an elephant off the diet-wagon. In the last decade an indoor pool, the dojo, the gymnasium, and the armory, not to mention scads of smaller structures for security and training, had increased the sixteen rooms to nearly thirty.

Knight, Inc., the family acquisitions and recovery company, generated ample funds for the upkeep. He'd soon take over the enterprise after his father, Colonel Bruce Knight, retired for the second time. The ex-military man's focus lay more in Washington these days than it did back home.

The television glowed mutely from a walnut cabinet. Tuned to CNBC, Senator Halley commanded the media's attention with a finger-pointing declaration of some sort. Drake didn't care for the man, an opinion based on the current feud between his father and the senator.

The outer door slammed, followed by echoing shouts in the large foyer. Drake clicked the television off, eager for the interruption. Only one person in the world entered his home like that. Stark.

From the thudding footfalls bearing down on him, he guessed she wasn't happy about Mexico. He adjusted his cuffs and unsuccessfully tried to control his smile. If there was anything more interesting than a pissed off woman, it was a pissed off Stark.

Fritz appeared, more friend than butler, his wizened face puckered with concern. Drake waved him back through the red oak doors. No one could stop a freight train with polite cajoling.

"Drake!" She shouted as she banged into the room. "Easy job? Why the hell didn't I know the mine was guarded?"

"Hello, Stark. It's good to see you," he said mildly. She hadn't stopped to shower or change after their pilot had returned her to Houston. Mine dirt clung to her clothes and the thick, golden braid down her back was dulled to an amber hue. But there was nothing dull about the snapping green eyes peering between the ragged locks of her bangs. "I take it Mexico was more difficult than you were prepared for?"

She flushed with pure ire. "Don't even go there, I did the job. Bruce trained me to handle myself. He also taught me never to let someone off the hook for a sloppy job. Where the hell was your Intel on this?"

For a moment, Drake saw the obstinate twelve-year-old who'd hit their home like a hurricane. At seventeen, he hadn't been prepared for an adopted sister so soon after losing his mother. As now, she'd disrupted his life in not altogether unpleasant ways.

"Time was of the essence, Stark." Drake rounded his desk and perched on the edge, sitting between her and the throwable objects littering its surface. "Had I known the Mexican government was interested in the medallion, I would have put that in the packet. The mine *was* supposed to be abandoned."

She glared. "From now on, I don't want to bypass our own surveillance. That was a bad call on your part."

Drake nodded. "I'm sorry that you went in there blind. I should've come along."

"You're damned right you should've come along." Her words were harsh, but Drake sensed the storm was over. She pulled a soft leather satchel from the back of her belt and tossed it to him. "The coins from Glasgow."

They clinked inside as he tested the weight. In a deliberate show of trust, he set the bag on his desk without looking inside. "Good work."

She shrugged and sat in the visitors chair. "And what have you been doing while I was out knocking skulls?"

"Until my father returns from D.C., I'm stuck here." He grimaced at his defensive tone. "If you didn't murder every computer you touched, you could stay here and lend a hand while I went on assignment."

Her expression softened with something close to amusement. Gaze locked on his, she lifted her legs and rested her crossed ankles on the teak surface of his desk. "Will you tell me who the client is? Or are you gonna keep me in suspense?"

He scowled at the crusted dirt on the heels of her boots, but didn't ask her to remove them. Stubborn Stark. She could be charming at times, and plain frustrating at others. Instead, he focused on the length of her legs and hunted for an answer that wouldn't get him...bruised.

"Drake." She drummed the arms of her chair. "Don't leave me hanging here. Who's the client?"

Muscles in his neck tightened. *Here it comes.* "I'm sorry, that's confidential."

She froze. "Then I guess the location of the medallion is confidential."

"You wouldn't." He stood. She never backed down when

she took that tone. "Stark."

She cleaned the dirt from beneath her short nails.

Bending, he planted his hands on the armrests of her chair and loomed over her. "You have no choice. The Colonel wants this done."

Her green gaze lifted and a humorless grin curved across her full mouth. Dropping her legs, she shifted to the edge of her chair and eliminated the last cushion of space between them.

He straightened quickly. Stark was off-limits. A sister to him, though no blood relation. His father had told him to befriend her, be a brother, be her family.

That had been fine when she was twelve.

She stood. The air crackled between them. He thought he saw triumph in the back of her gaze, but Stark wasn't a woman you could rely on to feel or think the way her body language indicated.

She forced him back until he hit the desk. Toe to toe, her chin tilted up to keep his gaze, she said, "The Colonel may want this done, but you owe me."

Like silk, her voice brought more to mind than he would confess to a priest. "All right."

She considered, then released him by stepping away.

He squared his shoulders, trying to regain a semblance of control. The Colonel had, in his own way, given permission to tell Stark if she pressed the issue. If she pressed any harder, more would crumble than his ability to withhold information. "I'll tell you who the client is. But first, the medallion."

"No way. Talk."

He shrugged and offered a smile to ease the tension. "It was worth a try. Sara..." He stopped at the use of her first name. Maybe it was safer behind his desk after all. He sat and began again. "This client needs to be kept confidential."

"Like I would tell anyone, even if there was anyone to tell." Sara waved him on.

"The client asked for anonymity–and considering who we think is behind the assignment, we felt it best to honor that. We were also concerned about your reaction."

"Reaction?" Stark rested a thigh on his desk and lifted the crystal penholder. He eyed it warily. "Listen to you. Stop beating around the bush. It's not like I'm some debutante you want to dump."

Drake ignored the familiar dig and resigned himself to the inevitable. "This is different."

"Who's the damned client?"

He braced himself for her response and said, "Victor Acosta."

"What?" Sara snapped upright so fast her spine crackled. *Victor Acosta?*

They sent me on a job for the man who killed my father?

"Let me explain," Drake began, but she shook her head. Betrayal stripped the armor from her heart. Cleaved in two, she didn't know what to think, which way to turn. She definitely couldn't stomach any sad sack excuses.

"Stark," he said, concern darkening his mahogany eyes.

How dare they use me this way. Volcanic with rage, she fast-balled the crystal penholder into the fireplace with a growling shout. She spun away to hide the sudden prick of tears.

Better to be angry, to shout and curse than to let Drake see her cry. Nothing on this hellhole of a planet could have carved through her as easily as this. Victor Acosta? Confused and too mad to speak, she strode for the door.

"Sara," he pleaded. "It's not what you think."

Hand on the brass knob, she glanced black, pleased she could muster a mutinous look. "No? What would you know about what I think? You have a father."

She slammed the door, the bang echoed through the cavernous foyer and inside her aching chest. Fritz held out the bag she'd dropped on entering and opened the front door. With a distracted thanks, she left the house she'd once considered home.

Every grain of dirt on her body turned to sludge in the muggy air. A nasty, overwhelming heat molested her chilled flesh. She wanted a hot shower, a cold drink, and not necessarily in that order.

The footpath across the back of the property led to one of the many converted cottages on the estate. She passed the more elegant one reserved for Drake's aunt and continued over the stones to her own, more comfortable home.

Each step punctuated a new knot in her neck and shoulders. *Lock it away, Stark, lock it away.* It didn't serve her purposes to be so greatly affected. But this time, the lock didn't work and grief, accompanied by fatigue, followed her inside.

A lamp glowed softly beside a heavy crystal glass, a silver ice bucket, and a bottle of Chivas. Fritz must have sent one of the staff to freshen her quarters. The comforts of wealth, and the emptiness of the abandoned and betrayed.

How could they?

She tossed the bag through the door leading to the gym–a new addition to the minimal cottage. Dead on her feet, emotionally depleted, she fell into her favorite chair. Glass filled, sans ice cubes, she sipped past an irritating knot of tears in her throat.

How long had she tried to convince herself having a family didn't matter? So what if her mother had died soon after giving birth to her? Who cared if relatives hadn't taken her in after her father's funeral? How many times had she risen in the night to confront ghosts of what should have been, only to face the reality of what was? To have all those years obliterated by two words made her feel weak.

Her father smiled at her from the military photograph on the mantle above the never-used fireplace. Memories of the American flag draped over his coffin, the startling noise of the Color Guard firing their weapons, and strangers dressed in black drifted through her mind. Then came the foster homes.

When Colonel Bruce Knight, liaison to the Department of Defense, had plucked her from juvie at the age of twelve, it had been like a fairytale. Daddy Warbucks rescues Annie. She'd left poverty and fear behind for a life of privilege. He'd even arranged to change her name to prove just how far behind her that life was.

She'd chosen Stark, an acronym for star in Starlight and the K in Knight. Why had he gone through so much damned trouble to help her forget and then accept an assignment from the one man responsible for it all?

The Chivas burned through the pressure in her chest and she finished the whiskey in one long swallow. She banged it on the table. The shower could wait. Only getting down and dirty would relieve this stress.

The gym boasted a long wall of night blackened windows and when she flicked the lights on, her doubled image bounced back from a dozen reflective panes. She shed her button-down shirt and boots, ignored her dirty t-shirt, and taped her hands. Metallica suited her mood best and as the opening harsh chords blasted through the speakers, she went to town on the heavy bag chained to the ceiling.

She drove her fists into the bag, reliving the childhood terror of waking in a stranger's house, the awkwardness of new schools. She delivered a roundhouse kick for the juvie guards tackling her when she defended herself and another for a foster father who had her arrested for arson, a fire he'd started to collect insurance money. The bag swung.

Halfway through her workout, sweat dampening the t-shirt at her spine and between her breasts, the tiny hairs on her nape bristled; she wasn't alone. She threw another punch and glanced toward the door.

Drake watched her, his arms crossed casually over a burgundy silk shirt. He'd deceived her. She never would have gone on that assignment if she'd known the truth. Breathing hard, but unwilling to allow him the power of interruption, she continued her assault on the bag. "What do you want?"

He straightened to his full height of six-three and strolled to the stereo like a man without a worry. Metallica stopped mid-guitar-solo. He turned mahogany eyes on her. "The Colonel's flying in tonight and wants to talk to you at breakfast in the morning."

"Oh, he does, does he?" Hands on hips, she gulped air. "He'll have to eat alone. What you both did was... inexcusable."

She stalked to the door, unable to remain stoic, and unwilling to have him witness the fault. Drake didn't let her sail past him. He grasped her arm. The contact unleashed her fury. Reversing the hold, she gripped him and bent, flipping him over her shoulder with a grunt. He landed on his back.

Drake swept her legs, but overextended and caught the low stool beside the door. It toppled as she hit the ground. She yanked him forward by a fistful of silk, and delivered a kick to the center of his chest. A satisfying exclamation of air burst from him. "Had enough?"

"Not by a long shot." They'd played this game for nearly fifteen years, he never gave up. He rolled until she was pinned beneath him. She held her instinct to damage the family jewels in check. Attacking Drake below the belt had always been off limits.

She wished they hadn't trained her quite so well.

Astride her hips, he trapped her wrists against the mat. "I didn't come here to spar with you, Stark. He wants us both there; he's got something important to talk about. I think you should listen."

Drake didn't smile, didn't plead, didn't try any of his usual charm tactics. Sara struggled for oxygen, but his weight made it impossible. "Get off me, I can't breathe."

He shifted his weight to his knees, but kept her pinned. "Not until I get your agreement."

"Would you believe me? You don't think I'd just say what you wanted to hear so you'd leave me alone?" She stalled, trying to decide if she wanted to follow the Colonel's orders, a man who had so recently broken her trust.

"Of course. You always keep your word."

Unlike some I know.

He smiled. That damned crooked grin of his. Although she couldn't be sure if it was calculated, all her arguments evaporated. She quivered inside. The old game turned into something completely...unfamiliar.

Her breathing didn't get any easier. His gaze shifted a fraction to where her t-shirt was stretched taut. When he raised his eyes, they settled on her mouth.

Warning bells rang deep in her mind. She tried to speak, tried to agree to join the Knight men for breakfast. Anything to end the dangerous electricity surging through her, but nothing came out.

The grip on her wrists relaxed. She didn't try to pull away, she couldn't. Drake searched her as he leaned forward, the distance between them closed.

Don't let him kiss me.

She felt open, raw and blamed that on him. His eyes smoldered.

Please, kiss me.

The tension, the *temptation*, was too great and she hooked the fallen stool around one ankle. With an effort, she sent it careening into his back. He grunted, surprised, but not injured. The angle had been too awkward to do much damage.

The air returned to normal, breathable matter she could use. On her elbows, she wriggled backward and out from beneath him. He stood with her, breathing too hard for the little bit of grappling they'd done.

"Tell your father I'll be there." Sara left the room without a backward glance. She'd had a warm drink, and now she needed a cold shower–a very cold shower.

CHAPTER TWO

Drake stepped out of the shower, shivering, and remembered he'd forgotten to get the medallion. If this thing between him and Stark continued to build, he'd need a lobotomy to keep his mind clear. Either that, or send Stark off on a mission far, far away–like another galaxy.

He toweled off and wondered if anyone else might take his mind off the woman across the back lawn. Not likely. Stark was one of a kind and his virile imagination created scenarios beyond his experiences with the society women he dated.

In his best James Bond, he whispered, "The possibilities are intriguing, indeed."

He ignored the pajamas Fritz had laid out and shrugged into his robe. The balcony offered a view of Sara's cottage and he wondered if she was still awake. Hot, damp air hit him as he stepped through the French doors.

The cottage crouched blackly on the lawn. He imagined her curled in bed, long naked legs tangled in sheets, and the humidity became oppressive. Abruptly he retreated into the air-conditioned interior. The scent of earth, alive and vibrant, and reminiscent of Sara, followed him inside.

"She's gonna be the death of me," he whispered and hung his robe on one of the four posters. He slid between the sheets, clasped his hands behind his head, and stared at the Fresco ceiling. The details offered him an alternative from...other thoughts.

His father would arrive at dawn, shortly before the meeting, and although he'd love to grill the old man for whatever secret he hid from them both, it would be useless. Bruce Knight did nothing until he was ready.

What could have prompted his father to take the assignment in the first place? Drake's own fear for Stark's safety had given him reason enough to withhold Acosta's name. No telling what she'd have done let loose with that information. But now he worried she'd think him guilty of outright deception. Perhaps he was.

He frowned, uncomfortable with the idea of betraying her. The alternative would have been to disregard his father's wishes. Not a good idea. After a rebellious time at university in London, he'd learned to respect his father. He trusted him. The old man must have an excellent reason.

Maybe it had something to do with Senator Halley. The senator's ongoing attempts to ramrod his bill through congress had his father outraged. But what did that have to do with Acosta? It didn't add up and Drake tossed the idea aside.

He considered a dozen different explanations, but could find none that justified what his father had done. As always, he missed his mother's perspective. But she'd passed away when he was fifteen, a short grief-filled year before Stark arrived. His mother's battle with cancer and her death were the reasons Stark languished in the state's care for four years.

Maybe if they'd known she'd become a ward of the state earlier, or if relatives had taken her in after her father was killed, she wouldn't be so difficult, so black and white when it came to trust. Stark didn't operate in gray areas.

Despite the questions and confusion, Drake yawned. One of his better talents, he thought, was the ability to sleep at any time, anywhere. He only hoped Stark would get a good night's rest. She deserved it after the back-to-back assignments. She would need it; the worst was yet to come.

Sara shook off the nightmare with practiced ease. Sound sleep just wasn't part of her routine. She swung her legs over the edge of the bed and stood.

Sun slanted through the window and picked out the details on the heavy, carved armoire across the room. She blinked and glanced at the clock. Seven-thirty. Breakfast was at eight. She'd have to rush to get up to the house on time.

The mirror reflected little evidence of her difficult night, only the tangled mess of sheets on the bed behind her, and equally tangled mass of hair on her head. In the bathroom, she washed the last of sleep from her eyes and the residuals of emotional overload from the day before.

Although she wasn't prepared to breeze into the dining room with a song in her heart, the overwhelming fury was gone. She'd learned to live with her past, to even embrace parts of it, and there was no way she would let the mere mention of Victor Acosta undo all she'd strived for.

No way in hell.

She buckled her watch in place and mentally prepared for the meeting. No longer Sara Sanders, orphan and delinquent, she was Stark, recovery and acquisitions expert. Treasure hunter to the elite–nothing intimidated her.

She dressed in her usual, white t-shirt beneath a chambray button-up tucked into black pants. Her belt and essentials in place, she glanced once again in the mirror.

Her hair needed dire help. She dragged a brush through it, braided it deftly, and secured the end with a very abused band. A strand fell into her face and with the silver scissors that went with the brush set, she hacked it off at eyebrow level.

From the nightstand, she dug out the pouch containing the medallion. What the hell did Acosta want with it? The damn thing wasn't worth one tenth what Knight, Inc. charged for finding it.

The palm-sized swirl of metal fit coolly into her palm. It wasn't close to being the aged artifact described in the packet.

To an untrained eye it might seem eons old. Someone had gone to the trouble of antiquing the metal. She closed her fist around the medallion. If Bruce wanted it, he'd have to talk first.

Five minutes later, the medallion safely hidden inside the lining of her boot, she entered the kitchen. Sizzling bacon made her stomach growl. She tallied the hours since her last meal. Eighteen, not good. With a strip of bacon in her hand, one in her mouth, she nodded to Fritz on her way into the dining room.

"Miss Stark?" Fritz stopped her, and when she turned, his lined face softened. "Be...careful, please."

"It's not me you need to worry about Fritz." Because he liked her, despite all the grief she caused him, she patted his forearm and whispered, "It'll be all right."

Fritz didn't look as certain, but Sara didn't have time to comfort him. Control of herself, control of the situation, those were her goals now. If only she could master that as easily as kickboxing.

The dining room, decorated a la Elizabeth Knight, gleamed with gilt framed oils of the landscaped acreage surrounding the estate. Imported golden silk covering the walls added to the luster. The rug, a dense Turkish marvel in russet, mauve, and ivory warmed those who dined at the large Victorian table.

Deep in discussion with Drake, Bruce commanded the head of the table like a king over his court. Sara felt twelve again and appearing for another stern lecture about *unacceptable behavior*. Two words she'd come to despise by the end of her first year. If only Bruce had known from the start what she'd needed, he might have bought stock in Everlast boxing equipment.

Bruce glanced up and her heart thudded. The lines in his face ran deep, his silver hair, always so neatly trimmed, appeared sparser. His mouth curved slightly down, as if the muscles were too exhausted to hold it higher. Lately, the Colonel had spent less and less time heading Knight, Inc. and it was no secret Drake would soon take over completely.

"Stark," he called and waved her forward. "Come sit. We've been waiting for you."

Drake smiled in her direction and she snapped her teeth into the bacon. *Ain't gonna be that easy, pal.*

"I trust you slept well?" Bruce opened his napkin and placed it carefully in his lap.

The next few minutes were crucial if she wanted to establish control. Sympathy for Bruce's obvious exhaustion or not. "Don't toy with me, Colonel. I waited all night to hear what you have to say."

His gaze went from care-worn to hard stone in the space of a heartbeat. Here was the man who'd fought and killed for his country. "Keep a civil tongue in your head."

The whispered command went straight to the obedient daughterly girl inside her and Sara stared at the Baccarat centerpiece. *So much for cool determination.* Fine, he could have that one, but she refused to apologize. Bruce needed to understand he couldn't betray her and expect no consequences.

The kitchen doors swung open and the M&M twins, Marge and Madge–local spinsters who argued constantly–served breakfast. They layered the heavy table with trays of food, poured coffee, and retreated.

No one moved to fill their plates. Drake finally broke the uncomfortable silence. "Stark, we'll need the medallion."

Of course he would demand her only leverage. A glance at Bruce made it clear a protest would appear childish. The chair rasped against the carpet as she shoved back from the table and dropped her booted foot between the syrup and the biscuits. She unlaced it enough to pull the medallion free and tossed it at him. Drake caught it before it could land in a bowl of gravy.

"Thank you," he said dryly, mouth twitching. He gave it

to his father.

Sara retied the laces, stomped her boot back to the floor and debated which donut to throw at Drake. *The jelly-filled? Or the chocolate-covered?*

"Stark!" Bruce barked as she reached purposefully for the jelly-filled, having decided not to waste perfectly good chocolate.

She dropped the sweet back on the tray.

"Enough. We've got much to discuss."

"Yes," she agreed and glared at Drake. "It is enough."

Bruce threw his napkin on the empty plate with a sigh that slumped his shoulders. He rubbed his forehead.

I will not feel guilty, I will not give in.

Sara used coffee to rinse away the taste of defeat and bacon. Who was she kidding? As much as she wanted to scold Bruce, the act was beyond her.

Bruce breathed deep and began. "First, I need to fill in the holes your father's file didn't cover. When I gave you that file, it was to help you understand that he was a hero, he died for his country."

Sara didn't believe the simple act of dying could make anyone a hero, but she did believe that Sergeant Major Greg Sanders had been a heroic man. His dying, and thereby abandoning her, had been dealt with years ago. Now, her anger, turned to hatred after fermenting for so long, centered on the man responsible for his death. She wanted to hear about Acosta, not rehash painful history. "I know this, let's move on."

"As you wish. Sara." The use of her first name told her how deeply important his next words would be. "As I mentioned, there are holes in the file, deliberate ones."

She clasped her hands tightly in her lap and avoided Drake's uncomfortable stare. He was just waiting for her to run out of patience.

"Sanders and I knew each other." Bruce sipped from his

water glass. "We'd met four years earlier in Grenada. Your father." He paused again, as if in pain and the last of Sara's resolve disintegrated. How could she remain cold-hearted when his regret was so obvious? "He was a good man. He simply had too much pride, not enough...humbleness, to rise in rank as I did. Too gung-ho, too rash. He never disobeyed an order, but it was borderline with him. When Noriega gave us such problems in Panama, I was asked to get involved."

"Go on." Sara slid a look to Drake. He didn't seem to notice her impatient tone; his attention was on his father.

Bruce cleared his throat. "What I left out of his file, what I didn't tell you, is I assigned your father to Panama."

Grief rolled off him in waves. She reached across the table to squeeze his hand. "You couldn't know he'd be killed."

Drake nodded. "She's right. It's not your fault."

Bruce shook his head. "Every man I sent there was my responsibility." To Sara, he said, "If Elizabeth hadn't been so ill, I would have found you sooner. I assumed you were being taken care of by relatives." He patted the back of her hand. "You wouldn't have suffered for so long."

"It's all right." Sara squeezed his fingers and withdrew her hand. "I don't regret my past. It's funny, but in a way," she paused, considering how to relate the sense of acceptance she'd gained, "everything I lived through made me who I am today. I can't resent anything that made me stronger."

"And Acosta?" Drake asked, openly surprised.

She narrowed her eyes. "Coming to terms with my past is one thing, but letting that murdering bastard off the hook for what he did is completely different."

Drake nodded brusquely, as if satisfied by the answer, even hoped for it. He turned to his father. "Go on."

"During Operation Just Cause, Sanders worked covertly for me under General Kray. While the official reason for the invasion was to unseat Noriega, your father's assignment was to watch certain academics Noriega had befriended, some who were on the verge of technological breakthroughs. Sanders worked in an unofficial capacity and reported directly to me."

"I don't get it." Drake frowned. "From what I understand, Noriega wasn't the sort who put much stock in higher thought."

Bruce shook his head. "Not many would think so, but his military intelligence training was impressive. The man was a public figure, but managed to act as a double agent, that takes finesse. From there...how shall I say it? He made it very comfortable for certain loyal doctors and scientists to continue their research. Men like Acosta."

"Acosta, did he...plan my father's murder?" She'd never had the courage, or the opportunity to ask before.

"No," Bruce said softly. "Your father happened to be in the wrong place at the wrong time when Acosta acted. I did not falsify the file I gave you, I simply withheld certain information regarding myself."

Relief swept through her and she leaned back in the chair. His motivation was understandable. If the Colonel had revealed to her his involvement in her father's death when she was still young, still untrained, still so angry, she might have hated him. Her trust renewed with caution however, there was still the matter of Mexico to deal with.

"So what does Mexico have to do with Acosta?" Drake asked and she was struck by how often he echoed her own thoughts. The toe of his shoe touched hers beneath the table for a fraction of a second. Whether accident or not, the sense of connection comforted her.

"Acosta was a professor, well-liked, influential. But he despised the fact Noriega was on the CIA payroll and believed he'd betrayed his country. To complicate the matter, there was an incident with Acosta's oldest daughter and a private on base, though we were never able to find out the truth of that."

Bruce's gaze dulled as his memories took him back to a time Sara imagined had, at the very least, been frightening. "When it happened, Acosta began to hate all things American.

During the occupation, there was so much happening. Civilians died. It was a very nasty time and I'm glad it's over."

The kitchen doors opened and Madge came through with a pot of steaming coffee. Their cups were barely touched, but she added a drop to each, raised eyebrows at the empty plates and retreated to the kitchen.

Sara watched her leave and wondered if working for the Knight family was similar to life in an occupied country. Were the constant evacuation drills and other security measures Knight employees endured in small part an echo of life in Panama back then? Thoughtful, she glanced at the table and spotted the medallion. "What does this have to do with Mexico?"

"I'm getting to that." Bruce waved a hand, casting a spell for silence. "I believe Acosta turned his hatred on the soldiers stationed in Panama. His involvement with the bombing was not only blatant, but announced in a letter sent to the media. What concerns us most are the dozens of his contacts all over the world.

"A year ago those known associates began disappearing. The last one, a scientist who specializes in developing military weapons, made the Department of Defense nervous and they asked me to investigate."

"DoD brought you in?" Drake straightened. "Do you believe this has something to do with medallion? How is Acosta involved?"

"Acosta's last remaining relative, his nephew, hired us."

"What happened to the rest of his family?" Sara asked, uncertain why she wanted to know, or even if she did.

"They were slaughtered during the invasion." Bruce fingered the medallion, turning it over on the white linen tablecloth.

Silence fell between them as they all considered the implications. Although Sara felt no pity for a man who would resort to terrorism as revenge for a military action, his evolution into the criminal he'd become followed a tragic kind of logic. If violent revenge could ever be logical. The last thought hit close to home and she shook off a wave of foreboding.

"And the medallion?" Drake urged.

"We're not sure why it's important to him," Bruce stated, turning to his son, "but he wouldn't risk sending his nephew into the hands of the Mexican government. Until you called last night, and described how the mine was guarded, we weren't sure if Mexico was in Acosta's back pocket. Now we know it's not."

In the corrupt ranks of Mexican law enforcement, a fair arrest and trial were exceptions to the rule. Execution was more likely. "So he hired us to place one of our own in jeopardy."

"That." Bruce nodded, "and I personally think he used our company to get at me. Even if the odds were against the possibility I'd personally take the assignment, Acosta would have a shot at someone under my supervision...again."

He sipped water and Sara was once more struck by how weary he appeared. "Aside from that, we believe the medallion was hidden in the mine after the shipment was first intercepted on its way to Acosta himself. Our hope was you'd stumble onto his whereabouts. We couldn't risk telling you who the real client was and I asked Drake to keep it confidential unless you pressured him."

Sara nodded again. "You couldn't trust me."

"No," Drake responded quickly. "We feared for you. If you knew Acosta was the client, we couldn't be certain you wouldn't go after him alone, without the information you needed."

Bruce said, "The fact is, we aren't sure where Acosta is. He could be in Mexico, but we suspect he's still in Panama. God knows you've mastered everything we've thrown at you, but there's more at stake than just taking down Acosta.

Whatever he's planning, whatever he's *doing*, may be larger than him."

"And there wasn't time enough to brief me before I left." She exhaled. Their loyalty had never faltered. She almost felt foolish for believing it had. *Almost.* "The medallion itself is worthless. What could he possibly want with it?"

Drake lifted the swirl of brass. He turned it over in his hands and peered closer. The false age didn't fool him. "Strange. I'll have the tech team examine it at the lab."

"Tell them to hurry," Bruce added. "We'll need to get that to Acosta's nephew by noon tomorrow. I've sent a team to follow him after the meet." He deflated and rested his elbows on the table.

Alarmed by the uncharacteristic display of fatigue, she asked, "How did Washington go?"

"Is Senator Halley still giving you headaches?" Drake sipped his coffee, eyeing his father over the rim of the cup.

Bruce nodded. "Now he's pulled together an emergency meeting of the Intelligence Committee. He knows everyone's down at Stennis Space Center. The bastard's gonna railroad his bill through if no one stops him."

"What's this about?" Sara shot a look at Drake. Why hadn't he mentioned this before?

"Senator Halley," Drake answered, "owns stock in Electronic Protections and Development Technology through a blind trust. EPDT provides electronics for the military. He's hoping he'll get a federal regulation passed to upgrade all civilian infrastructures. Making sure his companies get the contracts, of course."

Bruce ran both hands through his hair and straightened. "He's got his eye on the Presidency and if he's successful, it would finance his campaign."

Sara didn't see the problem. Maybe ugly ethics, perhaps personally reprehensible, but not unusual. "So? It's not as if these practices are anything new."

Bruce and Drake looked at each other and she fought the rush of heat wanting to warm her cheeks. What *else* didn't she know?

Drake said, "You haven't had a chance to catch the news."

Bruce finished, "Senator Halley's made headlines. Some reporter hired a hacker to peek at Halley's private emails to a young intern, a very pretty intern he's having an affair with."

Sara rolled her eyes and groaned. Democrat, republican, she didn't care. She only wanted to know one thing. "Please tell me he doesn't smoke a cigar."

"Thank God, he doesn't." Bruce looked heavenward and exhaled with exaggerated relief. When their chuckles faded, he said, "I've got some calls to make but I'd like to meet again this afternoon for a briefing."

"All right." Drake pocketed the medallion and asked Sara, "Are you sure this is what you want to do?"

She transferred a chocolate donut to her plate to buy time to think. This wouldn't be her first covert mission, but it would be the first time she would be emotionally involved. She wasn't such a fool she didn't understand the danger in that.

What *did* she want to do? There was only one answer. She gave each of the Knight men her most determined stare. "I want to nail Acosta to the wall."

An hour later Drake returned from delivering the medallion to the tech lab housed in their downtown offices. Unable to sit still, he went to the window. Eaves kept the window glass clear of the fine, heavy mist beyond. He stared across the expanse of lawn, past the cottages and the stable and tried to meditate the tautness from his muscles.

Stark, on the back of Lancelot, one of their prized mustangs, rode into view. She was likely just as anxious to discover what lay in store for them.

Her steed turned toward the orchard. Hat shoved down over her forehead to keep it from blowing off, shoulders hunched as she bent low over the mustang's neck, she careened fearlessly for the back of the property. Drizzle turned the landscape gray, except for the dull blue swatch of Stark's shirt and the blonde braid flopping against her back.

That was how it had been when she'd arrived. All the gray and grief of his mother's passing had been shoved back by the hell-bent kid with a wicked sense of humor.

How she'd pranked Fritz, he thought with a grin. After the episode with the bees, Drake had been sure he'd give his notice. But Stark had a quality about her, a charm that worked magic on everyone who had called her friend.

When Fritz told her she couldn't snack on an entire jar of honey, she'd managed to hijack a frame from the bee farm on the west end of the estate and shove it up the chimney in the master den. Drake still wasn't sure how she'd managed that feat.

As Fritz started a fire that evening, they'd erupted in an angry horde. If the wood had smoked more, Fritz might not have been stung so bad. Bedridden from an allergic reaction, Fritz had enjoyed visits from Sara, bearing tea, with honey, every night that week.

Now she would face Acosta.

Drake couldn't allow her to confront the monster alone, not when she was twelve, and not when she was twenty-five. Her magic had worked on him as well.

Stark was long gone from view. He turned from the window. As restless as a virgin at an orgy, he decided she had the right idea. Physical activity would prepare his mind and body for the meeting that afternoon. He'd visit his room to change and then go on to the stables. Who knew? Perhaps he'd catch up with her.

In the back of his mind, he recognized that catching up with her was the only reason a ride appealed to him.

CHAPTER THREE

Exhilarated from the ride, Sara dismounted regretfully at the apple orchard and tethered the mustang to a tree. The branches were heavy with fruit and at the opposite end a team of gardeners and hired help stripped the trees of their bounty. Lancelot helped.

She strolled down the center of the wide path. Rain soaked her shirt, but the hat's rim kept it off her face. She didn't mind. The shower was warmer than the one she'd endured the night before. Her thoughts turned from Acosta and settled uncomfortably on Drake.

His attraction was obvious, but her own feelings were still a mystery. She'd looked at him for so long as the older brother: the guy who would defend her and protect her when the world crept too close for comfort. Until he'd returned from abroad last summer, she'd never thought of him as a *man.*

A dangerous streak of jealousy lurked inside her. On the occasions he entertained one of his polished beauties at the estate, she always found a reason to interrupt the visit. Secretly, she yearned for him to *see* her. Not as a child, but as the woman she'd become.

Now that he'd begun to look at her in that special way of his, the look that made her bra suddenly very tight, she couldn't bring herself to act. It was as if she'd finally gotten the gift she'd longed for and couldn't quite bring herself to take it out of the box. What held her back?

No stranger to men, she enjoyed dating. She'd never

initiated any of her flings, or fallen in love, not really. They'd paled in comparison to the Knight men. Bruce had said once, that a man without an arsenal at his disposal would never capture her interest for long.

Drake had an arsenal.

She kicked at a branch in the lush grass and sent it flying into the trunk of a tree, far more than she'd intended. Was that her problem then? In her effort to learn, to please the man who at first allowed her to participate in Drake's training, then proudly arranged for her own instruction, had she lost her femininity? Did she have a heart to give? Or had the walls she'd built around that vulnerable organ become too sturdy for love?

The sound of drumming hooves distracted her and she turned as Drake rode into the orchard. He grinned, almost warily, and leapt from the saddle with an agility that tripled the rhythm of her heart. He tethered his mount near hers and waved as he stalked closer.

Stalked perfectly described his natural grace. No, the Knight men had definitely ruined her for the average Joe. She swallowed hard and tried to remember why she thought acting on their mutual attraction was a bad idea, then realized she'd never truly figured it out.

"I thought I'd find you here."

Why were you looking for me? Sara said, "I'll have to remember not to be so predictable."

"I like that I can find you when I need to," he answered slowly, falling in step beside her as she continued her walk.

"What did you need, then?" She tried to sound as if she didn't care, but even more, tried not to notice how the drizzle made his navy shirt cling to his biceps.

"I wanted to see if you were all right after this morning. I know how difficult this must be for you."

His arm bumped hers and she stepped further away. "I'm fine, Drake. Really."

"Stark." He stopped her with a hand on her elbow. "You may not believe this, but I do understand. I lost my mother, I know what it's like to lose someone you love."

She studied him. His wide forehead, straight brows settled over eyes outlined by thick black lashes, the hardly-there lump on the bridge of his nose–a flaw he'd received from Master Kwan at twenty–and the molded upper lip were all softened by genuine concern. She averted her eyes and forced her mind to recall what he'd just said.

He understood her loss. "I do believe you. But you have a family that supports you, cares for you."

"Did we fail so miserably?" Drake released her and back-stepped to a tree. He leaned against the trunk. "Don't you feel a part of this family?"

"You didn't fail." She shoved her hands deep into her pockets and stared at his riding boots. They were worn, but well oiled. She did feel comfortable, accepted. Maybe too much so. "It's just not the same. I have aunts, uncles, and grandparents who couldn't be bothered with me."

Sara felt a twinge of shame. Thousands of parentless kids were worse off than she'd been.

"Don't get me wrong, Drake, I appreciate all you and your father have done for me." She nodded once to show her adamancy and dispel the mistaken air of ingratitude. "You were like a brother to me."

"Were?" He grinned.

She set off for the horses. "Yes, you were. Now you make a good co-worker. At least when you're doing your job."

The struggle to keep her own emotions hidden from Drake's incessant scrutiny was too much after the last twenty-four hours. Besides, they had larger, more important matters to contend with.

Once mounted, she called, "We should prepare to leave."

Drake took his time straightening from the tree, but she didn't wait to rush back to the stables. There was more danger in acknowledging her attraction for Drake than there was in confronting the man who'd murdered her father. At least with Acosta, she'd not be so vulnerable.

The reason for her hesitation came suddenly clear. Drake would never commit, never tie himself to a wife. Something held him back, some secret reason he'd never been serious about a woman. Oh, he liked women, lots of them, maybe too many. But she couldn't gamble on a man who might get bored with her. Being orphaned once was enough.

If her backside wasn't so appealing, Drake would grow tired of always watching her run away from him. It didn't take a rocket scientist to understand there was more than sisterly love lurking beneath those verdant eyes. But it was also clear she wasn't interested in pursuing a deeper relationship. He admired her restraint.

All in all, he didn't regret soaking himself to ride in the rain and confront her. Her slip, calling him brother in the past tense, had told him what he'd needed to know.

How did he feel? He wasn't sure. The idea of sleeping with Sara had entered his mind more than once, but beyond that? It was impossible to imagine them sharing a bed and working together, and it didn't sit right with him that they could enjoy a simple fling. What did that leave?

Emotional entanglements, that's where.

He remounted. Unlike Sara, he didn't relish galloping, but rather enjoyed a slow, steady return. The damp didn't bother him as he mulled over this new complication.

With no immediate answer available, he decided it was a moot point. Sara either didn't want, or wasn't ready for, a deeper relationship between them. Hell, for that matter, neither was he. If he could only keep her out of his thoughts.

He found her in the kitchen, cheeks full as she devoured a plate of leftover breakfast and listened to a heated debate on yams and sweet potatoes between the M&M twins. She glanced to him once, but didn't speak; couldn't because of the biscuits and gravy in her mouth. He nodded to her and continued to his room.

In dry clothes, he laid his carry-ons across the bed and began filling them with what he'd need for their trip. Not sure where they were headed, he left some decisions until later and began with items for more tropical climes. Panama or Mexico, either destination would be sultry.

"Are you planning a trip, sir?" Fritz asked from the door, a stack of towels in his hand.

"Yes, we'll leave either tonight or in the morning."

Fritz placed the towels on the dresser and opened the top drawer. "You never pack enough socks, if you don't mind me saying so, sir."

Drake smiled, he hadn't thought to pack any yet. He accepted six pair. "Thanks."

He waved off the thanks. "Will Miss Stark accompany you?"

"Yes." Drake stuffed the socks into the second, nearly empty bag. "She and I will need our usual from the armory."

"I'll see to it. Would you like the Jaguar or the Mercedes?"

"The Jaguar, I think." Drake paused, relishing the idea of the car's speed in his hands. But there wouldn't be enough time. "Make it the Mercedes. I don't think we're going far."

"Straight to the airport, then, sir?" Fritz took the towels in hand and stood in the doorway to the bathroom.

"I should know for certain this afternoon."

"Is it...dangerous?"

Drake didn't mind Fritz prying. The old man cared for both him and Sara as if they were his own grandchildren. With a nod, he confirmed the exceptional risk in the assignment.

After a silence, the older man whispered, "Take good care of her sir."

That's the man who killed my dad.

Sara stared at the enlarged image of Acosta and seethed. His photograph, a surveillance shot of him in Panama, glowed brightly from the flat screen in the dim room. Regardless of what had happened to him and his family, he had no right to kill her father, or to involve her as a mule in his plans.

"As you can see," Bruce said, standing at the head of the long conference table, "the most recent Intel we have on Acosta was in the fall of 2003. He came above ground to attend a lecture at the City of Learning. The university is housed on one of our military bases left over from the occupation. General Kray believes some who work there are loyal to Acosta."

"Loyal to what?" Sara snorted, arms crossed over her chest, "Slaughtering those he imagined wronged him?"

"At the very least," Drake mumbled. In the darkened room he sent her an approving look.

The Colonel wasn't pleased. "Stick to the assignment. We'll worry about his reasons later. I have to leave for D.C. in forty minutes. Pay attention." With a click of the remote, the image turned to a man with the dark coloring of a native born South American. "This is Dr. Juan Salva."

The single shot was replaced by one of Acosta and Salva bent in conversation. Where as Acosta was tall and almost distinguished looking, Salva was squat with long hair oiled back from his heavy features. Bruce clicked to the next frame and the angle pulled back. Rolling hills dotted the landscape behind the refurbished army base. The two men were minuscule. It was a satellite shot, Sara would bet her next commission on it.

"When you're there, you'll need to download the memory files on Salva's computer. Our hope is that it will help us locate Acosta. If we're lucky, it might reveal a bit of what he's up to." Bruce forwarded the video to show different angles of the buildings.

Sara flipped through the pages of the file he'd given her. Between the photographs and the copied blueprints, she memorized the pertinent passageways, exits, and other areas that would help her navigate the grounds.

Most government buildings relied heavily on the same infrastructures–once familiar with those, it didn't take long to spot anything unique, such as the section that housed Salva's offices and those of his peers. Additions added early that year, they were little more than connected boxes.

"This is Salva's office," Bruce stopped and touched the screen, "here, and here, are hidden cameras placed by our people. Our time is limited by the availability of satellite minutes, only fourteen hours of tape a month. So far as we know, Acosta hasn't visited."

Sara absorbed the room and its contents; computer beside the filing cabinet to the left of the door, two ventilation shafts, one above the desk and one beside the bulletin board. They might provide an escape route if things went south in a hurry.

"Sara, you'll need to get cozy with Salva long enough to steal his computer card. The section he works in is well funded. They've developed a system that we can't reliably duplicate. Without that card, we won't be able to get in.

"You'll pass the card to Drake and keep Salva occupied long enough for Drake to download the files." Bruce stopped as Sara shook her head.

"It will be easier for me to move around. They won't suspect a woman."

Drake grunted. "You can't *turn on* a computer."

"So, you'll show me what I need to do." She didn't add that it was important for her to take the lead on this assignment. The Knight men might have assumed she wanted to compete with Drake for the glory, but that wasn't the case at all. She wanted to bring her father's murderer to justice.

"It's not a good idea," Bruce said. "They're holding a benefit tomorrow. VIPs from all over the world will be attending. The guard will be heavy."

"Why go in during the benefit?" Drake asked. "We could leave tonight, go in before the guests arrive."

"It'll be easier for you to get lost in the crowd," Bruce said, "and with Salva busy with the festivities, it's likely he won't be working in his office."

The revolving Knight, Inc. logo filled the screen and Bruce flicked the lights back on.

"So we go in as a couple." Sara flipped a page and checked her information. "Solely there for the thousand-dollar a plate grub and to hob-knob with the bigwigs. Drake watches my back as I slip in. I'm sure I can do it. You'll show me, and if something goes wrong, Drake can back me up. I'm sure the tech team can come up with something to make hacking in easier." She didn't outright plead, but came close. "Let me go in."

Bruce and Drake exchanged considering looks. Drake returned her expectant stare first. "All right, Stark, I'll stand watch and make sure you're not discovered."

"Are you certain?" Bruce tugged on his cuff links. "I really think it would be better for Drake to lead on this one."

"It'll be fine, Colonel." Sara straightened her shoulders to prove she could bear the weight of the assignment. Bruce nodded and she grinned broadly. She would not let them down. After all, what could possibly go wrong?

CHAPTER FOUR

Fritz held up two tuxedos. "The black, sir? Or the white?"

"Black," Drake said without hesitation. White would draw attention to him like a fire at a moth convention. "With the silver cuff links."

"Excellent choice, sir." Fritz zipped the garment bag closed, added the velvet-lined box with the links to an inner compartment, and clasped the bag in half.

"And Stark?" Drake couldn't help asking, "Did she make an excellent choice?"

He refused to be embarrassed as Fritz gave him a knowing look. "Why do you ask sir?"

"Only curious." Drake poked at the shoes he'd just packed.

"Wouldn't be interested to see the lady dressed as a...lady, would you, sir?" Fritz's words vibrated with suppressed amusement.

"Never mind," Drake muttered and battled the stuck zipper on the shoe pocket.

"I took the liberty of airing out the Versace the Colonel gave her at Christmas."

The zipper came free, catching the thick of his thumb and he bit his lip to keep from cursing. He didn't have to ask Fritz more, the black beaded number was unforgettable. He'd wanted to see her in it the moment the wrapping had come off. He sucked the blood-blister on his thumb, as Fritz busied himself by returning the white tuxedo to the walk-in closet.

The door opened. "Don't forget extra socks, Drake," Sara said as she entered and went to the bureau. She was dressed for her role in a tailored, lightweight black pantsuit and white satin top. She wore her hair braided as usual.

Fritz chuckled under his breath. "He has not forgotten socks this time, Miss Stark."

Drake sent Fritz a warning glare as Sara dropped the pairs back in the drawer and closed it with her hip. He locked his suitcase. "All packed?"

She nodded. "I called Carlos at the lab. He should be here shortly."

"Good." Drake kept his tone light, despite the continued mirth emanating from Fritz. "Bring the car around and have our luggage brought down. We leave in an hour."

"Very well, sir," Fritz said as he headed to the door. He paused and gave them both a smile. "Have a safe trip, *kinderlieb*."

He left, the door closing silently behind him. When Fritz resorted to German, it meant he was highly amused, or highly concerned. Drake believed it was a mixture of both this time.

Sara tensed noticeably, her eyes on the door. It occurred to him that they were alone, behind a closed door, in his bedroom. Her tension was contagious.

"Well..." She trailed off with a sidelong glance to his bed as if the hulking Georgian piece were a dragon that might sneak up on her.

Drake hated seeing her so unsettled. Stark was a rock, his anchor to responsibility. Aside from her, there wasn't anyone who needed him; not since his mother had passed away. His mounting desire for her was tempered by the great concern he'd hurt her, make her resent him. This couldn't get any more difficult. "Ready to go, little sister?"

She cocked a sideways grin and relaxed visibly, her shoulders falling to their normal position. "I'm not your sister, and the last time I checked, I wasn't very little."

He chuckled and couldn't resist a slow, appraising perusal of all five feet, seven inches of her. With a wink, he said, "You're right, you have grown."

For the first time, he witnessed an honest-to-goodness blush. He laughed outright as she placed her hand on the door. "Are you blushing? Is that a real blush, lil' sis?"

"Knock it off Drake. I don't blush."

He followed her into the hall. "Yes you do. You're practically hot pink."

"I said stop," she growled over her shoulder as they headed for the stairs.

"Why? Will you break an ant farm in my dresser again? Or will it be frogs in the commode? Or how about the baby raccoon? That was fun, finding that fur-ball in my bed."

She shook her head, and though he couldn't see her face, he heard the staccato exhalation of quiet laughter. "You deserved every one of those pranks, Drake, don't try to say you didn't."

They descended the staircase to the foyer. "Now you're definitely wrong, Stark. I beat you fair and square every time. It got so I didn't want to spar with you, afraid you'd find a bear, or worse, a skunk and let it loose in my room."

"You weren't so afraid that you would let me win, though, were you?" She stopped at the front door and aimed a charming smile at him. "You never let up on me."

"No." Drake paused, overwhelmed by an unexpected urge to kiss her. She backed up a step. Her alarm drained the levity between them. He'd have to show more control. Sobering, he said, "I never let you win, Stark. You did that all on your own."

The front door opened, interrupting whatever Stark might have said in reply. Fritz entered, the Mercedes parked in the drive behind him in front of Carlos's Buick.

"Sorry, sir," Fritz said absently as he cast an astute look

over them. The unspoken lingered in the air and the old man's face wrinkled with delight. "Mr. Martinez has arrived. Should I show him to your den?"

"Yes." Drake hoped that beneath the surface, Sara was as pleased as Fritz appeared by the prospect of something deeper between them. Carlos came up the steps and Drake put aside all thoughts not directly related to the assignment. He welcomed the interruption as much as he despised it.

"Hello, Carlos." Sara quirked a bemused eyebrow at him. The techie had become a good friend over the years and his startlingly puritan beliefs about women were always excellent ammunition for a good teasing.

Carlos, short, with honey-colored skin and ever tidy in pressed jeans and a polo pullover nodded warily at her. The urge to laugh was only squelched by her respect for him.

His first language was Spanish and when Sara had decided to learn, the poor guy had been at first astonished, then embarrassed by her persistence to learn all the language, including vulgarities. He believed it his duty to protect a lady from such rude phrases and it had nearly tied his tongue to speak the words his own mother likely didn't know.

"I brought everything." Carlos lifted his briefcase.

Fritz led them to the den and opened the door. Drake took his place behind the desk and she leaned against one end as Carlos set the briefcase on the protective mat.

"As I was told, Stark, you need to download the entire hard drive of a secured computer system. I'm not sure if you realize how difficult that is."

Drake nodded, "I thought it was odd."

"Not only odd, but you would need a good day and a boatload of CDs to do it right. So," he lifted a small box, one inch thick, four inches across on each side, "I named it the Scarferator, since she'll eat up all the data in about four minutes. Stark, all you need to do is connect it with this." He held up what looked like a telephone cord and pantomimed the insertion using the back of Drake's desktop computer. "Once you're hooked up, you have to type in the password to get you through security."

"The password?" Sara swallowed hard, proud she'd managed to sound casual. Tie her to a chair, arm her with a rusty screw, and send in seven men to battle and she was in her element, but make her hack into a computer for a password and she was Jell-o.

Carlos smiled. "Surveillance sent over the password. I asked how they got it, thinking we could get in the same way and download the files from here so you wouldn't have to do it manually. But no such luck. The password came from video of his keyboard entries."

Drake hefted the device. "Where you gonna put this, Stark?"

"That's for me to know, and for you to imagine." She grinned at the quick heat in his eyes and snatched it from his hands. The Velcro strap she'd planned to use to conceal her Ruger would work. The device would fit snugly against her inner thigh, the cord curled beside it. She asked Carlos, "The password?"

"Lower-case, ten letters, chupacabra." He spelled it.

Sara memorized the word. "What the heck does that mean?"

"It's a mythical creature from Puerto Rico, I think," Carlos explained. "Nonsense, like UFO's. Chupacabra means goatsucker. Tabloid sightings, mostly New Mexico, I think."

Sara exchanged a look with Drake who chuckled. "That's his password? Why would he choose that?"

Carlos shrugged. "*El loco*. Who knows? Maybe the Colonel? You could ask him."

"No," Drake said. "He's already left for D.C. on business."

"We have the password, that's all that matters." Sara

wrapped the cord around the device. "Anything else I should know about the Scarferator?"

"Nope," Carlos said, then shrugged. "If you abort before the download completes, you'll lose data."

"Got it." Sara smiled, and thanked him, in the best Spanish vulgarities she recalled.

"Stark!" Drake tried to sound stern, but the laughter in his voice gave him away.

Carlos turned red. "*No habla Espanol.*" He snapped his briefcase together quickly, gave her a scathing look that didn't quite hide the smile in his eyes, and left.

"We're going to have to have a talk about showing some appreciation to those who help you," Drake said.

"What?" Grinning, Sara led the way to the waiting Mercedes. "I did thank him."

The word chupacabra played in her head as the Knight, Inc. pilot flew them to Panama. Drake, as was his habit, slept across from her, music piped into his ears via the in-flight headset. The man hated flying. He didn't fear it, just hated the claustrophobic quarters.

She returned her gaze to the window and wondered what in the world mythological goat-suckers had to do with Acosta. After a long bout of musing, she gave up. It was like fishing for feathers–illogical.

In a few hours they'd land at Tocumen airport where a car waited to take them to the Marriott. As she stared at the blackness beyond the window, she breathed deep and reminded herself Acosta was irrelevant to this mission. Once they'd taken the files off Dr. Salva's computer, then she could think about him, his motives, and what his plans might be. Until then, they were working blind and assumptions were dangerous.

Drake murmured something unintelligible and stretched. His shoe rubbed hers and her thoughts were off and running on their own again.

It had been too damned long since she dated. Maybe if she got out more, Drake's nearness wouldn't be such a...distraction. Did they have a pill for that? Maybe the opposite of Viagra? She imagined herself asking their doctor for an anti-libido pill and stifled a chuckle. She didn't want to wake Drake and try to explain what was so amusing.

If she didn't care for him, didn't value his friendship, didn't count on him and his father to be her family, these new feelings might not matter so much.

Life as she knew it hung in the balance. One wrong step, and she'd plummet from the tightrope she'd walked since her father's death. Drake didn't have anything to lose.

A sigh, frustrated and weary, escaped her. She picked up a worn copy of Forbes, probably left by the Colonel when he'd last flown in the Jetstar, and flipped through the pages.

On page forty-four there was a spread on the City of Learning; its history, future plans, and immediate activities. The information was dry, old news, and less detailed than the file she'd nearly memorized that afternoon. One paragraph grabbed her attention though, and suddenly irritated by Drake's ability to relax, she kicked his outstretched foot. "Drake."

He opened one eye, and scowled. "Let me rest, Stark."

"Check this out." She offered the magazine.

With a grunt, he straightened, removed the earphones, and took the pages. "So? There's nothing here we don't already know."

"Look further down. Barbara Salinger's interviewed." The professor, one of Sara's earliest role models when she began seriously thinking of joining Knight, Inc., was a highly respected archeologist and expert on ancient cultures. Her adventures had painted a very colorful picture for Sara, who considered the professor to be a regular Indiana Joan. "Maybe she'll be at the benefit."

"Could be." Drake shrugged and handed the magazine

back. "Too bad you won't have time for an autograph."

Disgusted by his lack of excitement, and not sure why she had expected more, she tossed the magazine on the table. "Come on, if it was Sean Connery, you'd be hopping in your seat."

"Yeah, well, Sean's the man." Drake folded his arms and wriggled back into the plush seat. "You need to relax, Stark."

"Relax? I don't see how you can." Her life consisted mostly of strenuous physical challenges, dirty but mundane missions like Mexico–minus the guards, and very few white-collar jobs. This assignment would be a first. "Aren't you the least bit concerned we'll be able to pull this off?"

"Nope." He closed his eyes.

She kicked him his foot again. "Well, I am."

He peered at her beneath heavy lids and gave a frustrated sigh. "Don't be. If the Colonel didn't think you could do it, we wouldn't be on this plane. Now will you please be quiet and stop kicking me?" He moved his legs out of kicking range.

Sara realized he was right. The Colonel had simply told her to get cozy with the doctor and steal his key card. No hesitation, just complete faith in her feminine wiles. Sara wished she had as much faith. Talk about daunting, she thought. The heels Fritz packed with that damned dress would give her away the second she landed on her face.

Com chatter erupted from the cockpit as the co-pilot strode to the restroom in the back of the plane. Drake plugged the music back into his ears and closed his eyes decisively.

A headache settled across her forehead. Drake's hatred for planes seeped into her, except for her, the inactivity made the flight torture.

Sleep wouldn't come as easy either, it never did. If she did nap and Drake entered her dreams instead of remaining across from her where he belonged, jumping out of a perfectly good airplane might be her only relief.

Drake tossed Stark's bag on the sofa. After the flight, dealing with customs, and checking into the three-room suite at the Marriott, he was done for the day. Stark looked just as beat as she directed Chuck, a Knight, Inc. employee and their driver while in Panama, to leave the luggage in their respective bedrooms. Once they were alone, she fell onto the sofa with a weary groan.

"Drink?" Drake went to the bar set against the wall behind the sofa in the sunken living room.

"Yes," she sighed the word, head back, a hand over her eyes.

"They don't have Chivas, but there's some Jamesons."

"That's fine."

He fixed them both a drink on the rocks. When he returned, he paused behind her, noting the tension in her posture. She must have one doozy of a headache. Stark never remained still, or quiet, for this long. She accepted the glass and stared up at him through her ragged bangs.

"Are you going to sit down? Or stand behind me all night?" She tried to grin, but it turned into a grimace.

"Headache?" Drake set his glass on the end table as she nodded. He gently gripped her head in his hands and massaged her temples; her hair silken beneath his palms.

She murmured her appreciation and his thoughts turned toward the erotic, as they did so often lately. How would she sound in bed? This lazy, soft purring of a contented feline? Or the more untamed full-moon calls of a wild woman?

"Drake?" she whispered.

"*Hmm*," he answered, lost in the pleasant debate.

"What turns you on?"

His hands stilled, and so did his ability to think. He swallowed hard and told himself Stark could not read minds. Thankful for the couch between them, he asked, "Why do you want to know?"

She looked at him again, the angle of her face

emphasizing the pleasant, and striking, line of her jaw, and lower, the swell of her breasts against the white of her shirt. "For research. What turns you on?"

He frowned, trying to focus on her meaning. The assignment, of course. With Stark, it was always the assignment. He exhaled and found his drink. Stepping down into the sunken living room, he crossed the carpet. Back turned to her, he gazed at the Monet print above the fireplace.

"Drake?" She stood directly behind him, her voice full of amusement. "Did I make you blush?"

"No, of course not." He turned with a grin that was all show. Why did this attraction make him nervous? An image of his father weeping over the casket, the only time he'd ever seen his father cry, flickered through his mind. The pain of that moment, of not only losing his mother, but discovering his father wasn't super-human, that Bruce Knight could be struck down so thoroughly, tightened the muscles in his gut.

"Must be jet lag then." She gave him a quiet smile, as if she sensed the morbidity of his thoughts. "But will you answer my question? Or should I go downstairs and take a poll?"

The thought of her lounging with the lizards in the hotel bar struck a sour note with him. How in the hell had he gotten himself in so deep? He had vowed long ago to never love a woman the way his father loved his mother. Stark's penchant for danger made a relationship with her impossible. Still, as unfair as it was, he couldn't stomach the thought of Sara with anyone else. "I thought you were bushed?"

"I am, but I'll never get to sleep until I complete my...research." She stepped back, leaned against the sofa, and sipped her drink. "So, what's it gonna be?"

"I don't know how to answer that question, Stark." Drake consciously loosened his grip on the glass in his hand before it shattered. "If this is about Salva and your role tomorrow, I can't help you."

"What else would it be about?" Her eyes widened, her

gaze never wavered, as if daring him to speak the unsaid. When he remained silent, she blinked and asked, "Why can't you help me?"

"Because every man is different."

"So?" She continued stubbornly. "At least you could give me some pointers on what I should do."

What she should do? The possibilities were endless, and completely tempting. He swallowed the last of his drink and slammed the glass on the bar, startling himself. He'd only meant to set it down. "Just do what you did when you dated before. It's a no-brainer."

She blew her bangs back from her forehead. A look of great debate flickered across her features. "Unfortunately." She spoke so low he had to strain to hear, "I don't have any experience in that department. I've never needed to seduce a man. They always approach me."

Stunned, Drake stared. He'd always considered her choice in men odd, but it never occurred to him that the men chose her, rather than the other way around. To him, Stark would go after the man she wanted, rejecting all others. This revelation only complicated the dilemma.

From the moment he'd returned from London, he'd known things were different between them. He couldn't eat breakfast with her and not wonder what she'd looked like in bed. When she finished her laps in the indoor pool, he imagined what it would be like to kiss her wet lips. Every aspect of the day was hindered by the erotic fantasies he couldn't escape. Now, if things did go beyond the borders of their current relationship, could he trust it was what she truly wanted? Or would she only accept him out of a strange fear of hurting him?

"Drake? What are you thinking?" She sounded timid and it angered him.

"Nothing," he said more brusquely than he meant to and tried to soften the reply. "If you really want me to help, I will."

But who would help him?

"Thanks." She didn't smile, didn't sound pleased, instead, she sounded the way he felt, too damned nervous for his own good.

"So, how does a woman catch your eye?" Sara's heart pounded loud in her ears. She'd entered dangerous territory of her own volition, but couldn't force herself to turn back. Whether it was a weird sense of self-torture or an underlying need to test the depth of her attraction to him, the opportunity held her curiosity prisoner.

Drake studied the carpet as if it explained the secrets of the universe, then gave her a roguish grin, "Are you sure you want to hear this?"

"Yes." She set her glass down and leaned on the arm of the sofa. *Only business, nothing more.* "I really need to know."

"Okay." He paused and Sara resisted the need to shake it out of him.

Please don't drag this out. She trampled down the same embarrassment she'd felt the first time she'd asked a man to use a condom.

Drake continued, "With Georgia Jackson, it was her smile and Emma Danvers had a way of making eye contact that told you she wanted you. With Deb Maxwell, it was the way she flipped her hair over her shoulder–which was bare the first time we met."

"And? What did she say? What did she do?"

"Like I said, it's different for every man, but a confident woman, one who's ready to project a certain...carnal knowledge, is highly arousing to most."

Sara imagined herself projecting an image of carnality and scowled. "God, wouldn't it be easier to just clobber him and steal the key card?"

Drake laughed. "That's not very subtle and it would be rather conspicuous if Dr. Salva was found lying in the hall with a dented skull. The guards would figure out something wasn't kosher."

"All right," Sara said. At least her headache was gone. It helped to finally *do* something. "So, I have to be confident, and I suppose flirty."

Drake nodded, and an especially mischievous smile settled on his mouth. "Why don't you give it a shot?"

"What?" She stood abruptly, her heart rate hitting hyper speed. "Right now? Here? With you?"

"Don't sound so shocked, Stark. I promise to behave. What other option do you have?"

If he'd laughed outright, or even hinted that he would tease her attempt, she would have fled, but he looked serious, as if this was more than a test of her abilities. "Fine, but don't you dare laugh."

Drake crossed his heart and held up three fingers. "Scout's honor."

She rolled her head, cracking her neck, and shook her hands, loosening up as if she were about to launch herself onto the parallel bars. Eyes closed, she dug deep for a sense of sexuality, tapping the innermost feminine side of herself. When she opened her eyes, she was grateful to see Drake remained serious.

Subtle, she told herself, be very subtle, nothing overt. *A smile, he'd said.* She tried one on, a simple flip of the lips. *Eye contact, he'd said.* She tried that and lost all train of thought. His eyes turned into black magnets, tugging her closer. She strolled forward and wracked her misfiring brain for the next tidbit.

Hair over her shoulder.

But hers was braided. She yanked the tie off the end, trying to make it seem casual, and ran her fingers through the mess to untangle it. Drake sucked in a breath and she stopped in amazement. It was working, she could tell by the sudden tautness in his carriage; the way his shoulders both straightened and bent toward her. This time, her smile wasn't a ploy.

With careful *subtlety* she tossed the hair over her shoulder and again brought her eyes to his. He didn't move, didn't breathe as far as she could tell. She stepped closer, projecting as much carnal knowledge as she could, until mere inches separated them.

He lifted a hand, his fingers warm and tender on her face as he brushed a stray strand behind her ear. A shower of sparks shivered through her. The sensation, unexpected, brought her fears to the surface.

Drake doesn't have anything to lose.

To cover her reaction, she arched a brow and grinned. "Did I pass, *big brother*?"

He shuddered once and stepped back a step. "Admirably."

"Good." She was proud at how matter of fact she sounded, and pleased by his pained expression. "Now I can sleep. Goodnight, Drake."

She waltzed into her room, barely controlling the urge to make it a headlong dash. With the door safely closed between them, she leaned against it and consciously brought her breathing under control. Sleep was as unattainable as peace of mind around that man.

Drake doesn't have anything to lose.

Drake's preference for a new flavor every month frightened her. Yes, a week or two rolling in the hay with such a dangerously sexy man would be great fun, but what then? What if a beautiful social butterfly fluttered into his life? One that wasn't quite so prickly, so rough around the edges? Could she compete with the pampered and polished women he was used to? Not unless she went through a major makeover and a personality transplant.

She sat on the edge of the bed. If they acted on their attraction and he left her, she would despise him. He would be like every other person who'd abandoned her. No, she couldn't live with those consequences. Capturing Drake for a moment would be simple, but could she give him up for a lifetime?

She buried her face in her hands, emotionally wrung out. *Focus on the mission.* At least she could take comfort in her success. Whatever happened tomorrow, however Dr. Salva met her performance, if it was anything like Drake's reaction, she'd not only have access to Salva's computer, but his entire world.

CHAPTER FIVE

Drake checked his watch for the umpteenth time and set his teeth. They were supposed to leave right now and Stark was still upstairs. He paced the lobby, ignoring the flirtatious looks from the girl behind the counter. The air-conditioned hotel kept him from perspiring, but he was sweating it nonetheless. If they didn't leave soon to make their fashionably late entrance, they'd just be plain late.

Others dressed in finery that indicated their attendance at the fete had stopped exiting the elevators and entering waiting limos. Some had left as long as an hour before. Now, only tourists and businessmen occupied the rapidly emptying lobby.

The television carried news from the States and suited men stared, glassy-eyed as the media hype continued over Senator Halley's involvement with the intern. Drake shook his head. What had happened to journalism? If they were truly going after Halley, they had a ton of documentation to hang him on. Not juicy enough, he thought and returned his vigil to the elevator doors. He'd give her ten more minutes.

In five he was ready to go up and drag her down. He stood to do just that when she stepped off the elevator. Chuck, behind her with their luggage, took one look at him and scurried out the door. Drake started forward, ready to lay into her, but stopped short once he got a good gander.

She wore a wig. An abundance of red curls swung with each step. The black dress clung to every curve and shimmered beneath the bright lighting. Every head turned to her. The girl behind the counter sized her up with disappointment as Stark glided through the lobby, right toward him.

Heat spread through his limbs. Artful makeup accentuated her cat-like eyes and made her mouth a glistening temptation. Golden flesh flashed between the slip of a dress and the ends of the wig. She was so damned sleek; the slim muscles in her bare arms, the dress over her flat stomach and firm thighs, she positively gleamed with decadent good health. A coil of arousal tightened exquisitely below his belt.

She smiled. The intensity of his response to the new Stark frightened him, made it impossible for him to manage the vise-like control he'd struggled so long to sustain and he became angry. Stark hadn't dressed for him, she'd done this for Salva–the enemy. His lack of logic flared his temper to further heights.

"Waiting long?" Stark asked with a smile.

He scowled. "Yes, but I shouldn't be surprised."

"Why?" She arranged the low cut neckline of the dress to better reveal the heady swell of her breasts.

"Transforming from a lumberjack to a lady takes time."

She sucked in a breath and her eyes hardened, the same way his father's did when Drake over-stepped himself. "And if you'd had to change your attitude with that tux, I'd be the one waiting on you."

She turned on her heel and nearly fell on her face. He gripped her elbow and steered her to the door. Between gritted teeth, he said, "You can't even walk, and you're supposed to seduce Salva? Am I missing something?"

"Yeah, a brain." She yanked from his grasp.

He felt like a jerk. More than reproof glistened in her eyes. He'd injured her, but he couldn't quite bring himself to apologize, not while her backside was so blatantly detailed by the hugging gown, not while her bare back rippled with toned muscles. Her body drove him to the brink, as if his attraction, bottled too long, had turned to vinegar in the cellar of his subconscious.

Chuck waited patiently beside the limo having already stowed their luggage in the trunk. They would not return to the hotel and Drake thanked his lucky stars for that. Another night in seclusion with Stark and he'd either fall into a coma from unreleased sexual tension, or bust down doors to have his way with her–neither prospect appealed to him.

Chuck opened the door and, as she got in, Drake noticed the long length of her leg, to his disgust. First he was hot, then angry, now he was ready to reverse roles and seduce her. What the hell was wrong with him?

"You know, Drake," Stark said as he settled in beside her, "you can be such an ass."

"Yeah." No sense in arguing with the obvious. "You're right. I'm just..." *What? What am I*?

If his foot could reach his backside, he'd give himself a swift kick. He knew how she felt about the mission, how oddly unsure she was of herself, and yet he'd trampled on her confidence. Not only was that a mistake between them, but it could be detrimental to the assignment. He needed to repair the damage and hope to hell he succeeded before they arrived.

With an effort that burned like acid in his chest, he smiled and patted her knee. "Look, you'll be fine. Salva won't know what hit him."

She crossed her legs toward the window, removing his hand.

Easing closer, he gained a nose full of her perfume–a light sweetness that made him yearn to breathe in the rest of her. Anger receded into the swelling ocean of his desire. "Aww, come on, you still love me."

"Don't be so sure of yourself." She muttered. Her shoulders relaxed, but she continued stare out the window as the limo pulled into traffic.

Charming her wouldn't work, he thought, disgruntled. He

turned sideways, as much to address her directly as to put distance between. "I know this is a difficult assignment, Stark. I didn't mean what I said."

Gaze locked on the darkened windows, she said, "It doesn't matter, Drake. I understand."

"Understand?" he asked, confused.

She turned, and he was struck by how green her eyes appeared beneath the red wig. "Yes, I understand. You're angry that I've taken lead. You want to be in control, as always."

"No," he said quickly, then realized that to argue with her, he'd have to reveal the truth. How in the hell could he tell her that he was jealous? A sickening queasiness stole over him. *Jealous*. God, he was screwed.

"No?" Her agitation was obvious in the way her hands convulsed around the beaded bag.

Looking at her, no one would believe she could protect herself against five armed men without breaking a sweat.

"What then, Drake? You can't really be angry that I made you wait."

He shook his head and ran a hand through his hair, rubbing the back of his neck. How could he untangle this mess? Especially if he couldn't keep his mind on the mission. "It's the whole damned assignment. I think it's just nerves."

She looked skeptical. "Since when do you get nervous?"

Since the stakes were raised high enough to threaten the life of the woman I care about. "Acosta makes me nervous."

Sara nodded and relaxed fully, accepting his apology. The naked curve of her shoulder was lustrous in the dimly lit interior. He averted his eyes with a silent curse.

The view from his window was not much different than the meaner areas of Houston, but here, a tropical aura leant an elegance to both the opulence and the poverty. People were everywhere, driven from homes by nightfall and boredom. Horns honked furiously and traffic more or less hurtled in either direction with the same single mindedness of a stampede.

The city lights dulled as they hit less congested streets. Drake worked over their plan from all angles looking for holes, for avoidable mistakes, but his thoughts kept returning to the real concern. Stark was just too damned attractive in her costume. She'd surely succeed in making her first conquest.

How he wished it was him.

Stark remained silent, obviously preparing herself. The nature of the assignment called for mental acrobatics, not simply the physical demands they were both accustomed to.

Twenty minutes later, Chuck parked the limo in front of a guarded gate. The courtyard beyond teemed with well-dressed guests. Drake whispered, "Remember, once we're inside, you'll need to stay close to Salva. We can't afford for anything to get between you and him." *Even me.*

"I understand."

Her no-nonsense tone was a relief, though he wasn't surprised. She would do all right, she wouldn't fumble or allow her fears to confuse the mission. He admired her professionalism and it only deepened his determination for nothing to go wrong.

Chuck opened the door and wet humidity curled inside the cool interior. Stark stood, her ankles managing to keep her upright as Drake emerged. He wrapped an arm around her waist. "I'll help you inside."

"I'm fine," she said and shrugged his arm off to prove it. She took a few steps and managed them with the finesse of someone who lived in heels.

Surprised, he wondered about her earlier clumsiness. Of course, he thought, she was upset about his stupid comment. Guilt sneered at him. He wouldn't make that mistake twice. "Well done," he whispered and smiled. "I'm impressed."

Her responding proud grin dissolved the last of the discomfort between them and they joined another couple who'd just arrived. Drake was glad for their company. Better to enter with the pack, than arrive as a lone wolf sniffing out his prey.

Sara thanked heaven for the Velcro straps holding the Ruger and the Scarferator to her thigh. It helped her balance in the heels. The added weight of the device, and the tight confines of the dress forced her to glide, rather than stride, as she normally would. She inhaled the heavy, flower-perfumed air and glanced at Drake. She recalled his hand on her knee in apology and his charming, crooked grin. This did not help her effort to focus and she tore her eyes away to survey the battlefield.

Streams of white twinkling lights and paper lanterns lit the courtyard in a myriad of russets, oranges, and crimsons. They cast a fine sunset glow over the white linens on the tables, the standard white china, and the caterers dressed in their starched uniforms. Women captured the fall season in beaded gowns of gold, cherry, and the ultimate favorite, black. Drake fit in nicely with his black tuxedo, but to her, he stuck out like chocolate on a veggie platter–too scrumptious to be healthy.

Music drifted from the orchestra seated beside a small stage and podium. Sara glanced over the men, discarding sly and blatant stares alike until her gaze landed on Dr. Salva, his head bent in discussion with a man twice his age. Salva looked the same as he had in the photographs, if slightly more gray at the temples. The man was appallingly short.

"I'll leave you, but I won't be far. Don't approach him yet, let him see you first," Drake murmured and set off for the ornate fountain of sparkling champagne.

Sara gave him a sarcastic thumbs-up for the lesson on seduction etiquette. That had been fine when she asked for it, but now it made her feel like he had no confidence in her abilities. She found a tree to lean against and unraveled the spaghetti string of the clutch to hang over one shoulder.

Back protected, the guests in front of her, she waited for Salva to finish his conversation. She kept him in the corner of her eye as she searched for Professor Salinger. Nowhere in sight. Too bad. But it wasn't something she ought to be thinking about now anyway.

Drake meandered slowly back through the guests, pausing to talk with a statuesque black-haired beauty in a red, revealing sheath. Sara wasn't sure if it was the dress, or the woman herself, but she immediately straightened and debated swooping down beside Drake to keep his attention on the mission. *And her.* But he didn't linger, only nodded and continued at a snail's pace through the crowd.

What she wouldn't give for pants, a black stocking cap to hide her hair instead of the itchy wig, and to use the custom molded ear-mike in her purse to get through this mission. As close as she would get to the doctor, however, she couldn't risk his notice of the device yet and sighed with discontent. She checked on Salva. The older, white-haired gentleman smiled, patted Salva on the arm, and moseyed away. Time to begin.

Sara stepped from the tree, caught Drake's eye, and tilted her head toward Salva. Drake nodded at her, a warning of caution in his eyes. Not only would Sara have to convince Dr. Salva she was interested in him physically, but that her interest was sincere. A tall order for such a short guy.

She wound her way through the guests, inching nearer to the head table where Salva stood. With muttered agreement to a perfectly coifed women on the loveliness of the courtyard and a small laugh for the man who complimented her dress, she managed to appear casual as she zoomed in on her target.

Finally, Dr. Salva found her, and the last of her worries left. His stare was lecherous, his arrogance apparent in the way his chest swelled and chin jerked higher.

Eye contact.

Sara met his gaze and conveyed confidence, though inwardly she wanted to rip a cloth from the table and cover her bared skin from his gaze. She tried on the smile she'd used the night before and Dr. *Saliva* nearly drooled.

Sara reigned in her lethal imagination. Calling him Dr. Saliva in her head was fine *after* the mission, but to do so now might cause an irreparable blunder. After a moment of lip-biting debate, she decided that someone with as much force and pride as this man, would succumb better to a game of cat and mouse, something she'd had more practice with lately than she wanted to admit. Though, what sizzled between her and Drake could hardly be called a game.

She turned her back on Salva, ignored Drake's frown, and wove her way through the dancing guests to the six-person orchestra. Classical music was beyond her understanding, but not her appreciation. She'd been dismal at every fine arts class at the private school Bruce sent her to, but she could recognize most of the famous composers, if not the score.

"Lovely, isn't it?"

As soon as she heard the voice, she knew it was Salva. It came from too low to the ground to be anyone else. She turned with a smile and crooked one knee to shorten her own stature. "Yes. Vivaldi is always lovely."

The top of his head barely reached her eyebrows, taller than she'd guessed, but still a hindrance. He smiled, his thick lips wet. "I could say the same about you."

"Thank you." Sara laughed softly and turned shyly away, luring him in more than any lap-dance would have.

He placed a hand on her arm and as she pivoted back, she caught the thundering scowl on Drake's face where he stood six feet away.

"Please," Salva said with a thick, South American accent, his thumb caressing her arm. "I must know your name, or forever live in agony."

Proud she didn't roll her eyes, she replied, "It's Sara Cross, and you are?"

"I'm Dr. Ramon Salva. I am in charge of Advanced Environmental Studies at the City," he boasted, but didn't release her arm.

"Oh my, you must be very important," Sara gushed, praying she sounded sincere, though she sensed his ego would have lapped up even the most blatantly shallow comment.

"They could not manage without me." He smiled. "But you have no drink. May I have the honor of bringing you a glass of champagne?"

"I would love that," Sara said, thankful he'd finally let go of her. Realizing she might hang herself by revealing her dislike, she placed a hand on his arm. "But hurry back, I'd love to discuss your work with you."

"I will," Salva said, positively glowing with his apparent conquest. "Don't go away."

"I'll be right here." She wriggled her fingers in a toodle-loo wave.

Drake, having circled closer and placed his back to her, mumbled over his shoulder. "We haven't got all night. Watch yourself."

Understanding he thought her antics to be nerves, she chuckled. "No fear, he's already eating out of my cleavage."

Drake stepped further away, but she sensed his acute attention on her and tried to focus on the music, rather than the lingering scent of his light cologne. *Turn that energy toward Salva and you've got it made.*

When Salva returned with her glass, she accepted it with a smile and tossed the ends of the wig over one shoulder.

Salva's gaze flickered from her shoulder, to her breasts, then back to her face. "I have not seen you here before," he said, sipping from his glass. "I could not have forgotten you?"

She gulped a swallow from her own flute. "No, I've never been here before." Then to add some realism to her act, she said, "I read the article in Forbes and was just tickled by what y'all have done here. Plus, Panama, at this time of year is just lovely."

"It is, it is," Salva agreed. "Are you interested in our work with the environment?"

"I recycle." Sara shrugged delicately. "But I'm always interested in studies of every kind. There's nothing more glorious than an intelligent man. You can learn so much."

His eyes lit up as she playfully ran a finger down the lapel of his tux. He grasped her hand and held it firmly against his chest. "I'm an excellent instructor, if you're in need of one."

"Oh, that I am." She wet her lips, smiled, and gazed at him through her lashes.

Couples crowded them as the orchestra struck up a vaguely familiar waltz. A regal-looking woman announced it was the last dance before dinner would be served and laughingly asked the guests not to forget their donations went to fund the scientific programs, not to the caterers.

"Dr. Salva, perhaps you could begin your instruction on the dance floor." She grinned wickedly, suddenly enjoying her seductress role, though Salva's picture surely hung in the slime-ball hall of fame.

"Yes!" he cried, as if broken from a trance. "Yes, it would be my pleasure."

He took her drink and set it, along with his, on the tray of a passing server. In seconds, his hot hand blistered her lower back while the other sweated against her palm. He danced fairly well, but in seconds she felt like a tomato being tested by a savvy shopper.

To hide her disgust, she pressed her hand closer to Salva's neck, lightly toying with the curls at the nape. Salva, occupied with trying to see down the front of her dress, grunted with pleasure.

"I am grateful to have been sent such an angel," he murmured against her collarbone and pressed closer. "Do you know what your smile has done to me?"

It wasn't her smile he was staring at and to cover a snort, she gave him what she hoped was an erotic laugh. "Doctor's are so sexy. All that intelligence wrapped up in such a...nice package."

He expelled hot, harsh wind on her cheek as he turned his face upward. "My dear, I have a package just for you."

"Oh my, Dr. Salva." She heaved a breath to press her breasts against his chest. "Intelligent men must know so much more about...things, than the common man."

"We do, and you must call me Ramon." His frantic and impassioned plea preceded more wet air against her skin and she resisted the urge to rub the dampness away.

Sara considered searching his pockets for the keycard and slipping away before he knew it was gone, but without knowing which pocket it might be in, or even if he had it on him, she couldn't risk it.

The music ended and Salva ushered her to the head table. They settled in a dim corner while Drake watched her covertly two tables over. She grinned. The brunette had been replaced by the white-haired woman she'd spoken to earlier.

"Tell me about your work, Dr. Salv–Ramon." She nibbled on the food, too queasy to enjoy the lobster feast. "I would love to see your office. Or is it a lab?"

"I have both, but unfortunately, I cannot give you a tour of the lab without clearance." Again he puffed up with his own importance as he dabbed the corners of his mouth with a napkin, pinky-fingers in the air. "But if you're really interested, we can go to my office after we're finished here."

Home run. The crowd goes wild! She doubted shouting hooray was wise and smiled demurely. "I would love that, Ramon."

"Sara, may I call you Sara?" he asked and she nodded. "My work is the best, one of the reasons many attend tonight. Without my research, no one would care to see our wonderful City."

He waved at the guests. "They all come to meet me. Did I say I hold several patents? No? It is true. Mostly for the military. But I'm working on something quite special right now. Something that will change the world."

Chupacabra. The word rang in her head. It didn't seem to fit the smug man in front of her. "That's so interesting. Can you tell me about it?"

He shook his head. "I can tell you of the irrigation system I invented, though. It could change the Sahara to an oasis." Salva frowned and shoved dripping white meat into his cheek before continuing, "If I could only convince their government to fund the project."

Sara swallowed a bit of asparagus and wondered if he weren't seeking funding elsewhere, like through Acosta. She geared herself up to ask him about his military work when the microphone on stage squawked with feedback. The ceremonies began and she resigned herself to boredom until they could get away.

Speakers droned on while Salva groped her knee beneath the table. She endured the fumbling assault on her leg and scanned the grounds. Drake, two tables away, glanced in her direction every few seconds. In between, he politely nodded to the lady beside him and feigned interest in the speakers.

She caught his eye and jerked her chin to the right. He scanned the area she'd indicated and nodded once, but didn't make eye contact again. For the most part, the security measures were hidden from the guests; men in tuxedos lined the vulnerable points where gates and buildings allowed access to the courtyard, but to the right, uniformed men blatantly displayed automatic weapons. Sara concluded they guarded the most sensitive area of the City.

Time to get the party started.

She whispered an excuse, leaving for the ladies room. In a stall with the door closed, she extracted a lipstick tube from the tiny beaded purse. With a tissue, she popped off the creamy, rose-colored stick and shook the hollow base until her earpiece fell into her palm. The device, molded to fit snugly into her left ear would be concealed partly by the wig, and partly by keeping her right side to Salva for the duration.

The last item in her purse, a compact canister of body spray, was cold and heavy in her hand. She unscrewed the cap and shoved the extra magazine for the Ruger deep into her cleavage. It was icy, but she welcomed the shock. With the purse holding only empty items, she didn't want to carry it anymore, but Salva might notice and she slipped it over one shoulder.

The game was about to return to territory she understood. Her only concern now was to keep Salva's hands off her anatomy long enough to use the Scarferator.

CHAPTER SIX

Drake fisted his hands and waited outside the darkened building. Stark had been in there with the slimy doctor for over twenty minutes. What could be keeping her? He wanted to rush in and pummel the brazen bastard. But, without any knowledge of what was happening, he might create more trouble for her rather than rescue her from it.

He fingered the transmit button on the mike woven through the inside of the tux jacket, eager to contact her. Every minute of nauseating chatter, ever second of heavy breathing, made him wish he'd flown in an expert in acupuncture.

He imagined the dark man's hands on her skin, his mouth on her neck and shoulders and his blood pressure rose. Damn the consequences, he would go in and kick the living crap out of the good doctor. What had the Colonel been thinking to place Stark in such jeopardy? He stood, ready to dash inside. A uniformed guard walked by and he ducked back into the shadows.

"Stark," he whispered into the transmitter when the uniform had disappeared, "get a move on." She mumbled something unintelligible, clearly not meant for him. Again, he fought to control the instinct to break in and find her. He'd give her five minutes to appear.

Stark emerged in two, her red wig slightly tangled and a frown on her face.

"Are you all right?" He grabbed her shoulders and searched for oily handprints on her flesh.

She shrugged off his hands and held up the key card. "I'm fine, but we've only got a few minutes. I sent him to find a condom."

Disgusted by the errand and alarmed at how little time they had, he grabbed the key card and opened the outer door. "Why did you come back out here?"

"Because you sounded ready to storm the castle," she paused to give him a scolding stare, "and I need you to run interference. If he returns before I come back out of the office, keep him occupied until I'm done."

"How the hell am I supposed to do that?" Drake wanted to shake her, wanted to kick box with her, anything to avoid thinking of Salva kissing her, or worse.

"You'll think of something."

He followed her through the maze of corridors. While she'd been dancing with the idiot doctor, he'd been counting guards and lost track after twenty. They were all armed, all ready to shoot first and never ask questions.

She stopped in front of a door and pointed at the lock. "Open it."

"Wait," Drake said, "when he returns, he'll know he left the card behind, he won't be able to get in. You'll have to let me download the files and *you* keep him occupied."

She shook her head, a wave of disgust wrinkling her nose. "No good. I said I'd wait for him on the desk. He'll wonder why I'm not in the room."

On the desk? Drake imagined knocking out Salva's teeth the moment he returned. Maybe cracking his skull and just taking what they wanted was a better plan after all.

"You'll have to bump into him, drop the key card in his pocket. His right one, and then apologize." She brightened with an idea. "Ask him to talk to you about his work. He goes on forever about some irrigation system he designed. That should keep him busy."

"I hate this." Drake opened the door, but grabbed her

wrist to prevent her from entering. "It'll be easier if you just catch him outside, tell him you've got a headache, and then leave. I'll meet up with you out front after I do the download."

She stared at his hand until he removed it. "No, it won't be easier. The man is an octopus. Believe me, he won't be put off, he'll force me back into the office."

"Will you be able to get rid of him once I'm gone?"

She sighed, and whispered fiercely, "Drake! We don't have time to argue about this. Do as I say, for once!"

A door opened and closed, echoing from an inner corridor. Footsteps clacked on tile flooring, growing louder as they came in their direction.

"Fine." He pushed her inside, "but I'm waiting right outside this door. I'll keep him busy as long as I can. Do it and come right back out. Hurry."

Drake yanked the door closed and backed up ten paces. Salva strutted around the corner with a grin on his codfish lips. Drake's temper boiled as he lunged forward and stumbled into the doctor, dropping the key card surreptitiously back into the man's pocket.

"Oh, I so sorry," Drake slurred, pretending to be drunk. "I need a bathroom." He peered at the walls, the ceiling, "Iss there a bathroom?"

Salva sneered. "What are you doing in here? This is off limits."

"I didn't know." Drake clung to Salva's coat to keep him stuck to the wall. "Door wasss open. Hey..." He trailed off, gearing himself up for the performance of a lifetime. "You're that guy, that doctor guy, with the irritation system."

"Irrigation, you baboon." Salva pushed on Drake's shoulders to force him away. "Now, if you don't mind..."

But Drake did mind, he minded a whole hell of a lot. "Oh gosh, I sorry." He wavered on his feet and fell against Salva's office door, seemingly oblivious that it was precisely where the doctor wanted to go. "Will you autograph my invitation?" He patted down his coat and looked inside the tux blearily. "I have a pen here somewhere."

"Here." Dr. Salva sighed with frustration and produced his own pen.

"Thanksss." Drake fought the need to stab the horny fool and continued to pat his coat down. "Now where'sss that invitation?"

Another exasperated sigh and Salva removed a card from his tux pocket. "Here, I'll sign this for you." He scribbled quickly, and handed the card to Drake who promptly fumbled it to the floor.

"Ooopss." He took his time bending over to retrieve it and urged Stark to hurry. He didn't know how long he could keep up the charade. Salva was a rutting boar. No way he'd let that animal near Stark.

He straightened and wondered if four minutes had ever passed so slow in his life. "Thanksss, What insspired your infection, ahh, I mean invention. Is your lavatory here?"

"Please, I do not have time for this." Salva turned red with agitation.

Drake unclenched his teeth to ask the question torturing him, "Wasssa matter, you gotta hot date?"

"That is none of your affair." Salva puffed visibly. "But if you must know, yes, and I do not want to disappoint her."

Drake loathed him. "She gotta sissster for me?"

"No," the doctor, shouted, and pointed behind him. "There is a bathroom down the hall and to the left. Use it and return to the party."

"Ahh, bathroom..." Drake closed his eyes, pretending to pass out. Silently, he screamed at Stark to finish.

"You must leave now." Salva tugged on his coat and cursed liquidly in Spanish.

Drake opened one eye and scowled. "Hey, lay off the tux."

Salva's black eyes went beady with rage and he shouted

into Drake's face. "Wake up, you cannot sleep here. Wake up or I will have security remove you."

"Fine." Drake slapped at the doctors hands. What the hell was taking Stark so long? "I'll go." He half-straightened, then pretended to slump back once more. *Call security, you pervert, let me take you down.*

"Move!" Salva yanked on Drake's tux again and his head hit the door with a thud. They struggled with each other, Drake skidding his shoes on the floor and using the door to hold himself up.

Seconds later, the door opened and Drake fell back to see Stark standing over him, and a good deal up her dress. Momentarily stunned, he stared at the finest set of thighs on earth, complemented by the sleek blackness of her Ruger and the pale shape of the Scarferator beside it.

"Sara." Salva sounded as if he'd been caught doing a tango with Drake. "I tried to hurry, but this buffoon would not leave."

She nudged Drake with her toe to move and stepped out of the office. "You know, Dr. Salva, I don't think I have the stamina to entertain someone of your...abilities tonight. I'm sorry, but I have to go. My limo turns into a pumpkin if I'm not back in ten minutes."

"But, but..." He looked apoplectic with disappointment. "I would have come back sooner, but I couldn't find my keycard." As he spoke, he put his hand in his pocket, as if to prove it wasn't there, but pulled the hard plastic out and looked dumbly at it for a moment. His eyes filled with dawning realization.

Drake found his feet and saw the computer was still on through the open door. The screen flickered, in the process of shutting down. His mouth went dry and he moved in front of Stark, but it was too late.

"What are you doing with my computer?" Salva looked startled and pushed past them to stand in the middle of the room. "What the hell's going on?"

"Nothing, I...I bumped it with my knee waiting for you." She gave Drake a wary look.

A moment before, Salva had appeared an old, sex-driven paunchy fool, but as he turned to them, his eyes glittered malevolently, his skin darkened and his lips settled in a firm line. "Who are you? CIA? NSA?"

"I don't know what you're talking about, Doctor." Stark backed further into the corridor.

Drake cast off his drunken act and straightened behind her. Their cover was blown. He reached inside his coat for the Glock as Salva darted toward a box on the wall.

"Don't move," Drake said, icily.

Stark dropped the little purse she'd been clutching and bent, reached beneath the hem of her dress. She straightened with the Ruger out in front of her. "Hold it right there, Salva."

They froze in a suspended triangle of wills. Drake concentrated on the man. Sweaty drops beaded on Salva's forehead and his eyes shifted sideways. The doctor would not remain motionless for long. "Don't do it."

Salva dove forward. Drake fired, Stark a fraction after him, as Salva's hand punched the alarm. The doctors forward motion saved his life; Drake's bullet slammed into his shoulder, Stark's round into his hip.

The blaring foghorn alarm startled them into action. Drake yanked her through the door and into the hall, their footfalls echoing in the empty corridors. Sara kicked off her shoes and instantly matched his pace.

He urged her ahead and cursed himself for not retrieving the key card. They would be forced to navigate the building without the ability to open doors. A red light pulsed over the door they'd entered. It banged open and four armed guards raced into the corridor.

Stark spun around, retreating the way she'd come. Drake followed. Shouts for them to halt, in both English and Spanish, accompanied the enormous boom of gunfire in the tile and cement hall. A bullet blasted a chunk of concrete from the wall where Stark's head had been a moment before.

He raced down another hall. Against a legion of armed backup, they didn't stand a chance.

As he feared, the door ahead of them opened and more uniformed men rushed into the building. Led by a man in a tux who spoke rapidly into his headset, this group numbered eight and Drake turned cold with fear for Stark. He fisted his hand tighter around the Glock–the entire grounds would be teeming with armed men looking for them now.

Stark led him into the tail of a T-junction. Drake kept his body between her back and anyone who might aim for the bare skin between her shoulder blades. If anything happened to her, he would never forgive himself...or her.

"Here," she yelled and aimed her pistol at the keycard swipe. The computer board blew inward in a spray of sparks. Another round from her Ruger destroyed the plate between knob and frame.

Drake kicked the door open and they rushed through a haze of ozone scented smoke. Stark ran to the vent on the opposite end of the room and fired twice, once at each of the top screws. "Kick it in."

He did, the grate bending inward until it flattened. Boots on tile thundered closer. Stark dropped to the floor, shoved the Ruger into the front of her dress, and crawled through the opening. Drake followed her as automatic fire perforated the wall over his head. He hoped to hell she knew where she was going.

The aluminum buckled and popped beneath their hands and knees. Their rapid breathing sounded harsh as they sweltered in the enclosure.

"This way," she muttered when they came to a juncture.

Gunfire rattled into the enclosure, forcing them faster. There was no telltale sound of buckling aluminum behind them–the guards had not entered the shaft. He hoped that wasn't a bad sign. "Do you know where this leads?"

She nodded, bumping her head lightly on the ceiling and glancing over her shoulder at him. "Yes, it goes to an outside access vent. But we're going to the roof."

He grinned. The guards weren't following. They believed he and Stark would escape through that exit. One guard stayed behind to make sure he and Stark didn't return the way they'd come, while the others ran outside. He could kiss her–and her backside would be his choice right now, as it wriggled enticingly in front of his face.

He loved watching her go.

Sara's ears rang from firing the Ruger in the enclosed space, but the rooftop grate had been stubborn. After the inferno of the shaft, the breeze rushing across the roof cooled her heated flesh. She yanked the wig from her head, allowing the wind access to the damp hair at her nape. Her ponytail fell to tickle her shoulders and gooseflesh spread down her arms.

"Good work." Drake tugged her to the roof's edge.

Below them, guards raced about like mice in a maze. Sara felt as vulnerable as a tasty bit of cheese. They scrambled through courtyards, rushed in and out of buildings, and made it impossible for her and Drake to climb down without being detected.

"What are we gonna do?" she asked, frustrated by their lack of options.

He pointed past the low wall separating the grounds from the street. "The limo's there. We only need to get that far. Let's check the other side of the building."

They checked, but it was the same on that side, and the other. On the fourth, Sara almost didn't want to look. The guards would eventually figure out they weren't going to emerge from the ground vent and would search for them on the roof. But the fourth side of the building gave them the exit they needed and she thanked heaven for the glass encased catwalk ten feet below.

"You go first," Drake said, aiming his Glock at the empty gangway below. "I'll keep you covered."

Sara eased over the edge and dangled, the further four foot drop was simple, but she was exposed, Drake her only protection should a guard come into the narrow passage. She glanced up, and she caught her breath. Drake's face had darkened with concentration, his eyes glittered blackly as he watched for a threat, and the danger emanating from him thrilled her in a way it shouldn't.

She dropped, and the domed glass was cool beneath her ruined stockings. She pulled her Ruger to give Drake cover as he followed. Careful not to slip, she worked across the glass and pressed her back firmly to the opposite building.

He was barely over the edge when a guard raced into the catwalk. A black beret shadowed the guard's face and the fluorescent lighting glinted of his weapon. She held her breath and motioned for Drake to stop where he was. He saw the guard and stilled.

The guard continued forward, but the shouts of his comrades rose in volume and drew her attention to the east corner. If they were discovered in the open like this, it would be a Wild West shootout.

She cast her gaze downward. The guard had gone through without seeing them. Drake dropped with a heavy thud that vibrated the thick glass.

She gestured him forward with relief, grateful they were both merely yards from escaping. A shot punctured the brick beside her head; a fragment of stone streaked across her shoulder and she winced.

Drake cursed. "Get down!"

She dropped to her knees, preparing to slide over the opposite side of the tunnel and fired instinctively at the opening between the buildings.

Drake hunkered low five feet to her left and fired at the uniformed guards on the ground. The men ducked back behind the building. Alerted by the shots, the rest came running, including the guard who'd passed through the catwalk.

He spotted her above and aimed at her. She fired through the catwalk and prayed it didn't shatter. A hole appeared first in the glass, then in the shoulder of the guard. The gun tumbled from his deadened fingers. He fell and backed toward the building she and Drake had just left.

A deadly and ear-splitting blanket of gunfire descended on them. Drake emptied his Glock at the group clogging the gangway and Sara joined him in driving them back. More bullet holes chinked through the glass they sprawled on and to her dismay, spider web cracks stretched upward and out. The splintering sound of the structure was loud beneath their combined weight.

Dreading the fall almost as much as she dreaded getting shot, Sara braced herself. "Drake!"

He grimaced as the domed roof caved in. There was nothing to grab, nothing to hold on to, and they spilled into the tunnel. The safety glass, though thick and dull, nicked Sara's flesh everywhere as she rolled to a stop. The crunch of glass beneath Drake was loud as the weapons fire ceased.

The guards below could not get a line of sight on her and Drake, crouched as they were on the carpeted floor. Drake reached her in a crab-like walk and glanced at her bare feet.

Guards raced into the building. Drake flicked his gaze to the path ahead, littered with wicked shards of glass and tossed her over his shoulder. Her breath expelled in a woof, her solar plexus pressed into the hard bulge of muscle between his neck and upper arm as he dove into the next structure.

Shots rang behind them, but the running guards couldn't aim well at moving targets. Their bullets thunked into the floor, ceiling, and open door. Sara reloaded the Ruger from the magazine in her bra and fired back.

"Keep going!" He shouted as he dropped her on glass-free terrain and pushed her forward. She glanced back as he reloaded and fired at the oncoming guards.

Sara made a left and sprinted for the public entranceway to the City. She smashed the long metal bar downward to open the glass doors, but it wouldn't budge. Locked. She cursed and stepped back into the lobby. Why did everything have to be made of glass?

The Ruger erupted in her hands and the door shattered, covering the floor with torturous shards, lethal enough to cut through a tendon. She braced herself for the dash across and an arm wrapped around her neck, cutting off her air and trapping the scream of surprise in her throat. Her attacker dragged her toward the corridor leading away from Drake, who's back was turned as he lay cover fire to keep their pursuers at bay.

Hands locked on the arm strangling her, Sara waited until he pushed her closer to the wall and lifted both legs. She pressed the soles of her feet against the concrete and shoved with all her might. They tumbled backward and the man behind her let out a grunt as her weight landed on his belly. With a shout of anger, she smashed the back of her head into the bridge of his nose.

He howled and the arm disappeared from around her neck. Before she could find her feet, Drake was there, yanking her out of the way. The rage on his face was frightening, and wonderful. He lifted the guard, smashed a fist twice into the man's already broken nose, and then dropped him like a used oil rag.

Sara didn't have time to thank him. The guards from the catwalk reached the entrance to the lobby. She fired, forcing them to retreat into the hall for cover. Any second now, black clad men would be scurrying over the front lawn like cockroaches in a suddenly bright room, sealing off their exit.

Drake didn't hesitate to use her cover to lift her, one-armed, off her feet. He squeezed awkwardly beneath the metal bar and dashed down the steps while she continued to fire behind them to cover his back. Once on the grass, he shoved her ahead of him.

Guards spilled out from inside and between the two buildings. Their automatic fire, a tough weapon to aim accurately with, sprayed rounds at her feet. Drake raced sideways, firing and continuing to buy them a narrow margin of bullet-free space in which to run. Tufts of dirt flew up from rounds that missed their mark. Any second now, Sara expected to be thrown forward by a bullet.

Drake shouted a curse and stumbled, but didn't falter in their mad dash for the low wall a mere ten feet away. Chuck waited on the other side, trained and ready to speed them to the airport.

Drake grasped the top of the wall in one leap and Sara emptied her pistol at the oncoming guards. He held his hand out for her, but without a running start, she had to scramble up the concrete, scraping her knees and tearing the skin on her right foot before managing to gain the other side.

They landed on the sidewalk. The street was remarkably quiet on the opposite side of the wall. The guards stopped firing once they were out of sight. The limo's back door hung open and Chuck revved the engine. Sara dived inside behind Drake and slammed the door. Drake breathed heavily as they careened down narrow roads toward the airport.

"Are you all right?" She knelt on the floor, wincing at the sting of carpet rubbing her scrapes and cuts. She ran her hands across his body, up and down his arms, legs and torso, searching for a bullet wound.

"I'm fine," he said through gritted teeth.

His left leg was hot, slick, and when she pulled her hand back, it was red with blood. "No, you're not. You've been shot."

She found the hole with trembling fingers and ripped the

leg of his pants apart. "Turn the overhead on."

He did as she asked, and she almost wished he hadn't. The blood was awful. She swallowed hard. Blood didn't bother her, never had before, but *Drake's blood* was another matter all together.

"How bad is it?" Drake sounded casual, as if being shot wasn't a big deal.

"Don't know." Sara reached up and yanked the decorative handkerchief from his pocket. She dabbed at the wound, still unable to see where the bullet had gone in. The driver took a sharp turn and she was thrown, face forward, into his lap. He hissed at the pain, but chuckled as she removed her face from his groin.

"Some bedside manner you got there."

She grinned. "Don't get used to it."

The small fridge contained a bottle of spring water and she used it to cleanse the wound. She sighed, relieved. "It's just a graze, deep, but not major."

"Good," he said and dropped his shoulders against the seat. "It didn't feel too serious."

"I should have known it was okay," she mumbled as she continued to clean the wound. "You vaulted that wall like you were going for the gold."

"Close enough." He grimaced as she blotted the worst of the blood away. "Did you get the download?"

"Yep, all of it. I heard you bang on the door and thought it was the all clear, or I would have waited for the stupid computer to finish shutting down. I should have just put a bullet in the thing and saved us the trouble." She removed the barely contained the Scarferator and tossed it on the seat. The Velcro strap worked well to secure the handkerchief over the wound.

"It would have been better if Salva didn't know." He cursed as the limo swung around a tight turn and he was thrown to the right.

Sara rocked backward, bracing herself against the seat and bit her lip in pain as her injuries scraped across the nylon fibers of the carpet.

"Are *you* all right?" Drake asked, raising his brows in concern. "Were you hurt?"

"Just a couple nicks and scrapes, nothing bad." She eased onto the seat and he leaned over, running his hand down her calf to lift her leg. Where her wounds had ignited on fire a moment before, they now throbbed with the delicious sensation of his hand gently touching her skin. She pulled her leg back. "I'm fine."

"There's some bad ones there," he whispered and grabbed the bottle of water. "Let me at least wash them off."

She didn't speak as the cooling liquid coursed from knee to toe. A pulse began to pound at her core–native drums in a sweltering jungle. She tingled, everywhere. A pleasure filled sigh escaped her and she clamped her lips closed. He took off his coat, stretching his shirt wonderfully taut against his chest and arms. With the silk cummerbund, he gently caressed the dirt from her legs.

Then he began to tear off her stockings. She thought she'd go through the roof when his hands brushed her thighs. Once, twice, three times was all she could stand and she shoved him away before he could damage the tenuous hold on her self-control. "Okay, that's good, thanks."

He lifted his head, his eyes dark and thoroughly *erotic* in the tiny space. If her heart thudded any louder, he'd be able to hear it. She swallowed hard, but couldn't drag her eyes away.

The limo stopped suddenly, throwing her forward and into his arms, exactly where she wanted to be, exactly where she couldn't be. He lowered his head, his breath warm and sweet against her face. She parted her lips, wetted them with the tip of her tongue. With a mental fist, she knocked the alarmed warning of her subconscious into oblivion.

God, she wanted him.

His hands were large and strong on her back, on her neck. She was dizzy from the stroking caress of his thumb on her nape. Her breasts warmed and she arched, against her will, to press them to his chest, wanting more. Oh, how she wanted more.

His eyes; she could drown in them, was drowning in them. Her gaze fell to his lips, the molded softness of them tantalized her. He groaned deep in his throat, a luscious, vibrating sound. His mouth covered hers gently, the press of flesh to flesh a shocking exhilaration. His tongue flicked against her sensitive lips, probing, gentle.

I'm in heaven.

He worked his mouth against hers, not entering, simply tasting, exploring. She opened her lips, inhaled his soft breath and it seemed as if his essence traveled to the junction of her thighs, settled in the moist heat generated by his caress, his kiss, and the drums pounded louder, heavier until she wanted to strip her clothes away and feel him against her.

The limo door opened and they both jerked back, startled. Chuck politely turned his head away, but the moment was broken. She shook everywhere, her body screaming for release from the pressure he'd built in her. Drake growled, a frustrated sound she totally agreed with.

I'm in hell.

Sara extracted herself from Drake's arms, feeling clumsy as she perched on the seat, and covered her face. The full consequences of the kiss stumbled around in her head like confused elephants. She refused to give them credence, couldn't give relevance to the damage caused by her lack of self-control. A kiss was nothing to get herself worked up about, damn it. Just a kiss. It wasn't as if it meant anything, *right?*

"I had no idea the airport was so damned close," Drake muttered, grabbed his coat, and left the limo.

Chuck, busy with transferring their baggage to the waiting

Jetstar, didn't look her way as she emerged, and she appreciated his consideration. She was a mess; her stockings torn away from mid-thigh down to her bare feet, her hair tangled and wild, and her entire body littered with cuts and scrapes. How she yearned to appear the polished debutante, but after the fiasco at the City, it was hopeless. In the brighter lights inside the plane, Drake would see her as she was and her confidence winked out like a candle in a tornado.

Drake wrapped his coat around her shoulders, a gentle reminder a line had been crossed. Both had declared very loudly the attraction between them could no longer be ignored. She would have to deal with it and decide once and for all to risk losing him for good, or to strive for greater control in the future. She disliked both options equally.

Sudden tears burned her eyes and she was grateful for the whipping wind, the loud hum of the Jetstar engines, and Drake's determined stride to the waiting plane. Her tears were foolish, nonsense *girly* idiocy. It was silly to be so distraught. It was downright ludicrous.

But she couldn't help feeling she'd just lost half her family.

CHAPTER SEVEN

They traveled in silence all the way home. Drake thought of broaching a subject, any subject, to break the dense tension between them. But every thought went where he couldn't go without invitation; Stark's feelings for him. Even sleep evaded him. Stark kept her nose buried in one magazine after another, but he could tell she didn't read a word; she rarely turned a page.

Once home, he showered, shaved, and stood on his balcony while he tried to decipher his own thoughts, his own feelings. Stark...Sara... he couldn't let her go. He couldn't forget the kiss and how wonderful she'd felt in his arms. How far would it have gone if they'd not been interrupted?

The moon, full and hazy, cast a surreal glow over the lawn and he imagined himself crossing that lush carpet of greenery to her bedroom doors. He imagined opening them, slipping beneath her sheets, and doing to her body what he fantasized about every waking moment.

He was aroused, and exhausted, and restless all at once. Dreaming of what could be in the future didn't make anything better in the present and he turned away from the window.

Fritz. The old man's wise face, care worn and comforting, came to mind and Drake left his room to see if the butler was prowling the kitchen as was his habit.

Drake found him in a robe and hand-sewn leather slippers, sitting at the large butcher-block island. The lights were off, save for the one over the stove. He hated to disturb such a peaceful setting, especially with what might be idiotic schoolboy jitters.

Fritz saw him and stood abruptly. "Is anything the matter, sir?"

"No, no." Drake waved for him to sit. "I can't sleep. Thought I'd see if you were awake."

Fritz remained standing. "Can I get you some tea, sir? A glass of warm milk?"

"I can tend to myself." Drake shook his head and chuckled. "Warm milk? When was the last time I drank that awful stuff?"

"I think you were about eight." Fritz smiled and sat, sipping his tea.

"Well, I'm definitely not eight anymore, and I've got a hell of a lot more to worry about than that soccer bully."

"Brad Farwell." Fritz supplied with a knowing grin. "How you worried over him."

"That boy was a menace." Drake dismissed the discussion with rueful shake of his head and poured himself iced tea. For a moment, he debated spilling his guts then and there, then decided he didn't need the humiliation. Careful questions would give him what he wanted. "Tell me, how are things with Stark?"

Fritz raised an eyebrow over the rim of his cup. "She's her usual self, sir."

"Does she...talk to you at all?" Drake settled in a stool across from Fritz.

Fritz shook his head. "She confides in no one."

Drake frowned, disliking the sound of that. "When I was away in London, did she date much? Make friends? That sort of thing?"

"No, sir, she worked very hard." Fritz gave him a meaningful weighty stare. "Are you thinking of changing things?"

Drake swirled the cubes in his glass. When his mother

died, he hadn't been certain which hurt worse; losing her, or seeing the effects of her death on his father. Without Elizabeth in his life, the Colonel wasn't the same. Yes, he was tough. Yes, he worked hard. Stark's arrival had brightened his eyes again, but Bruce Knight was never quite as invulnerable.

The Colonel didn't date and never considered remarrying. For him, Drake's mother was the only woman he would, and could, love. Drake found it increasingly worrisome that his father would spend the rest of his life alone, surrounded by big business, foreign hotshots, and a museum of a house.

Could he walk that same path? Could he love another so strongly that if she were to die, he'd die with her? Stark, she thrived on danger. It was all so impossible.

"Sir?" Fritz asked. When Drake lifted his gaze, the elderly man continued. "If I may be so bold, I think that as long as your intentions are honorable, and I have no doubt they are, what the future may bring will not change how you feel today. You can't throw away the possibility of happiness in order to avoid heartache."

Drake shook his head. Fritz made it sound simple, but it was more complex than that. *Wasn't it*? "I don't know what I'll do Fritz. Play it by ear, I guess."

"Sir," Fritz said, "If I were you, I'd make that young woman my own and hold tightly with both hands. She's your match."

"Bring the Jag around, would you Fritz?" Sara called as she entered the house, the Scarferator gripped in one hand. "Where's Drake?"

"Good morning, Miss. He's in his study." Fritz touched her elbow as he passed her. "I'm glad you returned safely."

She paused long enough to squeeze his hand and smile. "It's good to be back."

He nodded and left. Sara strode to the den and flung the door open without knocking. Drake, bent at the waist, in the middle of retrieving a paper from beneath his desk, thunked his head. He straightened and scowled at her. "Damn, Stark, can't you knock?"

"Good morning to you, too, Drake." She crossed the faded rug. Over the last few months she'd spent more and more time in this room, reminding her that Bruce would soon retire and Drake would become her boss. Which only added to the problems orbiting the memory of the kiss that shouldn't have been.

He rubbed the back of his head and looked as if he wanted to strengthen that memory. Her heart hammered. How fast he could make her react. She moved to the opposite side of the desk to place distance between them.

"Did you sleep well?" he asked.

No, I dreamed of you all night. "Yes, fine, and you?"

"Good," he mumbled and she sensed he lied as well.

"How's the leg?" she asked, hoping for a subject other than that sparking between them.

"A bit stiff, but otherwise I'm fine. How about your cuts? Are any of them deep?"

"Band-aids took care of the worst. Are you coming with me to run this data through the tech lab?" She waved the Scarferator.

"Yes."

A stack of messages on his desk offered her a new distraction from his dark, searching gaze. "Any interesting calls?"

"We've had a request for an assignment, but it can wait. The Colonel rang to see if we'd returned safely, but otherwise it's mostly junk."

She fell silent, struggling to avoid any mention of what had happened in the limo, but she couldn't think of anything besides how his hands felt against her bare back, or the way his mouth felt on her lips. The skin there yearned for a repeat performance. She frowned at the Scarferator.

"Sara," Drake whispered and when she met his eyes, the intensity of his stare made her aware of every molecule in her body. "What happened last night, between us, I mean, was–"

"–an accident. I'm sorry if I gave you the wrong impression." She lifted her chin to hide her confusion. She wanted him to believe her, yet hated that he might.

He frowned in consternation, as if he'd not expected her to apologize and appeared insulted she could dismiss him so quickly. "We really need to talk."

"No, not yet, not until after we get Acosta." She refused to look at him again and stared at the Scarferator. Yes, she thought, focus on the assignment, on the Intel. *Don't fool yourself.*

It suddenly seemed overwhelming; being in charge of such an important assignment, dealing with her need for Drake, and trying to honor her father's memory by being strong. She was trained to do exactly what the assignment called for, but she was also a living breathing person, not some superwoman who could take down the bad guy with a flick of her wrist.

But what was the alternative? To let someone with perhaps less experience, or less knowledge, less *heart* take over? Only she, with Drake's help, would never stop hunting for justice. She'd never give up. There was no going back.

There never was.

"Sara?" Drake had come around the desk and she hadn't noticed until she felt the heat of his body on her arm. "Are you going to be all right?"

She nodded and stepped away, the temptation to melt in his embrace too great. "Let's go see what's in this thing."

Before he might try hacking his way into her thoughts and perhaps coax a confession from her, she brushed past him and headed for the door.

The lab was sterile white, fully equipped, and strangely busy for a Saturday morning. His father must have ordered the entire tech lab to keep working. Drake held the door open for Stark and put his game face on.

She'd insisted on driving, and her performance behind the wheel kept him occupied with trying to breathe naturally as she maneuvered through traffic like a stockcar ace. Windblown tendrils framed her flushed cheeks and she smelled like sunshine as she dipped past him into the room.

Game face, Drake.

They followed the familiar path to Carlos's workstation. He stood over a busy printer beside the three computers cluttering the wide horseshoe counter top. He looked up as they approached.

"Hey, there y'all are. I was wondering when I'd see you." Carlos tore the paper from the printer. "Interesting things have been going on. The Colonel should be here shortly. He'll want to brief you on what we've discovered." His glance fell to the band-aids on Stark's bare arm. "Panama go okay?"

Stark nodded and handed him the Scarferator. "Worked like a charm."

"What's going on?" Drake gestured to the computers and the printout, impatient for the details.

"Let me show you." Carlos sat and swiveled to his computer. He clicked open multiple windows on the monitor. Pictures of several medallions flashed into view. Captions, in different languages, followed by an English translation, sprang up beneath each image.

"The medallion you recovered in Mexico is one of seven. The other six..." he paused and selected a picture, "are from different museums around the world. Like this one. It's from Moscow. Each of them was shipped via inter-museum exchanges to the Museum of Natural History in Mexico City."

Drake nodded. That was smart, he thought. The usual shipping routes would have been subjected to all sorts of foul-ups, not to mention the dismal delays of customs. "So, the nephew picked these up at the museum then?"

Carlos shook his head. "No. Mexico City has no record of receiving them. He got them in route."

"How'd the delivery go?" Stark asked. "Our team still on his tail?"

"They lost him." Carlos raised his hands in a gesture of helplessness. "What can I say? The guy's slippery and Mexico ain't exactly cooperative with American's posing as bounty hunters."

"What about the others," Drake said, nodding to the screen. "The other medallions?"

"There's only these that we know about."

"All six have already gone?" Stark asked, leaning over to peer closer at the monitor.

"Yes, the last shipment before the one you recovered was two months ago." Carlos rolled back, knitted his fingers behind his head, and grinned. "But that ain't the juicy part."

Drake raised his brows and glanced at Stark who remained cool looking and vibrant against the white fluorescent lighting. He wished he could feel as composed. To Carlos, he said, "Tell us what you found."

"It's better if you see for yourself," he said and stood.

Drake followed him, Stark at his side, and again he caught the scent of sun and *woman* coming from her. He exorcized that lustful demon from his mind and focused instead on the Cray supercomputer Carlos and his team used for more advanced work. Drake searched for and found the name of the man bent over his keyboard. Mark was one of their earlier recruits from MIT.

"What's this about?" Stark asked, arms crossed as she stared at the code on the screen.

"Wait." Carlos behaved like a kid on Christmas morning, bouncing on his heels and grinning. "Run the program, Mark."

The screen changed from an indecipherable log of code to a blown up photograph of the medallion.

Carlos began to narrate as the view zoomed in closer.

"We were afraid to use a standard x-ray to see if there was more in the metals, so we used a computerized microscopic program Mark and I developed." He paused, pointing at the screen as the shot went deeper. Green jagged scales faded to reveal a minuscule red line.

"We found this vein, here. It runs through the entire shape of the medallion. Go ahead Mark, put the rest through. When we followed it and removed the top layer of brass," Carlos beamed with delight, "we found this!"

Drake sucked in a breath. The tiny square was unmistakable. "A computer chip?"

Stark straightened, excited. "What's on the chip?"

"In," Carlos corrected, grinning at the chance to pick on her English. "In the chip."

She waved her hand at him. "Don't bust my chops, Carlos. Tell us what you found."

Carlos led them to a bulletin board covered in sheets of printed paper. "That's the tricky part. We're not exactly sure what we found. After some finessing, I was able to get the content in a readable format. I'm hoping the Scarferator will give us a program to run this code through."

"Do you have any ideas?" Stark asked.

Drake frowned at the list of numbers, the balance of characters to code, the arrangement of data on the paper. Bells rang in his head. "It looks almost like NASA code."

Carlos nodded. "That's what we thought at first, but it's not precisely the same. NASA code is complex, but this has anomalies we can't decipher. That's why the Colonel's on his way here."

"I'm already here."

Drake turned with the others to greet the man behind them. His father appeared tired. Not a good sign. He would have to think carefully about moving up their plan for his retirement. Though he loathed to see the day come when the proud man stepped down, he wouldn't risk his father's health.

Stark kissed his cheek. "It's good to see you."

Drake stifled a sudden burst of illogical jealousy. God, he was turning into a lunatic.

The Colonel smiled, a soft caring expression that didn't touch the stern lines of his face. "You both did well in Panama."

Drake scoffed. "I could have controlled it better." He waved to the board. "Have you seen this already?"

Bruce nodded. "In flight. You gave him the device?"

"Yes." Stark turned to Carlos. "How long do you think it will take to run the data?"

"About an hour to bring it up, but much longer to study it completely." Carlos shrugged. "I have some idea what we're looking for, based on what we know already. Two, three hours and I should have an initial report for you."

"Good. Make it two." Drake clapped the man on the shoulder. "Why don't you get started?"

"Had lunch yet?" Stark asked the Colonel and when he shook his head, she smiled. "I'm starving. Let's eat and then come back."

The Colonel nodded. "It's a plan."

"Sounds good." Drake would grill him until he found out if he was pushing himself too hard. "You have my cell number Carlos?"

"Yes, I'll call right away if anything comes up."

They left Carlos to his work and rode the elevator down. Outside, the sun hot against his skin, Drake watched his father walk arm and arm with Sara to the car.

The easy comfortable friendship they shared, based on mutual respect, made him wonder what he was doing. Sara was like a sister, without that secured relationship with her, he risked destroying their bond forever. Did he really want to pursue more and risk everything?

Hell, yes.

"Drake?" Stark stared at him from the front of the Jag.

"*Hmm*?" he asked, understanding he'd missed what she'd said.

She raised an amused brow. "I asked if you'd like to go to Irma's?"

"Oh, yes, sure, great, Tex Mex, perfect." He sounded like an idiot.

"Drake, are you all right?" His father frowned and put a hand on his shoulder. "Something on your mind?"

Drake wanted to say yes, to pull his father aside, and confide all to the man. Though he usually turned to Fritz for a sounding board because he was more available, Drake generally felt more comfortable making an ass of himself in front of his father. "No. I'm fine. Let's eat."

With a wicked grin aimed at Drake, Sara slid into the driver's seat. Her look dared him to protest so she could tease him about his fear of her driving ability. He didn't have the heart to confess his amusement at her antics behind the wheel, though he admitted she took risks he wouldn't. But, with the Colonel in the passenger seat and he in the back, it was his father who'd have the brunt of the ride.

"Go easy, Stark," Drake drawled as he folded himself into the back seat. "Dad's ticker ain't what it used to be."

"My ticker's just fine, thank you son." Bruce sounded disgruntled.

"Maybe *now* it is." She grinned, slid her sunglasses on, and revved the motor.

Rubber squealed as she yanked the vehicle into traffic, shifting at the last possible second in order to get a full growl from the engine. Horns honked, but she only chuckled and continued swerving around cars at breakneck speed.

Drake had a good view of his father's hunched shoulders. With Stark behind the wheel, he was safe. Not many could unsettle his father and it was moments like these, he absolutely loved her.

It was amazing what sunshine and a good meal could do for one's spirit, Sara thought as she wiped her mouth with a cloth napkin and leaned back in the chair. They sat in a private area reserved for meetings and small parties. Through the meal, talk had been mostly about the chaos and ineptitude of some who worked in airports, hotels, and the travel industry in general. Each had their own experiences with lost luggage, directionless taxi drivers, and customs agents who thought they were God.

Coffee had been poured all around and the mood turned serious. It was time to discuss what had happened in Panama and what Bruce had discovered at DoD.

Bruce stirred sugar into his black coffee and sipped the steaming liquid. "General Kray doesn't have any new information."

"No? Isn't that odd?" Drake leaned back in his chair, the front legs popping off the ground as he stretched his injured calf. Sara wondered if it bothered him more than he let on. "Are they still investigating Acosta?"

Sara agreed. "Shouldn't they have at least some knowledge about where he is by now? I mean, if we can read the license plate off a car in Timbuktu, how hard can it be to find one man?"

Bruce said, "I don't know. But you're both correct. He should have had something to tell me. My only guess is that there's more here than I understand. I had the sense, when I spoke with him, that he's holding back, something the brass wants kept quiet."

"That doesn't make sense." Sara ran a hand over the back of her neck and leaned forward, elbows on the table. "Didn't they ask you to investigate? Why would they keep intel from you?"

"I don't know," Bruce said again, his voice dropping low as he pondered the question. "I'll get to the bottom of it though. Kray said I was on a need to know basis, the usual macho blather from someone who's lost his authority."

Drake asked, "What do you mean?"

"I mean that Kray was pulled from active duty." He waved the topic off as unimportant. "They're nervous about Acosta, but it's a peripheral threat. They think he's nothing more than a lone man with a few screws loose. Dangerous, but not worrisome enough to take official military action."

"So Kray's pissed that he's been given this assignment?" Sara asked, unable to dismiss Drake's question as easily as Bruce. Something wasn't right. She thought of Noriega and wasn't sure why. "What did Kray have to do with Operation Just Cause?"

Bruce gave her an appraising look. "Very good, Stark. I should have guessed you'd put that together. Operation Just Cause was Kray's albatross. He...disobeyed orders to save the lives of civilians. I believe he should have received a commendation, but instead, he was quietly made unimportant."

"Is there a possibility he's withholding information because he wants to sabotage us?" Drake asked.

She kept her attention riveted on Bruce and caught a fleeting glimpse of deep concern. The break from his usual commanding confidence worried her. A glance to Drake, and she saw he'd caught the Colonel's look too.

Her gaze dropped to Drake's mouth of it's own volition. The memory of the limo made her wet her lips. Drake flicked his eyes her way and his expression darkened. She felt the heat of that look pass beneath her clothes and touch parts of her that had no right to be awake during this conversation.

"No," Bruce said adamantly, snapping her back to the task. She straightened, ashamed by her lapse. "Kray has been my friend for years. I know him too well. There's nothing he wouldn't do for his country. He cares as much for the American people as he does for the system that protects them. He wouldn't deliberately do anything to jeopardize this assignment. If he knows something, he has a damned good reason for not telling me.

"Or," he broke off in thought, "perhaps information's being withheld from *him* and he hasn't found out why, or what, yet. When he does, I'm sure I'll be the first to know what he discovers."

Sara relaxed a bit, but her trust in Bruce did not extend to Kray and she wanted to see this man in person, to gauge for herself if he dealt with them honestly. It was a moot point now, however. To go behind Bruce's back was not an option, nor, did she believe that it would be fruitful. Kray was inaccessible as long as Bruce remained his contact.

"Did you find out anything at all?" Drake asked. His tone mirrored her frustration.

"I did discover that Dr. Yusoff, a top Russian engineer, has disappeared. He and Acosta were tight *before* Operation Just Cause. Yusoff never returned from a six-month stint in the Antarctic." Bruce drank more coffee, as if the very word had chilled him. "This, and what Carlos uncovered about the origins of the medallions proves Acosta's plan is global."

Sara stared at the reflected light in the spoon on the table. "Global." The word frightened her deeply and again doubts wormed its way beneath her skin. Could they handle such a monstrous assignment? "Colonel, do you think we need help with this? I mean, can Drake and I cover this alone?"

He nodded. "I believe so. David defeated Goliath alone and you have each other. I believe our success lies in appearing uninterested in Acosta's plans. A show of force would drive him further underground."

"And Salva?" Sara wished she had done more in Panama to ensure the doctor's silence. "Will he warn Acosta?"

Drake shrugged. "Most likely, but what will he tell him? That two guests at a party managed to look at his computer? He can't know why we downloaded his files. He may not even know that we had the password and gained access."

"That's true," Stark said with relief. *Chupacabra,* a myth, like them, just an urban legend.

"Yes," Bruce continued. "Salva doesn't know who you are either. He might believe that you're rivals who wanted only to steal his inventions. Acosta is an arrogant man. He won't believe that two people, no matter how skilled, could take him down."

"How do you know?" Sara wanted to believe him.

"Acosta surfaced to attend a lecture, of all things, and he got away with it. That takes balls." Bruce grinned. "And it's our job to neuter him."

Sara chuckled. "Never quite thought of myself in those terms. 'Castrator for Hire'."

Drake winced and hissed between his teeth. They all laughed, but the Colonel's robust chuckle was an especially welcome sound.

"Speaking of snipping the hairy round ones." Drake delivered the image with a crooked grin, "how are things going with our gigolo Senator? Were you able to stop his emergency meeting?"

Bruce shook his head. "No, but that's all right. I called in a few favors and they trounced him. Halley's not the sort to give up easily though and I'm going to have to keep an eye on him."

Sara sipped her coffee, discovered it was cold, and set it down with a grimace. "Well, at least he'll lose public opinion points with the scandal and all. Should make your job easier."

"You'd think so." Bruce shrugged, a far away look on his face. "But that's not the impression I had when I saw him last. He seemed even more determined to shove this thing through."

"What is it, exactly, he's proposing?" Sara didn't understand why it was such a big deal to upgrade electrical equipment–aside from the cost factor. But that in itself didn't seem enough to gain this much opposition from Bruce.

Drake rolled his shoulders, leaning back in his chair. "Halley's interested in implementing the TEMPEST program on a civilian level. Before you ask," he held up a hand and offered another of his charming grins, "the TEMPEST program is a security measure to insulate computers and such from outside interference–hackers, that sort of thing."

"It's not what he's proposing," Bruce interjected, "it's that he really has no interest in implementing the security measures, it's all a financial chess game."

Sara nodded to show she understood. Halley wanted his cash cow to be milked exclusively.

"I'm fairly certain we'll be able to stop him. Now that we've intercepted his emergency meeting, our opposition is public. Others will follow our lead." Bruce pulled his wallet out. "It's under control. Things might have gotten spotty in Panama, but we're on mission. I think we can safely move forward with the rest of the plan and bring this thing to an end."

His confidence was inspiring and Sara said, "Let's go see what Carlos dug up."

CHAPTER EIGHT

Drake leaned against the table, arms crossed as he waited patiently for Carlos to finish typing in a series of commands. Stark, restless, paced the lab behind him, while the Colonel remained as stoic as a bronzed statue. They'd been back for a half an hour, watching Carlos work feverishly.

Carlos jabbed the enter key and stared at the screen. The sudden silence after the clacking keys was forbidding. He exhaled and rolled back from the desk. "*Dios mio...*"

Drake turned at once and Stark and his father joined him at the computer. It looked as if someone had punctured Carlos and left him a deflated mess in the chair. Drake's instincts revved into full alert. "What is it?"

"This." Carlos pointed to the bottom of the screen.

Drake swallowed hard. He couldn't believe what he saw. "Is that what I think it is?"

Carlos and Bruce nodded together.

"Will someone tell me what's going on?" Stark sounded frustrated and frightened.

He couldn't blame her, she obviously sensed their shock, but he didn't know where to begin.

Bruce cleared his throat. "The intel in the device, matched with the chip from the medallion, show partial satellite uplink codes."

"For a nuclear warhead," Carlos finished.

The following silence cocooned them in a menacing chrysalis of mortal threat. Stark gripped her elbows, hands flexing compulsively. If Drake thought she'd welcome it, he would wrap her in his arms and pull her close.

Bruce leaned to the screen, touching a series of code as if the digital data were brail. "A U.S. Nuclear warhead."

"One of ours?" Stark asked, disbelief in her tone.

"Yes," Drake answered and turned to Carlos. "What else?"

"This," he pushed a button, "a partial, but very detailed map of the mining system and underground caves in Mexico, and a topical graph of the Pico de Orizaba mountain range."

Stark breathed beside him. "He's planning to launch a nuclear bomb? Where is it targeted?"

"We don't know if he is actually planning a launch." Carlos shook his head. "The data's incomplete. But I'm running a program from the Scarferator that should give us more details. Right now, there are no coordinates, which means he might be interested in stealing the bomb, rather than detonating it. It'll take time to find out for sure, there's so much information here."

Stark released his arm. "I don't get it. Why all the scientists? Why the elaborate exchange of the medallions? Why does he need the code if he's only going to sell the damned thing?"

"The scientists," Bruce began, "are all familiar with nuclear energy, satellite systems and the language that supports them. If he's found our launching codes, it will raise the price of the bomb. Essentially, he'll be giving our enemies not only the means, but the technology, to turn our own defenses against us."

Drake scowled at the screen. "DoD didn't know? They have no idea that this is happening?"

Bruce shook his head. "They likely know, but whatever Acosta is doing, they must believe it's impossible. There's a standard protocol to launching a nuclear weapon that can't be duplicated, or falsified, by any hacker."

"He must have figured out something," Stark said. "This is too elaborate, too *planned.*"

Drake agreed. "The threat is real. We need to know where he's going with this. Carlos, you think there's enough there to uncover who Acosta might be working with? A possible buyer, or partner?"

"I think so. There are a few personal files that I haven't looked into yet. They could contain names." Carlos pulled his chair closer to the computer. His hands visibly shook as he began typing. "But it's going to take time."

"Work fast, but do it right," Bruce ordered. "We need to know as soon as possible. Dismiss the rest of the team except for those you absolutely need. The fewer who know about this, the better."

"Right away." Carlos picked up the phone and the speaker system in the ceiling crackled.

As he ordered those in the low-clearance teams to finish and depart for the day, Drake looked at his father. Worry etched the Colonel's features into a road map of crevices, indicating how dire the consequences would be should they fail.

He and Stark could make no mistakes. If things went bad, it could be the lives of many, and perhaps, life as they now knew it. A bomb, detonated in any major city, would kill millions, if not hundreds of millions, and stop commerce, perhaps shut the entire country down. The chain-reaction would be devastating.

Stark looked pale, her green eyes a shot of color against the alabaster of her skin. Her voice cracked when she spoke. "Drake..."

She didn't finish, but he understood her. It was up to them and quite literally they had the weight of the world on their shoulders. To Carlos, he said, "When can we expect the information?"

"Later tonight, maybe early tomorrow," he mumbled,

distracted. The screen flickered constantly as he worked through the massive data released from the guts of the Scarferator and the chip. "I'll work through the night if I have to."

Bruce nodded. "Call us as soon as you know more."

Drake led the others out, each of them silent, trapped in their thoughts. They joined the throng heading for the elevators; men and women who worked for Knight, Inc. Blondes, redheads, brunettes, young, old, thin and round. They were Americans, each and every one. They had children, spouses, and parents. They went to homes furnished with the income Knight, Inc. afforded them. They were his responsibility, and now, hundreds of millions had been added to that list, each one just as important, just as valuable.

Stark stared at the unsuspecting men and women and he saw the disbelief, the concern and heartbreak on her features. Like him, she recognized what these people represented; a smidgen of those who needed their protection, who needed them to solve the riddle and stop a madman, either Acosta or his buyer, from destroying their country and murdering those they loved. Drake wrapped an arm around her shoulder as they rode down in the elevator. She did not shrug him off.

Sara swam for the opposite end of the Olympic sized pool. By the tenth lap, she was winded. It was difficult to sustain physical activity when your insides felt coated with steel shards. She reached the end, dipped backward to pull her hair back from her face, and lay her forehead against the cool tiled curb of the pool.

Aside from the gentle lapping of the water and the delicate sounds from the plate-glass waterfall in the corner, the room was silent.

This can't be happening.

It was like a bad episode of the Twilight Zone that she couldn't escape. Salva, Acosta, all those scientists. There was more going on than just a simple nuclear sale. There had to be.

What does he have planned that he'd risk snatching, or luring, those scientists into his fold? She closed her eyes, blocking out the blue and white Italian design. *Think Stark! What is he up to?*

But her mind yielded nothing, not even the distant glimmer of an elusive theory. Angered by her inability to find an answer, she pulled herself from the pool and wrapped the plush white towel around her.

The Houston skyline, lit by the setting sun, shimmered through the back windows of the indoor pool. A haze hung about the buildings and it didn't take much for her imagination to change those structures into broken fingers of concrete reaching for the sky in a lake of fire. She shuddered the vision away and prayed it was not prophetic.

Normally, a good swim relieved the tension in her shoulders, but not today. She decided to relax in the sauna and let the heat work on her muscles.

She padded barefoot to the wide wooden door. It opened outward, rather than in, to avoid the central pit of rocks. She slipped her swimsuit off beneath the towel and kicked it onto a low bench. The chlorine in the fabric would mingle with the steam and work against the relaxing scent of the rose stones. The towel firmly tucked in place, she went inside.

Golden wood surrounded her and replaced the awful image of destruction with the illusion of a dimly lit cabin. The heated stones in the central pit appeared deceptively cool, their gray surfaces universally round. She tossed three of the rose stones from the basket near the door onto the heap and ladled water over the mound.

Steam hissed, releasing the healing, floral scent. Sara settled with her back to the wall and waited for the heat to do its work. Head back, eyes closed, she drifted as the taut muscles in her body began to unwind. As usual, when her thoughts were banned from work, they settled on Drake.

She wondered what her father would have thought of him. Would he have approved? The similarities between the men were obvious, but so were the differences.

She recalled sunny afternoons at a park on some long forgotten government facility. She recalled soldiers at her birthday parties and the nannies her father hired to watch after her, each one as wonderful and caring as the last had been. His choices obviously made after careful consideration.

Drake insisted she have the best of everything as well; trainers, equipment, everything a girl could want. He exhibited the same loyalty and care as her father had in seeing to all her needs, being both father and mother to his lonely daughter.

She used the edge of the towel to wipe the dampness from her face. Where Drake and her father differed the most was in their appetites for women. Her father had enjoyed the company of women, but not on the scale Drake did. At eight, she would have been kept from knowing her father's social agenda, but had he been as energetic in such pursuits as Drake, she would have known. Drake didn't have an unsatiated bone in his body.

After Houston's nightmare version of foster care, she'd come to understand much about the relationships between men and women, most of it unhealthy. When Bruce brought her home, she'd watched in fascination the string of polished socialites who appeared constantly at the dinner table.

Drake left for college soon after and returned only for holidays. Once he graduated, she'd expected him to stay at the estate, but he'd gone on to London, repeating the same ritual of visiting only for special occasions. She'd been so envious–filled with silly girl notions of country-hopping freedom.

Then suddenly he was home, and the women were too. In hindsight, she understood the envy had turned to jealousy. Those women took him away from her, stole his time, and oversaw every moment he wasn't at work.

She frowned. In the last six or so months, Drake hadn't

dated much at all, and in the last three, she couldn't recall one woman who dined at their table as his guest. The part of her that believed in the tooth fairy when she was a child, hoped his lack of female companionship meant his interest had centered on her. The grown woman in her, laughed cynically at such nonsense.

All this conjecture was pointless. In the end, Drake would leave her, everyone did. Sara wasn't meant to have a *happily ever after* in her life, history had proven that. But if she were fated to live alone, wouldn't she rather have the memory of being in Drake's arms, in his bed, to keep her warm in the cold nights of her future?

If she grew to love him, to make her heart vulnerable by depending on the return of that love, and then that bond was broken, would the heartache color those memories too painful to live with?

Frustrated by not finding satisfactory conclusions to either of her dilemmas, Sara straightened and ladled more water on the stones. The sibilant steam pressed her back onto the bench, but she wasn't relaxing. How she hated this feeling; the silt of memory and fear of the future all churned together until she felt muddy inside. There wasn't a soul to talk to.

She couldn't go to Bruce, didn't know how to broach the topic of his son without looking foolish. Fritz was kind, but he was still a man, and she knew he was loyal to Drake. Drake himself was out of the question. Every time she came near the man her brain turned to oatmeal.

Stumped, her thoughts and anger turned to Acosta. Drake may be dangerous to her sense of emotional well-being, but he made an excellent security measure against physical harm. He wouldn't let Acosta hide in the dark like a rodent waiting to strike–he would hunt the vermin down and exterminate him. She would be there to see the bastard get what he deserved.

A thud sounded loudly from somewhere nearby. Drake must have finally hired the men to repair the damaged wing.

One of their live-round exercises had demolished most of the decrepit furnishings in the unused portion of the house. Another loud bang thundered beyond the door. That wasn't any repairman busy at work. That was a gunshot!

Startled she ran to the slim window in the door and peered out. Whoever had fired a gun was close, very close. Was Drake practicing target shots beyond the windows of the pool?

A flash of black on the opposite end of the room doubled the pace of her heartbeat. Drake wouldn't be dashing about the estate dressed in black.

Her mind raced. The pool was vulnerable; they'd always known that, it had too many windows, too many access doors to the outside. They'd placed a guard shack near the back, extra security cameras in the vicinity, but if someone with experience wanted to get in, they could circumvent those security measures.

She twisted to hide herself while trying to find the dark clad figure. Face pressed against the wood, she spotted him rushing toward her. She gripped the doorknob, removed her hand, wiped her sweaty palm on the towel, and gripped the knob again. The thud of his footsteps placed him along the narrow walkway between pool and sauna.

She twisted the knob silently and held her breath. A face, long and strange to her, loomed for a fraction of a second in the window. He'd seen her, but that didn't matter. She opened the door hard and fast. The wood snapped against the stranger's face and he went down, stunned, but conscious. She followed with an obliterating stomp on his windpipe. He immediately rolled, grabbing his neck, gurgling and wheezing as he fought for air.

Unarmed, bare beneath her towel, Sara looked for another threat. Icy air attacked her sauna heated skin, raising gooseflesh on her arms and legs. He'd come in alone, but a man dressed for stealth, carrying an automatic weapon, didn't usually travel alone.

She yanked the gun from his shoulder and swung it like a Louisville Slugger. It connected with the bulbous nose beneath his one long eyebrow and he lost consciousness. A walkie-talkie strapped to his belt confirmed he had comrades. She took it from him, flicked it on, and waited. Nothing.

The towel slipped a bit and she tucked the end more securely. She felt exposed, her body unprotected from assault or sight, but she couldn't bother with that now. She set the walkie-talkie on a bench, grabbed the bleeding man's feet, dragged him into the sauna, and backed out. With the automatic–which was ready to fire–firmly in her hands and the door closed between her and the infiltrator, she felt better.

What to do? Should she sound the alarm? Or call Drake and Palmer, the head of security, quietly so as not to alert the bleeding man's buddies? She felt the rush of time, the seconds flying rapidly away. She decided to call Drake and see if the security cameras showed any other breaches. Perhaps the man in the sauna was merely recon.

She picked up the walkie-talkie. Three steps toward the in-house intercom, the glass wall opposite the pool exploded inward. Glass rained into the pool and onto the far walkway.

Sara changed directions and headed for the alcove behind the waterfall. The estate was under attack. She should never have hesitated. Chips of tile whistled past her head as automatic fire ripped the wall behind her to shreds. She slapped the security button and alarms, blissful, grating sirens, erupted all over the house and the grounds. She cursed as she turned and depressed the trigger on the borrowed gun.

Short bursts, she reminded herself, though her instincts wanted to hold that trigger down until the enemy, a horde of men dressed alike in Kevlar vests and black padded assault uniforms, lay sprawled in a lake of red chlorine. They rushed through the opened wall, moving in a well orchestrated formation. Whoever these men were, they were highly trained.

In spurts of no longer than one second, she was able to

send them scrambling for coverage. Automatic weapons were difficult to handle and were not her favorite. After the initial rounds, they tended to arc high, wasting ammunition as it punched into ceilings and walls. The east wing was evidence of that.

Her feet slapped the wet tile as she raced for the opposite end of the room. That door led to the hall, which led to the armory. There she could find clothes and equip herself for the invasion. One more burst from the weapon would be her last, she knew, before the men hiding behind the wide columns would fire from their cover.

As bullets erupted from their weapons, she slipped–an action that likely saved her life. The floor was still wet from where she'd emerged from the pool. She slid six feet over the tiles, turning the gun toward the enemy, spraying them in a sustained round as she went. From the floor, she could afford the high arc of the weapon.

Her slide ended three feet from the door and she scrambled, one hand holding her towel in place, the other laying down more cover fire to get her safely into the hall. The waterfall became a slide of broken glass as enemy fire laid it to waste. Her gun emptied, became a liability, and she threw it away as she dove through the door.

The incessant wail of the alarm siren was a good sign. Those left in the house knew the threat to be real, not just another drill, but the noise drove her crazy, fueling the adrenalin already slamming into her system. She raced for the end of the corridor and the armory. A door midway down the hall opened.

A man charged through, but hesitated as if startled to see a half-naked, wet woman in a towel hurtling toward him. She didn't give him a chance to recover his wits, kicking his legs out from beneath him. Desperate to keep her towel in place and save her own neck, she attacked him with a viciousness that allowed no room for retaliation.

A quick downward thrust broke the bone in his nose and blinded him with an automatic rush of tears and pain. Another punch to his windpipe cut off his ability to breathe, but unfortunately, not his ability to kick.

She grunted as his booted foot caught her in the belly and threw her back. Her own breath stolen by the thrust, she wondered again who the hell they were. The man was nearly blind, couldn't breathe, but his boot had found her solar plexus–they were too damned well trained.

Curled on her side, ribs throbbing, she forced oxygen-deprived limbs to move, to get up, and drag her to safety. The door at the end of the hall opened and the men she'd fended off by the pool filled the corridor. Sara staggered against the wall, trying to make herself a small target as she moved backward and closer to the fallen man.

Had he stayed were he was, she might have died, but he'd recovered sufficiently, quicker than she would have thought, and he was angry.

"Bitch broke my nose!" He hollered and grabbed a fistful of her hair, yanking her head back, unknowingly saving her from enemy fire–they would not shoot while he stood so close.

"My pleasure." She ignored the pain and clutched the towel tighter.

He snarled, teeth orange with the blood flowing copiously from his nose and raised a brutish fist.

Sara recognized a bully, a man who undoubtedly got his kicks from beating women and drunkards on a regular basis. The look was unmistakable and foster care had taught her well. She ducked the fist, drove her hand into his groin, and twisted with all her might.

His eyes opened wide with surprise and a girlish scream burst from his lips. She yanked the revolver strapped to his hip from its holster and threw an arm around his neck. She placed the muzzle of the Magnum against his head.

"Get back!" She shouted to the staring men. They didn't

listen, but continued creeping closer. The bully started to tug on her arm, as if he would flip her, and she cocked the hammer back on the gun. "Don't."

He stilled immediately, and thankfully. Her towel was slipping and she didn't like the idea of getting covered in his blood, but he'd leave her no choice if he pushed it. Closer to the door, she was nearly to the armory now.

Once she went through, she could slap the emergency panel and steel doors would slam in place, locking her inside a safe room that could only be opened from the inside.

Using the bully as a shield, she inched her way closer. The alarm finally died, someone had shut it off from central command. She only prayed it was Drake or Bruce, not one of these men. How she wanted to question them, find out who they were, who'd sent them.

They were Americans, full-blooded red-white-and-blue men with military training. Where the hell had Acosta found these guys? There was only one reason they were here; they thought the computer chip had been hidden somewhere on the estate.

The door hit her back and she smiled. The men kept their weapons trained on her as they matched her pace. The hall, lit only by two long fluorescent lights, boasted no outside windows. It was her only chance.

In rapid succession she fired, not at the men, but at the ceiling. They were plunged into darkness. The bully turned on her as she dropped to her knees, certain that with the lights out, the men would fire. A fist caught the side of her head, but in the dark, he'd missed his true mark and the blow was glancing.

Before he could register what had happened, she'd gotten the armory door open and his comrades opened fire, missing their target and taking down one of their own in the blackness. Apparently, bullies didn't inspire much loyalty.

CHAPTER NINE

Sirens rang again, reactivated by the security door. Steel panels slid closed and lights popped on over the large garage-like room. Sara rested her bare back against the steel doors, breathing hard. She set the Magnum aside, disliking the feel of a dead man's gun in her hand.

Half her towel was wedged outside the door, half inside. Naked, and uncomfortable, she needed to find something to wear and a headset to see if she could raise Drake. Protocol dictated he find one of the others placed about the property. If Drake hadn't, it meant he was in trouble.

Hopefully, the men entered only through the poolroom, and nowhere else on the estate. Dimly, she heard the pop of bullets hitting the steel door and grinned. They couldn't get through that and as long as they were occupied with a futile effort, they weren't elsewhere hurting her family.

On her feet, she first switched the mind-numbing siren off, then searched through the duffle bag Drake had left after their last exercise. Sara found a pair of his workout shorts, a towel, and sunglasses. Why did the man have to go shirtless for every exercise? The drawstring, pulled tight, held the shorts up.

She cast around for something else that might contain clothing and went to the heavy steel cabinet full of weapons and equipment. Inside, she found a headset and put it on. Immediately she heard Drake.

"Stark! You there? Answer me!" he whispered, fierce with concern.

"I'm here," she said. "I'm in the armory. Where are you?"

He inhaled at the sound of her voice, but didn't answer right away. Seconds passed, and if she hadn't been able to hear his breathing in the quiet room, she would have been concerned. "I'm nearing the kitchen. Are you hurt?"

"No, you?" She rummaged through the drawers and held up a roll of black electricians tape. Makeshift bra? She shook her head and threw it back in the drawer.

"I'm all right." He was moving now, his footfalls vibrated in his voice. "Have you seen my father?"

"No." Where had he been when she'd gone for a swim? She paused, hands hovering over the bulletproof vest hanging beside a pair of infrared goggles. Then she remembered. "He was in the library, doing research, but he asked if I wanted to go for a ride. He could be in the stables."

Again, silence.

"Drake?"

He shushed her and her heart lurched. He was in danger. She couldn't hide in here anymore. She threw the vest over her head and strapped it in place. It covered the front of her breasts, but not the sides.

So much for modesty.

"Drake," she whispered into the mike. "I'm coming to you."

Shouts, not Drakes, came through the headset. She pictured the kitchen and where Drake might hide. A standing freezer, complete with high-polished steel doors, stood between the pantry and the wall, leaving a one-foot space. She pictured him pressed deep into that shadowy gap.

"Are you armed?" She belted on shoulder holsters, snugged two Rugers into them, and picked up Drake's P239 Sig Sauer.

"Yeah, though I'm almost out," Drake finally replied. "But don't come here, I'm on my way to you."

She nodded, as if he could see her and scowled. *Focus,*

Sara, focus! "Good–use the north door, the south is occupied."

"Will do," he whispered, "I'm going silent, keep trying to raise my father."

"I will," Sara promised and the headset went dead as Drake shut his off. She worked quickly, strapping holsters to her thighs and filling them each with the sleek stainless steel slide-action 9mm's she used for intense combat drills.

What else? Two sets of Hellstorm tactical gloves to save her knuckles and give Drake protection, and the night-goggles. She couldn't be certain how long she'd been in the room, hadn't bothered to check the time, but the sun was setting before she went into the sauna and it would be dark by now.

Fully armed, she went to the monitors set against the interior wall, and flicked them on. Her heart sank. Men crawled all over the house. She counted fifteen before she gave up. They hunted, clearly intent on finding them, if not the computer chip, or maybe the Scarferator. Two ransacked Drake's study, another three tore through the empty library. Where the hell was Bruce?

"Colonel. Bruce. Are you there?" She played with the outside camera controls. The direct link from the stable wasn't available in this room, but two high-mounted security cameras on the back path offered a fairly good view of the structure. She panned left and right. No sign of him, or the enemy. Knight, Inc. guards crept close to the house, but hung back as they'd been trained to do, waiting for the invaders to be captured by surprise on retreat.

Perhaps Bruce hid inside the stable, or was riding on the grounds. She turned rapidly from the screens and went to another cabinet. Inside she found a pair of soft boots meant for scaling rock faces. Not much protection, but better than bare feet. She put them on.

"Bruce. Answer me." Again and again she tried to raise him, almost without thought, and with rising concern.

Another check of the monitors showed Drake on the run,

alone, and three rooms away. Though his pursuers weren't visible, the enemy occupied a room Drake would need to pass through. She wished he'd turn the headset on so she could warn him. But then, she might distract him at the wrong moment, or worse, cover any sounds someone sneaking up behind him would make.

She held her breath, stifling the need to shout uselessly at the monitor. Her stomach rolled, and she touched the screen, gently tracing a finger down his vulnerable back. Strong, handsome and smart, didn't make Drake bulletproof.

He pressed his ear to the door like a firefighter might feel for heat. He backed away and she exhaled. The cocky men inside the room didn't bother with something as basic as tactical silence.

Drake turned the doorknob and she watched both screens breathlessly. The camera inside the room didn't quite show the door, but on Drake's screen, he opened it a mere half inch. The invaders didn't notice. Drake raised his gun and kicked the door wide, not hard enough it would fly back and close, but quick enough to startle the occupants.

He fell, as they'd both been trained to do, and shot from a crouching position. The men dropped like knickknacks in an earthquake. Sara grinned with a silent cheer. Two more rooms and Drake would be there.

An industrial garage door built into the wall at the back opened onto the side lawn. Made of rippled steel, the door slid back against the ceiling. She removed the tarps from the two Kawasaki's she and Drake would use to escape and hopefully, find Bruce. The keys dangled from the ignition, just the way they'd left them. The rattle of the door retracting was exceedingly loud and she couldn't risk alerting the attackers until the last minute.

Annoying tendrils of nearly dry hair fell into her face. She couldn't afford the hindrance and went back to the climbing cabinet. From the second pair of boots she pulled a shoelace free and used it to knot her hair back.

The distant thunder of gunfire rumbled through the north door and she raced back to the monitors. Almost to the room, Drake ran flat out, men clearly on his tail. She rushed to the door, thrumming with adrenalin while she watched the screen, hand poised over the switch. Drake fired, turning sideways to shoot behind him. She heard it clearly now.

A second before he reached her, she flicked the switch and the steel panel slid up silently. He rushed inside and she sent the door on its swift downward glide. Alarms clanged around them again. The noise dissolved to a minimal drone in the haze of her relief. Drake's stare fell to hers.

Sweat trickled down his face and dampened the locks on his forehead. His eyes, dark and fearsome, still in battle-mode, drank her in. Why hadn't she ever noticed how tall he was before? His shoulders blocked the monitors and cast her in shadow.

Before she could think, before she could tell herself not to, that this wasn't the time, she threw herself into his arms. They opened at the same moment and he caught her. She buried her face into his shirt. He'd lived; he'd fought his way to her, and she felt something give inside, a wall crumble, a fear die.

He was hers, she couldn't hide from it, could no longer deny it. She didn't care if he went through women the way a kid went through chocolate. None of that mattered anymore.

Drake's hand wound through her hair, cradling the back of her skull. The heat of one arm pressed against the exposed side of her breast. His barely-there stubble rubbed lusciously against the bare skin of her jaw and neck as he bent his head.

His lips touched her ear, her cheek, and his mouth slanted over hers, capturing her, devouring her soul. He pivoted until she was rammed against the wall and the kiss became a full-body event, his male hardness a rush of immediate promise that made her feel weak and powerful at once.

Her hands roamed over him, pulling, tugging, caressing,

and kneading his hard, muscular flesh anywhere and everywhere she could find it; inside his collar, beneath the short sleeves of his black t-shirt.

When she thought she wouldn't be able to stay on her feet a moment longer, when she thought she'd faint from the strength of the erotic monsoon flowing through her veins, he pulled back.

His eyes were glazed, dark bottomless depths that drew her in like music from a snake charmer's flute. She couldn't tear herself away, couldn't draw back from him, not ever again.

Her headset erupted with static. In the stillness, Drake heard and cocked his head, listening as he stepped away. Cold air demolished the intimate heat between them.

"Drake, Stark."

It was Bruce. Drake turned on his headset. She straightened from the door, her blood chilling at the defeated sound in Bruce's voice. "Where are you?"

"I'm pinned in the west guard shack."

"Dad," Drake whispered. "We're coming. Hold tight."

"No time," he said, breathless, and Sara's heart wrenched. "Get the data from the lab and take it to Kray."

"Hold on!" Drake yelled, searching the room as if a solution hid in the corners. He yanked weapons from the armoire, slid inside a Kevlar vest, and slung shoulder holsters on as he walked. Gunshots rang through their headsets and Drake's face darkened.

One last worried glance at Drake, and she said, "We're coming, Bruce."

There was no reply.

Sara started for the motorcycles when a voice ground through the speakers of her headset.

"Acosta will be in touch." A pause. "You have something that belongs to us. Now we have something that belongs to you."

"Who the hell is this?" she shouted.

Drake pressed the set to his ear. "You touch my father and it'll be the last thing you ever do."

They stood stock still, waiting for a reply. Shattering glass goosed them both toward the motorcycles.

Sara handed him the Sauer, gloves, and visor. He moved fast. She punched the button to retract the door as he started the Kawasaki's powerful engine. She hopped on the second one and together they snapped their infrared goggles in place.

The door shivered upward with a metallic grinding rattle. She revved the idle, eager to be off. The wait was excruciating. The slow progress of the door dragged every second out until she wanted to explode and blow the damn thing off its hinges.

Drake was silent, focused, determined beside her. As soon as the opening offered enough clearance to race out, they turned on the goggles, bent low, and squealed for the exit at top speed.

The moment they hit open air, weapons exploded around them. Two bullets pinged off the reinforced steel of her motorcycle. The Kawasaki's headlights remained off, allowing them to blend better with the night-dark landscape. Drake drew away from her, splitting the enemy's target. Hunkered low, Sara pulled a 9mm from her thigh holster.

She fired rounds rapidly, twisting to aim across her throttle arm while maintaining control of the beast between her thighs. Their attackers were everywhere. Drake's weapons erupted further away but were nonetheless loud in the hot, still air.

They rode, the scent of burning fuel and churned up grass mingling with the scent of freshly-ignited gunpowder. A bullet, fired from too far away to cause damage, hit the back of her vest and she lurched forward.

Glowing green, the Knight, Inc. guards, rushed forward. They used hedges and outbuildings as cover to draw fire away from her and Drake. She spun the bike to make herself a hard target as the guard shack loomed ahead.

The shack was a ruin. The door hung off its hinges, the glass window nothing more than a jagged swag over the darkened interior. Drake swooped in first, sliding off the motorcycle without bothering to park it. It continued across the grass on its side, the engine cycling into a disgruntled idle.

"He's not here!" Drake screamed over the sound of her engine.

Her back wheel shoveled dirt and sod into the air as she swiveled, searching for heat sources in every direction. They'd left the enemy far enough behind she didn't worry about gunfire. Where the hell had Bruce gone?

"There!" Drake pointed at the same instant she saw the SUV parked on the gravel access road.

The unmistakable shape of a man kicked to his knees, the butt of a gun landing on the back of his neck as the four surrounding men worked to get him inside the vehicle flared in the green glow of the goggles. It was Bruce.

She revved the idle on the Kawasaki and jerked her chin for Drake to hop on. He landed in the seat and fired over her shoulder, the report of the bullet passing from chamber, to muzzle, to target, deafened her. She raced for the road as the men scrambled to get in the SUV.

The cycle hit gravel. The wheels fought her, wanting to slide on the uncertain terrain. But she bent low, allowing Drake a better line of sight on the men around his father. One fell, another slammed back against the SUV, but the others pulled the wounded men, and Bruce, inside. The emerald shape sank to a forest green as they closed the door.

Taillights flashed bright in the goggles and the back end of the SUV lurched to the side once before it sped toward the feeder road. Stark pursued, unwilling to back down until they had Bruce back, unwilling to give up, to let them get away with the man she loved like a father.

Drake was silent, gripping her sides as she put her muscle behind the motorcycle, compensating for Drake's weight in the back as the gravel became looser, less packed on the little-used road. Dirt flew, creating sandpaper between her gritted teeth.

She kept her eyes trained on the back of the SUV, watching for it to turn off the road. Drake's grip became painful. She gassed the engine, full throttle, but couldn't spare a glance from the road to gauge her speed. They were gaining on the SUV. They were going to get Bruce back, they were going to win, she could sense it. The bastards would not get away.

The back window rolled down and one of the men inside fired. Drake raised his gun, the metal a glint in the corner of her eye. She was about to shout a warning to not fire, to not risk hitting Bruce or disabling the SUV. At this speed an accident might prove fatal. But Drake lowered the gun on his own.

The kidnappers didn't have that concern, however, and a hole appeared in the front shield on the bike a fraction of a second before she felt the impact of a bullet driven into her vest. Slowed by distance, and the safety glass, it nonetheless felt like she'd been hit in the chest with a sledgehammer.

She rolled her shoulders forward, tried to remain in control of the bike as blackness crept into her vision. Stunned, she couldn't catch a gulp of air to right the damage.

"Stark!" Drake yelled and she looked up.

They were leaving the road, the motorcycle trained on a tree beyond the shoulder. She corrected their direction, but it was too late. They'd lost speed and the SUV pulled far ahead. Behind her, Drake grabbed the handles of the bike and added his strength to her feeble effort to keep the cycle upright.

They came to a halt, the SUV gone from sight. She sighed on a sob, unable to grab enough air to give it full justice. Tears of frustration and failure rushed from her eyes. Her lungs finally cooperated and she inhaled a cry. "Drake...I'm so sorry."

He rubbed her bare upper arms and when he spoke, his

voice was tight, strangled, and filled with terrible rage. "We'll get him back, I promise."

It sounded more like a threat.

CHAPTER TEN

Drake stormed into the lab, Stark fully-dressed and fully-outfitted on his heels. They were both shaken by the abduction of his father. He felt cold inside, prepared to do whatever it took to get him back and determined to not rest until he did. Fritz had called ahead to place the lab on alert and the pilots were already preparing the Jetstar.

After they'd returned to the estate to find it badly damaged and Knight, Inc. guards in control, Sara had gone to dress, but not before Drake noticed her purpling bruises. Further incensed to make Acosta and his men pay, he worked fast to replenish their ammunition. Sara offered no argument when he took the driver's seat in the Jaguar and raced to the lab at top speed, slowing only once when radar picked up a patrol car.

He found Carlos and stopped, sucked in a calming breath and reminded himself that this man wasn't his enemy. Stark's quiet presence was a welcomed anchor. He wouldn't lose his composure while she remained in control. "We need the data now, Carlos. Give us what you have."

"Drake." Carlos stood, the pages he'd been marking with a blue pen fluttered in his wake. He glanced over their weapons with alarm. "They put us on alert, but didn't say why. What's happened? Is it something to do with Senator Halley?"

"No. The senator?" Stark shook her head, her tone flat and vicious. "The Colonel's been taken. We're getting him back. We need what you know."

"What? How? Who's got the Colonel?" Carlos asked, his

tone warbling high.

"Acosta's men took him about an hour ago." Drake fought the urge to shake the man. "We don't have time to explain, give us what you got. Now."

Carlos remained frozen, mouth working as if he couldn't decide which language to speak in.

"Now!" Drake shouted, all patience gone.

Stark put a hand on his arm, and turned to Carlos. "Just give us what you have."

He nodded and started moving, to Drake's utter relief. Carlos rushed back to his computers, landed in his chair, and typed madly for the next thirty seconds. Printers scratched into action, the paper rolled through the machines, but still, it wasn't fast enough for Drake.

"Talk to us," Stark said to Carlos. "Why did you think this had anything to do with Senator Halley?"

"A man showed up about an hour ago looking for the Colonel here. Said he couldn't get through to the estate."

"What for?" Drake asked.

"Don't know. He left an envelope with the receptionist and she brought it to me for safekeeping." Carlos turned, but Drake waved him back.

"Keep working." Drake didn't care about the senator or the damned envelope.

"I'll get it," Stark said. "Where is it?"

"On the desk." Carlos gestured toward the door.

Stark found the manila envelope, gave it a cursory glance, and shoved it deep into the back pocket of her pants. Her gaze found Drake's. "We'll give it to him in person."

Silence fell over them as Carlos continued to work. Drake leaned forward, sweat cold on his brow. "What are you printing?"

Drake studied the computer screens, searching them for a clue where the invaders had taken his father. Carlos sped on the wheels of his chair between his station and the Cray.

"I think we finally nailed the coordinates, though they don't make sense." Carlos stood and tore the pages from the first printer. He ruffled through the information, folding the stack back to a list of numbers.

Drake scanned them. Carlos was right, the coordinates didn't make sense. "Are you sure this is right? This is an aerial location. Is it St. Louis?"

"No, it's Kansas City. We've checked it backwards, forwards, and sideways." Carlos yanked more paper from the printers and stacked the data into a neat pile. "But I haven't uncovered anything that explains what those numbers are for."

Stark fingered a bruise on her arm as she contemplated the papers in Drake's hands. Although banged up, she hadn't uttered one word of complaint. "Is it the coordinates for a bomber drop?"

Carlos shook his head. "If that were the case, it would read more like a flight plan and not so...encoded."

Drake closed his eyes, breathed deep, and swallowed his frustration. "Right now, I don't care. My father is obviously not dangling in midair over Kansas."

Stark straightened with unmasked chagrin and addressed Carlos. "We need the chip. It's not safe here."

Excitement infused Carlos's features. "I've got something to show you." He strode to the door adjoining the next room. "We were developing this for you, Stark," he said as Drake and Stark followed him into the tactical gear development lab. Carlos lifted a box from beside a cluttered desk covered with screws, wires, and tools. "They just finished it last night."

Stark accepted the box and opened it. "A barrette?"

Drake looked over her shoulder at a gold and silver filigree designed hair clasp. Though clearly not a work of art, the ornament wasn't ugly.

"Not just any barrette." Carlos lifted the metal clasp from the box and turned it over, springing the clip. "If you connect the two wires and depress here, it becomes a miniature bomb.

And..." He paused as he led them to a secured steel box. "There's a compartment here, perfect for the chip. This is made completely of undetectable alloys. You should be able to go anywhere, including airport security, without it setting off any alarms." Carlos retrieved the chip from the box, added it to the barrette, and passed it to Stark.

Drake grimaced at the idea of Stark wearing a bomb on her head. "Is there any chance that thing could go off without connecting those wires?"

"No," Carlos said with a grin. "The crew had a *blast* testing the mechanisms and it works like a charm."

Stark untangled what looked like a shoelace from her hair and secured the barrette in place. "Thanks Carlos, this is great."

"Thought you'd like it," he said with a proud smile.

Drake turned his attention back to the fat file and wished the answers would jump off the pages. "Did you come across any intel about their motives?"

"No, that remains a mystery." Carlos, his humor gone, shoved printed pages into a file.

"Like chupacabra," Stark whispered.

"Salva's password?" Drake struggled against the urge to rush her out of the room, into the Jaguar, and after Acosta.

Stark nodded. "Yes, it's been bugging me. This is like that, isn't it? A myth, mystery, something obvious we're missing."

"Maybe General Kray will tell us something." Drake inserted the stack of readouts into the file Carlos gave him. "We'll have time to figure it out, but right now, we need to get to the airport." He clapped Carlos on the shoulder. "Good work. Go home, get some rest."

Carlos nodded. "Be careful."

"You can count on it." Drake strode for the door.

Carlos called behind him, "*Vaya con Dios.*"

Stark matched Drake's speedy pace to the Jaguar parked

outside. They'd gotten a ticket and he shook his head in disgust. His father was in the hands of the very man who wanted to destroy the system under which a cop had given him this ticket. He crumpled the copy and tossed it into the back seat instead of in the gutter where it belonged. With his luck, he'd get another ticket for littering.

Stark buckled in as he brought the engine to life. She didn't speak until the Jaguar eased into traffic. "Did you notice the men at the house were American?"

He nodded. "Yes, and whoever sent them knew their stuff. They had military experience."

"I caught that too." Stark sounded royally ticked, and he cast a sideways glance at her.

She wore a white t-shirt covered by a new Kevlar vest and he recalled the glimpse of creamy curved flesh of her breasts beneath the previous one. He quickly focused on her face. Bathed in the green glow of the dash lights, determination and concentration hardened the contours of chin and cheek. It occurred to him how comforting it was to have her by his side.

"I know this sounds dumb," she said, "but that password keeps playing in my head like a stupid song you can't get rid of."

"I don't know, Stark," Drake said as he downshifted for a red light he'd almost raced through in his haste. "There's more going on here than just Acosta. He's behind it, but he's got someone bigger backing him."

"Who?" Sara asked, more to herself than to him. "It could be anyone. The Iraqis, the Columbians, hell, even the Russians."

"But those were American soldiers." Drake shook his head, drawing conclusions he didn't like.

"You think one of our own is behind this?" Stark whispered, appalled.

Drake shook his head again and slammed his palm on the steering wheel. Would the damned light ever turn green? "I don't see any other possibility. Do you?"

She was silent, contemplating. A flash of the kiss they'd shared in the armory came back to him. While he'd been kissing her, his father had been running for his life. Guilt thrummed in sync with the powerful engine. The light finally changed and the Jaguar leapt forward, growling as he shifted.

"No, I can't think of another possibility," Sara said to her folded hands. "Who could gather that manpower? And the satellite codes? Who would have that kind of access?"

"It has to be someone involved with Operation Just Cause, someone who hates my father, someone who was either reprimanded, discharged, court marshaled, someone with a personal reason to betray his country."

"Someone like Kray."

There it was, the accusation Drake did not want to make. He tried to find a reason *not* to suspect the General. "Kray is not a traitor, he's my father's friend. We have to trust that."

In her silence he sensed her disagreement.

"We can't do this, Stark." Drake flicked the blinker on briefly as he hugged a tight right turn. "We can't afford to settle on Kray. If it's not him, then we'll waste our time and allow the real bastard to get away."

"If it is him?"

"Then I'll hang the SOB myself." Drake glared at the road ahead. There had to be someone else, it just couldn't be General Kray. Regardless of what Stark thought, Drake had met the man before and knew the curmudgeon to be as honest as Lincoln himself. It didn't fit.

The glimmer of a memory struggled to surface. His father, sitting beside his mother's sickbed, his eyes dark and far away as Drake came in. But the memory shivered, than collapsed back out of reach without presenting any reason for coming to mind in the first place.

He sighed heavily. It was like trying to do a jigsaw puzzle upside down and backward without a picture. "Let's get this information to Kray and see what he has to say."

Stark nodded slowly in the darkness, her eyes averted to the scenery whipping past the windows.

Drake respected her judgment, her assessment of the situation, but he couldn't take any chances. His father's life hung in the balance. Everything centered on getting to Kray and combining their information. Until then, they'd be in the dark, where a hulking monster without a face waited for the opportunity to pounce.

Surprisingly, Sara fell asleep on the plane. Her entire body ached–her bruises pulsating reminders Bruce Knight was in danger.

She dreamed. In her sleep she raced through a darkened institution in a hospital gown, the kind worn when sentenced to isolation in juvie. Unseen pursuers chased, gaining on her.

This was her dream, her burden, the one which haunted her regularly. In the past, the search had been for her father. Now she hunted for Bruce. The two men became intermingled, a faceless persona of fatherly love stripped from her life. She sensed another presence and understood it to be Drake.

Barefoot and frightened, she hunted for a weapon. In slow motion she ran, unable to lift heavy legs, though her enemies neared. She turned, shoved through a door, the thud of a heartbeat booming through the walls, the floor, her body, ringing in her ears.

The room, bathed in a bright golden aura, momentarily blinded her. She lifted a dream hand to shield her eyes and an indistinct shape took form in the glow. The light dimmed, faded, and Drake stepped forward. His eyes, as they had been in the armory; filled with need, with desire and...danger.

He came to her, lowered his head, and pressed his mouth against hers. The thundering heartbeat reverberated through everything. She wanted to kiss him, to strip him, to cover his body with her mouth, to taste the flat of his stomach, to hook her hands into his pants and release him, to strip herself and feel his nakedness against her own flesh.

But danger was coming.

Fear clawed up her spine, and she pushed Drake back. In the doorway, a beast with the elongated fangs of a tiger, the demonic head of a ram, and the torso of Goliath, held Bruce off his feet, those terrible teeth buried deep in his throat. *Chupacabra.* Silver flashed in the evil eyes and the beast's face curved in a leering, sadistic grin.

She jerked awake, the scream in her throat strangled into a muted cry. Drake was beside her in an instant. She couldn't look at him, couldn't reveal her weakness.

Practice had given her the ability to shake off the reoccurring dream, but the subtle differences this time made it tenacious and her body refused to comply. The weight of Drake's arm around her shoulders helped, but didn't completely steady her quaking nerves.

"*Shh*," he murmured in her ear. "It's just a bad dream. We're safe."

She shook her head and lifted her face. "Are we? There's a madman out there with your father, with the technology to detonate a nuclear bomb and angry enough to use it. How can we ever be safe again?"

Drake didn't answer; he only folded her in his arms. She laid her head against his chest, the pound of his heart loud in her ear and a reminder of the dream. He rubbed lazy circles on her back and stroked her tangled hair. "It will be all right, Sara, I promise."

She prayed to heaven that he could keep that promise, that fate would smile on her for a change. The need for air and peace from the darkly erotic thoughts Drake's scent and body inspired made her pull away. She couldn't bring herself to leave his side though, he was too vibrant a reminder that life was precious. If human nature harbored malice and ignorance, it also was home to a great expanse of love, joy, and compassion–a complexity she was just beginning to understand.

The Jetstar landed, taxied onto the airport runway and as they disembarked, Sara wished she would have worn something heavier than the thin windbreaker. Washington was much colder in the fall than Texas and the wind bit through her clothing. But the chill refreshed her too, chasing the fog from her head.

A soldier emerged from a jeep and strode to them. He stood stiffly. "I'm Lieutenant Masterson, General Kray is expecting you. I'll ask you to leave your weapons on the plane."

Sara exchanged a nervous look with Drake, but what choice did they have? Eight guns, two knives, and Sara's Tazer later, they were declared 'clean'. The co-pilot took the weapons on board.

They followed Masterson to the jeep and Sara found herself comparing the two men. Although in uniform and humorless, the soldier appeared to be little more than a glorified boy scout beside Drake's tense carriage. She'd rather meet Masterson in a dark alley any day. Conversation was impossible in the presence of the soldier as they drove to the Pentagon.

On arrival, Masterson led the way to a nondescript door, opened it, and stood aside at attention. General Kray waited inside the short hall. Her first impression was that a slimmer George C. Scott might have studied him for a role.

He was the epitome of every General she'd ever seen–salt and pepper hair shorn close to his scalp, his uniform perfect in every regard, the decorations on his coat an indication of the sacrifices and bravery for his country. He gleamed with the power of the stars and stripes.

Her convictions that Kray was behind the assault on the estate and Bruce's kidnapping faltered, then dwindled. Drake had been right, this man reeked patriotism. He was crisp, comfortable in his command as he ordered them inside.

"We think we know who's behind Knight's abduction." Kray's voice carried enough grit to make one think he'd done time in the desert.

"Who?" Though Drake asked–he made it sound like a demand.

Sara sensed Kray would not respond well to orders and fought the urge to caution Drake–he would construe the warning as an insult. Kray abruptly halted, proving her instincts correct.

"I will tell you what I can," Kray said, "but remember where you are."

"My father's been taken from his home." Drake's voice rose. "We've brought our own intel to share, and expect you to do the same. Tell me who is behind this."

The file Drake carried was his leverage, but Sara didn't imagine it would go far with Kray if Drake didn't calm down. She put her hand on his arm.

"In here," Kray said and took three steps further down the hall to an unmarked door. Chairs surrounded a long conference table. A file rested on the table, almost identical to the one Drake carried, only much thinner. Sara hoped that was not an indication of how much Kray actually knew. Drake placed his file beside the other, dwarfing it in comparison.

Her eyes flicked to the flag drooping in one corner of the room. Memories of her father's funeral filled her with an angry grief and she turned away. Dangerous thoughts could skew her judgment, and at the moment, she needed to be objective.

Kray sat at the head of the table, Drake and Sara occupied the chairs flanking the distinguished General. She cleared her throat. "It's imperative that we learn what information you have as quickly as possible. We need to find the Colonel right away."

Kray nodded. "I agree. We believe a man named Browning lead the attack on your home. He was discharged for conduct unbecoming, convicted on a slew of other charges, and spent six years in Leavenworth. After he was paroled, he formed The Dulce Patriots. They're ex-military, mostly from the disciplinary barracks at Leavenworth. The DP is a dangerous faction of mercenary extremists. Browning is for hire and it's likely Acosta used him to attack the estate."

"Wait!" Drake sat straighter, brow furrowed. "Dulce? As in sweet?"

Kray shook his head. "Through what Intel we have on Browning, we believe he's referring to the Dulce Base in New Mexico."

Sara said, "What, exactly, is the purpose of the base?"

"Nothing really, unless you believe in all that UFO blarney." His grin was ugly, leering, and instinctually, Sara knew he lied. "It's a load of horse puckey if you ask me, but Browning thinks it's why he was convicted."

"What does that mean?" Drake asked as Sara fought to focus on the information and add it together. She remembered Carlos saying, *"Nonsense, like UFO's, chupacabra means goat-sucker."*

Kray's face returned to an impassive mask. "Officially, Browning was tried on assault and disobeying a direct order."

"And unofficially?" Sara held her breath, knowing this answer could finally be the link she needed.

"I'm not at liberty to speak about that." Kray tapped the folder. "You may find more in here, though."

Sara swallowed a grunt of frustration and flipped the folder open. The pages inside were covered in black, only three or four sentences available on each sheet. Whatever Browning had been into, the government obviously didn't want anyone to know the truth. She turned the folder on the table to show Drake and then leveled what she hoped was a scathing look at the General. "Are you going to help us, or play games with us?"

Kray's features didn't change, but his hands tightened

perceptibly around each other. "Knight is my friend. I want him back as much as you do. I've never served with a finer man and I hate that he's been taken. But, I can only help so much. My first obligation is to my country, first and foremost."

Drake slammed the folder closed, his anger returning in a fine, pale sheen. "My loyalty is to my father. Don't waste my time and don't play games with us! Chupacabra, UFO's, who gives a damn!" Drake rose and leaned over the General. "Tell me where my father is!"

Sara recoiled. What the hell was going on? Dulce base, Dulce Patriots, Acosta.

"Sit down." Kray didn't rise, didn't shout, simply glared power into his command.

Drake did not sit, but turned abruptly and kicked his chair into the table. With his back to the room, he muttered under his breath. Sara caught only two words, time and kill. She felt exactly the same way.

Kray sighed deeply, as if gathering himself. "All right, this is what I know. Acosta is in Mexico. We intercepted a radio transmission from the Pico de Orizaba mountain range to Los Alamos, which is connected by an underground system to the Dulce Base. This is why we believe Browning was hired by Acosta."

Relief swept through her. They had a location. Bruce had to be there. Drake returned and gripped the back of the chair. He didn't speak. Sara turned her attention back to Kray.

"And Salva?" Sara asked, wanting to confirm her theory, "His password was chupacabra. Is there some black ops project they may have all been involved in? Something we should know? Anything that will help us figure out what Acosta's objective is?" She slid the fat folder they'd brought with them to Kray. "Look, inside you'll find what we uncovered from Salva's computer."

"I can't discuss anything of that nature." Kray opened the

folder and turned slowly through the pages as he spoke. "I can tell you what you're referring to is a false assumption perpetrated by the media. In the '80's some reporter connected hysteria-induced suppositions that alien creatures, the chupacabra, were released from Los Alamos–pure urban legend, completely untrue."

"There's a truth in there somewhere." Drake jabbed the thinner file with a finger and raised his eyebrows skeptically. "You speak of myths, but aren't we really talking about a military cover-up?"

"Don't be so dramatic," Kray muttered as he continued to page through the file. "It's just media hype."

"Is it? Or is the media hype planted by the government to disguise the truth?"

Sara gaped. "You don't believe in UFO's or anything like that, do you Drake?"

"No, of course not. But think about it. Politicians hide behind spinning the truth. If we're knee-deep in a sensitive operation, they might concoct a story to divert attention from the real project." Drake paused, his stare intense as he tried to convey some meaning to Sara that she didn't quite get. "They say the devil pulled his best trick when he got the world to believe he didn't exist."

The connection which had evaded her since the beginning overwhelmed her. She exhaled. Everyone associated with this assignment was connected in some way to a government cover-up. It wasn't a coincidence that Salva chose that password. Acosta held a grudge against a government that had turned Noriega into a double agent and then invaded to cover-up that fact. Salva had been involved with allegedly stolen nuclear arming codes, while Browning was likely jailed to cover-up a Los Alamos project.

It was possible the nuclear codes hadn't been stolen at all, but purchased outright and now they were embroiled in a cover-up.

What was Bruce's involvement? Did this have anything to do with Halley and his company EDPT? Did it go back to Operation Just Cause and her father? Kray had been derailed from active duty because he'd tried to do the right thing, according to Bruce, which, she believed was simply a way of keeping Kray in a low profile. This answered one question, but left her floundering in a new sea of questions.

She thought of asking Kray, but he'd made it clear he wouldn't speak about sensitive issues and she didn't want to waste her breath.

She stood. "I think we're done here, General Kray, unless you have a more specific location we can search for the Colonel?"

Kray slapped the thick folder closed and rose. Drake collected the thin file with a look of disgust and she couldn't blame him, the folder was practically no help at all.

"Look at the end of the file, it's the best I can do," General Kray said.

Drake remained stiff. "Am I right to assume we'll get no help in retrieving him?"

"That's not my call." General Kray sighed and surprised Sara by placing a comforting hand on Drake's shoulder. "I regret deeply that I can't help you more. Find Bruce and I'll do my best to send in backup. I can't promise anything, but with a precise location, I can do a hell of a lot more."

Drake stared at the man, measuring him. Sara willed herself to remain still and not interfere with the silent exchange. Kray wasn't the enemy.

"I'll let you know the moment we find him." Drake shook the General's hand when Kray offered it. "Stark? Ready?"

"Yes." She stopped at the door. Although she couldn't bring herself to thank him for keeping his secrets, she shook his hand and said, "We'll be in touch."

Masterson was waiting, alert, and ready to return them to the Jetstar. She strode behind the two men to the waiting jeep.

They had the key to Acosta's motives, but now had to figure out which door it opened, and what lay on the other side.

CHAPTER ELEVEN

Drake waited impatiently while the new flight plan to Mexico City was pushed through, via help from General Kray. At least, he thought, the trip wasn't a total waste. Once the Jetstar left the ground, he studied the thin file on Browning and the known whereabouts of Acosta.

"Remember the guards?" Stark asked, her head bent over the folder in his lap. "The ones at the mine?"

Drake nodded. "I was thinking the exact same thing. We didn't know about Mexico's interest in the medallion because there wasn't any. Those guards had to be there for a reason though, and my guess it's to protect Acosta, or something he has hidden there."

She grasped his knee and squeezed gently. "We'll get Bruce back, Drake. Your father is a strong man, he'll make it through."

Drake recalled the exhaustion on his father's face and his graying hair. "I hope you're right."

"I am." She sat back. "He's seen worse than this. They won't harm him, not if they want the chip."

He closed the folder. He couldn't focus on the scant data between the blocks of black. Each darkened page angered him. How dare Kray keep him from knowing the full truth when his father's life depended on that knowledge?

"Want some coffee?" Stark asked as she stood. "I'm gonna make some for me."

"Sounds great." He tossed the folder on top of the

magazines and closed his eyes.

Acosta had hired the Dulce Patriots to retrieve the chip, had scientists working on something that used uplink codes for a nuclear warhead, aerial coordinates that didn't make any sense, and the bastard had his father. Between that and what Stark had theorized about the cover-ups, he would bet his teeth Browning knew something, or was involved in some way, with Operation Just Cause.

The aroma of freshly brewed java and the heat of steam opened his eyes. He accepted the mug as she settled across from him. The steady hum of the Jetstar engines filled the cabin as he studied her.

She was holding up remarkably well. Aside from the dream she'd had earlier, she appeared virtually unaffected by recent events. He scanned her bare arms, the thin flesh-colored band-aids, and the nicks she hadn't bothered to cover. Mottled bruises peppered her silken skin and a band of discolored flesh circled her throat. She'd been through hell.

The trenches of his mind projected images of her bleeding from gunshot wounds, eyes blank with death. He swallowed a large gulp of coffee, and felt the heat leave a trail down his gullet. Death was a nasty replacement for his past fantasies.

Stark, elbows on her knees, clasped the hot mug between pale fingers. "What are you thinking?"

"That I want you to be extra careful when we land." He set his cup down and leaned forward until the space between them became mere inches. "I mean it Stark. I'll do anything to get my father back, but I don't want you taking any unnecessary risks."

"I never do." She sounded disgruntled.

"Maybe not, but just promise me this time you definitely won't." He wanted to explain, to tell her that he cared too damned much to exchange her life for his father's, that he would rather die himself than to see her killed in their effort to get his father back. But the words wouldn't come and he sighed heavily. "Just promise, Stark."

She stilled, then nodded. "I promise."

"Thank you." His head suddenly seemed too heavy to hold up and he allowed it to drop. His throat closed.

Was it already too late? Was his father dead somewhere, his only mission now retribution, and he didn't even know it? Was it too late for him to protect himself against Stark? Did he love her already too much to avoid the same fate his father endured? Would another woman ever be able to fill the gap Stark's death would leave in his soul?

Caught in his torment, he barely heard the clink of china as her mug joined his, the rustle of clothing, as Sara knelt. Hands ran through his hair, caressing, assuring. She offered him solace and comfort.

He gathered her into his arms, burying his face in the crook of her neck. No other woman could know him so well, no other woman could touch him the same way. He grasped her tighter and her arms gripped him just as fiercely.

Her skin warmed the side of his face. Tea Roses, he thought, and recalled she'd been in the poolroom, probably in the sauna, during the invasion. He could have lost her then.

It all came crashing in on him. He wanted to cherish her, to experience her, to feel alive in her arms. Her hair, pulled back carelessly in the barrette, pooled over his arms and he plunged his hands through the mass, balling it in his fists–willing her essence into his palms.

He urged her gently, lifting her upright on her knees, tugging her closer until she leaned against the seat between his legs. His cheek brushed hers and he discovered it was wet with tears. Without thought, he kissed the salty skin, tasting her cheek, and finally, her lips.

She opened for him with a gasp and he explored the inside of her mouth. The sweet of sugar and cream, the velvety softness of her tongue pushed his blood faster into every throbbing place in his body, forcing away images of death from his mind.

He cradled her face in his hands, holding her, not allowing her to escape. Overcome by the desire to feel her living heart beat against him.

Her fingers fumbled on the straps of his vest and he found the closures holding hers in place. The armor dropped away from them with a dull thud he hardly noticed. Skin flushed, her eyes darkened with the reflection of the hunger surging through him. She straddled him, knees on either side of his thighs.

"Sara..." he whispered, and grasped the back of her head, pulling her closer yet and resuming the kiss. He wanted her; he wanted to be in her. The fabric of her pants, stretched against the hot, soft flesh of her inner thighs, enveloped his rigidity in a delicious promise of what might be, what *had* to be.

She teased him, grazing his lip with her teeth and he growled low in appreciation. He wound his arms beneath hers, circling her waist and sliding them inside the back of her shirt. She purred in reaction, pressing her backside against him, and it still wasn't enough. Hands on her shoulders, he pressed on her until she ground into him, a friction that created hot, red lust.

His tongue mated with hers as she pressed her lips rhythmically over his again and again. He fumbled with her bra, shoving it out of the way until his hands could explore the roundness of her breasts. His thumbs found the hardened buds and she tossed her head back with a soft cry of pleasure.

He kissed the line of her chin to her throat. Her hands fisted into the fabric covering his shoulders and she leaned back, granting him access. He shoved her shirt higher and covered one puckered rosette with his mouth.

She gasped as he flicked his tongue over the hardened flesh. She gripped the back of his head, knotting her fingers in his hair to press him closer. He suckled, the sound of her heart, her pulse, melding with his own in a rapid rhythm.

"Drake," she called, her voice thick with passion.

He grabbed her backside, filling his palms with the derriere that had tantalized him for so long. She felt so damned good.

"Drake," she said again, her voice rising.

He spread kisses, gently, across the bruise on her chest and paid homage to the other glorious breast. She arched her back, telling him without words she wanted him to continue. He was happy to oblige.

"Sara," he whispered, overwhelmed. "I need you so much."

She replied by pressing her pelvis against him again. He groaned low in his throat. The pleasure bordered on painful, his pants a strangling hindrance. He tugged her to him once more, wanting to taste her mouth again. She acquiesced readily, claiming his lips with an abandon he'd never known. Her kiss was bold, adamant, not the timid groping of a spoiled woman.

"Drake, we can't, not here."

With an effort, Drake understood her. The Jetstar wasn't the place for this. They could be interrupted at any moment. He eased away from her and dropped his head to her shoulder.

She kissed his hair, sighed, and tugged her shirt back down. When he glanced into her face, her eyes were heavy-lidded, her mouth crimson against her glowing skin.

He whispered, "Do you know what you do to me?"

A slow, languid smile spread over her face, "Exactly the same thing you do to me."

She scooted back to lay her head against his heart, curling into his arms. They breathed hard and in unison, her back rising and falling with each of his breaths. He closed his eyes and waited for the inferno inside him to recede into a muted flame.

So now he knew. There wasn't any way to keep his distance from Sara, emotionally or physically. He frowned over her shoulder. What of her? Did she want him just as deeply? Or was this her attempt to comfort him?

He'd known women who gave themselves without regard for their own desires–out of lack of self-esteem or some misguided attempt to hold onto something that might not be. He didn't want Sara on those terms, he wanted her willingly and because she needed him as badly as he needed her.

She heaved a breath, as if having trouble finding air and he shifted so she could straighten. Her head lifted, but settled back on his shoulder. She toyed with the collar of his t-shirt, running her finger along the edge. The unconscious caress made it difficult to rein in his desire. He clasped her hand in his and kissed the smooth skin of her palm.

He lowered her hand between them. "Are you okay?'

She chuckled. "I should be asking you that. I hear it's...painful to...and not..."

He saved her from having to clarify. "Yes, it can be, but I'll survive."

He would, but would she survive the future? If she didn't, even God wouldn't be able to save Acosta.

Sara fell against the door. The wait for the rental car, the wild ride through traffic, and the delay getting to the room had done nothing to assuage the massive fireworks exploding in her belly. Every time Drake brushed against her, whether he was holding a door open, lifting her luggage, or sitting beside her, the misfiring hormones inside her went ballistic. Now she was in their room, alone with him, and to her utter disbelief, the hotel only had one double bed available.

Drake, a few feet to her right, stood with his hands on his hips and stared at the furniture in question. This was supposed to be the best the Sheraton had, well, at two o'clock in the morning, it *was* the best they had. Sara didn't want to consider the ramifications of the one bed. Her girlish desire wanted it to be fate, another part of her felt more sinister entities might be at work here.

Drake cleared his throat and cast her a sheepish grin. "Don't you dare say I had anything to do with this."

"I won't." She smiled in a way that made her feel like an idiot. Her heart pounded in her chest simply from the flash of his white teeth. *Oh, girlfriend, you're losin' it.* "But I'm gonna take a shower. You want to see if you can get room service to deliver something hot?"

"Good idea, I'm famished." He looked relieved to have something to do and went to the phone.

She slung her suitcase on the end of the bed and retrieved another white t-shirt and the pants she'd planned to wear tomorrow. At the estate, she'd been too flustered to think of pajamas and knew Drake hadn't packed any either. He'd likely forgotten socks as well.

She did, however, remember her bath kit–a toothbrush, hairbrush, and hand cream. The bathroom stock of mini-shampoos, soaps, and conditioners would have to do. She removed the barrette with the chip and tucked it deep into an inner pocket of the suitcase.

Hot water sluiced over her, erasing the dirt of the, long, arduous day. The kiss with Drake had emerged from the need to comfort him, and be comforted by him. Regardless of her intentions, she realized now the kiss had been reckless and ill-timed.

Bruce was God knew where, being treated God knew how, and she was molesting his son instead of working the problem. Soap slid into her eye and she welcomed the burning punishment.

One bed or not, she would have to keep her distance from Drake. This was the worst possible time to test their relationship. The bar of soap flipped from her fingers as it occurred to her that the question was no longer if they would be lovers, but when. That is, if they made it out of this alive. The possibility remained that one, or both of them, may not survive the next day.

The little devil inside her whispered fiercely that if this was her last night on earth, did she want to spend it in prideful purity–in fearful frigidity? She hung her head beneath the pounding spray and cursed at her toes.

Who was to say that Drake would even want to continue what they'd started on the plane? His father, after all, was missing. He had bigger things on his mind than her. How presumptuous to think he'd even want her in his bed at a time like this.

Neither should she be thinking of him in that regard. She turned the water to cold and shivered for five minutes. The icy water helped. She would curl up in one of the large armchairs, read the folder through, snack on whatever he could get room service, and leave it at that.

When it came time to go to bed, she'd send Drake on, declare her need to keep reading, and then bunk down on the floor after he was asleep. He couldn't play gentleman and order her to take the bed if he was already dead to the world.

With that plan firmly set, she shut the deluge off and stepped out of the shower. She grimaced at her reflection in the wide mirror. She looked awful. The bruise on her chest was green, purple, and yellow around the edges. The other nicks and scrapes she'd gotten in Panama glowed pink from the water. To top it off, the ugly ring of blue and pink around her throat gave her the appearance of a Hollywood zombie.

With a white courtesy towel pressed against her breasts, she turned in the mirror and glimpsed another bruise on her back, where a bullet had hit the Kevlar vest. It looked as if she'd been caught in a hydraulic press, then roped like a rodeo calf.

Who would want to sleep with the bride of Frankenstein? She was daydreaming. Drake wasn't truly interested in her. He'd needed comfort on the plane, and accepted it, nothing more. His appetite for carnal encounters was well established, and therefore, any contact with a woman probably threw him into overdrive. She'd been wanton enough to allow it.

She dressed hurriedly and wrung her hair inside the towel. The Colonel should be in the uppermost of her thoughts, yet here she was, going on and on about Drake. Frustrated, mentally, emotionally, and worst of all, sexually, she prepared herself to face him again. A knock at the door startled her and she dropped the hairbrush with a clatter.

She opened the door wide enough to poke her head through. "What?"

"Food's here," he said with a smile. His eyes dropped to her chest for a second before returning to her face, his grin was gone. "Heard the shower go off and thought you'd like to come get it while it's hot."

"Be right there." She started to close the door again, but he blocked it with a foot.

Again his eyes flickered to her chest. "Don't you want to know what I got?"

"Sure." She wished he'd let her at least finish making her hair look halfway decent.

"Taco salad, those little tamales you like, and four orders of mozzarella sticks with marinara sauce." His eyes flicked to her chest again.

She felt decidedly ogled now, but gave him an approving smile. "All my favorites. Good work. I'll be out in a minute."

This time he allowed her to close the door and she turned to the mirror. Her face flushed red as soon as she got a good look at herself. The ends of her wet hair had dampened the white cotton of her shirt and her nipples were clearly outlined against the thin material. How the hell was she supposed to go out there now? Frantically, she blotted the front of her with dry towels, but it didn't help.

The hotel provided a hair dryer, hung on the wall beside the sink. She turned it on high and pointed at her breasts. *Oh cripes, that's hot!* She alternated between her hair and her shirt, drying each until she felt comfortable enough to leave the bathroom. But her face was bright red from sitting in the furnace blast for so long. If she wasn't so hungry, she would have waited until her coloring returned to normal.

Better red-faced, than wet-shirted, she thought, and left the bathroom, her soiled clothes in one hand. Drake waited for her at the table. He'd turned all the lights down low, aside from the one over the little sitting area.

He was munching on a mozzarella stick as he flipped through the file Kray had given them. The spiced aroma of good, hot food assailed her and her stomach rumbled loudly.

She curled up in the chair across from him, heels of her feet on the edge of the seat, knees squashed against her breasts. The laundry crackled as she tossed it to the floor and she recalled the envelope she'd shoved into the back pocket of her pants. She retrieved the pants and pulled it out.

"Hungry?" he asked, looking up from the pages with one of his entirely too handsome grins.

How was a gal supposed to hold out against him? She could see why he was rarely without a woman. "Yes, starving."

His smile fell as he noticed the envelope she tossed on the table. "Is this from the lab? From the senator?"

She nodded. "From the lab, but I don't know if it's from Senator Halley or not, it only has Bruce's name on it."

Drake touched the edges. "You think we should open it?"

Sara shrugged. "We could, but I don't know if Bruce would want us to."

"I think he would." Drake lifted the envelope decisively, tore out the single sheet of heavy paper inside, and began reading. His face revealed no reaction to the contents.

"What's it say?" Sara attacked her tamales, too hungry to wait.

"It says my father's been appointed as an independent expert and will be subpoenaed to testify against Senator Halley." He tossed the letter aside. "I hope they have better luck serving him than we are in finding him."

Mouth full, she thought about the possibilities while filling the hollow place below her ribs.

"If Halley's going on trial, there's got to be more going on than just a fling with his intern," Drake muttered absently, glancing to the paper once more before turning back to the open file. "We can't do anything about that now."

"We can," Sara muttered around half a mozzarella stick. "We can get your father back in time for the trial. Did you find anything new in the file?"

Drake shook crumbs from his fingers onto a napkin. "No, nothing. We know more than they do, according to what's left in here. I guess they don't call black ops black for no reason. Three quarters of this file is inked out. I don't know what Kray thought we'd get from this."

"Let me see." She turned the file on the table. Kray had mentioned something about the end of the report and she flipped until she got to the last page. There was some Intel there, but she couldn't make it out. "What's this? Some sort of computer program?"

Drake spun the folder back toward him and frowned. "No, these are readouts of RF signals. This is odd."

"How so?" Sara shoved away the last of the food, pleasantly stuffed.

"Well, look at this," he pointed to a paragraph on the previous page, "these give the same aerial coordinates we uncovered in the medallion, but these RF signals are for much higher..." He paused, and she didn't speak, allowing him the time to think.

He leaned back in the chair. He'd untucked his shirt from his jeans and left them open at the top. She quickly averted her eyes and focused on the nap of the plain beige carpet. "All right, let's look at we have. Satellite uplink codes for a nuclear weapon, RF signals, aerial coordinates, and one seriously screwed up bastard."

Drake sighed, rubbed his palms into his eyes. She felt a yawn coming on as well. It was after three in the morning. His gaze followed hers to the clock. He grunted and sat up. "I don't know, Stark. It's right in front of me, but I can't see it. What the hell would RF signals have to do with a nuclear weapon? The only thing remotely close to it are those supposed high-energy radio frequency, or HERF weapons. But they're very limited... damn, I can't think."

"It's late, Drake." Sara hated to see him so frustrated, especially because she knew how he felt. "Why don't you get some sleep? I'm going to stay up and study this a bit more. We'll go over everything later. Six hours? You think that'll be enough?"

He nodded. "Six hours should do it. But you need to get some rest too. We both need to be at our best tomorrow."

"I'm fine." She waved at him and sat straighter. "I slept on the plane, remember? And I had a shower, so I'm okay. I'll catch some sleep in a little while. Go on, I'm good."

Drake stared at her in the way that made her insides melt. She was turning into a puddle of lust and it was so damned distracting. She blew her bangs out of her eyes and pulled the file to her. *Please let him go so I won't be tempted.*

He stood, his shadow dark across the pages in front of her.

"Sleep well, Drake."

He hovered near, demanding her attention without uttering one word. She recalled the sensation of his hot mouth on her breasts and felt heat rise into her cheeks.

Rattled, she barked, "What?"

"There's only one bed." He quirked an eyebrow.

"Yes, I noticed." She tried to sound like it didn't matter, but her voice warbled and she cursed herself. With a noisy, throat-clearing growl, she turned back to the file. "Why don't you make some use of it while you can."

Instead of walking away, he came closer, running a hand up her arm. "I'd love to."

She tingled everywhere from that one sensual caress. Gooseflesh trailed his hand as he stepped behind her chair. His fingers danced to her shoulder, to the back of her neck. He kneaded her muscles, and despite herself, she closed her eyes and sighed with pleasure.

"Sara," he whispered her name, bending low and planting a kiss on her jaw where it met her ear. "Do you want to share the bed with me?"

She recoiled, and uncoiled at the same moment. The sensation was tantalizing and confusing. What about Bruce? Could she do this while he was probably suffering? Could she give in to her desire to have Drake between her thighs, holding her, until she cried out for his touch? The native drumbeats returned in full force and she squirmed on her seat while inside she waged a losing battle with her conscience.

"Drake, we need to sleep. We shouldn't..." She trailed off as his lips grazed her earlobe and worked wondrously along her flesh to the back of her neck.

"Shouldn't?" he murmured against her nape, his breath stirring tiny tendrils of hair.

Her whole body quaked and curled her toes around the edge of the chair. "Drake, we can't. The file...your father... we need…"

He moved her hair further out of the way and he continued caressing her with his hot hands. It was like being enveloped by the sun. "I know...but we need this too." He breathed against her skin. "Sara...I've waited too long for this."

He continued his tender assault, his hands moving down the front of her shirt, over the fabric, until they cupped her breast. She grabbed his hands to push them away, but couldn't bring herself to do it. Instead, she held them tightly and hung her head. He whispered, "Tell me to go away, and I will."

The words formed in her head to do just that, but the only thing to come out of her mouth was a lusty moan. His thumbs rubbed her nipples into hard nubbins. The pressure made her throb. His lips were magical, searing her skin one moment, then cooling it as he expelled breath.

She couldn't turn him away. It *had* been too long. Their attraction had simmered, boiled, and now it exploded. She slid her hands up his arms, over hard muscles and rounded biceps, beneath his shirt.

Sara twisted in her chair, tugging him closer for a kiss. Her entire being wanted his lips, but her mouth and heart needed them first. He obliged and the world slid, blurred, and disappeared. The only thing left in her universe was the delectable man behind her.

He eased her to her feet. She was dimly aware of the folder sliding to the floor. It didn't matter, nothing did. Her only anchor in this tempest was Drake, and she wanted him. Right now.

She turned in his arms and he grasped her, crushing her breasts against his chest. Passion passed from her to him and back again, gliding on a current of their mutual need. Sara couldn't breath, but she didn't want to. Let her die in his arms if that's what was meant to be, but she wouldn't deny him. Not now, not ever.

Drake wound his hands into her hair and tugged gently until she tilted her head back.

"Do you know how extraordinary you are?" he whispered, kissing the center of her throat, crouching as he moved down. She didn't answer, couldn't answer. He lifted her, holding her tightly in his strong arms and the sensation was exhilarating. She could barely think, and didn't want to.

He carried her to the bed. She went down, guided by his strong arms. He tugged her shirt up and his smile was sweet, tender as he drank in the sight of her.

Blessed heat shimmered intensely through her as his mouth lovingly teased her nakedness. She threaded her fingers through the silken waves of his hair. He nestled his hardness against the sensitive juncture of her thighs. It was all she could do not to rip his clothes off and release him.

Wild sensations rushed through her, electrifying every nerve ending from head to toe. She pulsed, felt swollen against him.

"Drake," she muttered, tugging on his shirt.

He grasped her fingers to still them. "Not yet," he said, and undid the snap at the top of her pants. He pulled them down, dropping kisses on the extremely sensitive line of flesh above her panties, on the inside of one thigh.

She was wet for him, ready for him, she didn't want to wait. For so long she'd denied herself the luxury to dream of him in this way, but beneath it all, her every moment had been consumed by a yearning for this. He tugged her higher on the bed until she was pressed against the center of the mattress.

His weight was delicious, her only protection a thin wall of cotton. She pressed her arms against his back, rubbing her breasts against his chest as his mouth created magic against hers. He held her in place by firm, yet gentle, fistfuls of her hair, pushing her into the pillows.

She hooked a leg around him. The pressure at her core was delicious. She gasped for air, dizzy and elated by his touch.

His paused to remove his clothes. Open-mouthed kisses drifted down her torso, across each breast and over the well of her belly button. A swirling mist of eroticism enveloped her. He freed her hands, but she couldn't move. Then he pressed his mouth at her center and she could do nothing but pray she didn't go insane from the sheer pleasure of it.

She pressed her face into the pillows until she couldn't stand the wonderful torment. "Now, Drake, now, come to me."

He refused to be rushed, leaving hot, damp kisses across her belly, pausing at her breast, grazing the nipple with his teeth.

She saw the dark glory of his sensuality revealed in the contours of his face and wrapped her hands around his neck.

When he pressed into her, she lifted her hips, taking his full length in one powerful thrust. He gasped and grit his teeth.

"Drake," she whispered, lost to the power between her thighs, feeling him deep within her. Neither of them moved. They were one, his body part of hers, she an extension of him. Joined together in the most intimate way, he'd not only invaded her body, but her soul.

He rocked back, then thrust forward again and she closed her eyes, giving into the carnal tide. They moved in unison, faster and harder. She relished it, met him at every thrust with an almost desperate need, deeper, harder.

Sara rose in the bed, grasping his back until they sat, entwined. Drake growled with pleasure, a sound that wove into the thread of her pulsating blood. She matched his thrusts, elating in the realization that neither dominated the other. They were as one, joined in equality.

She clung to the muscles of his shoulders, her hair spreading between them. Then it came, the explosion of her universe and she threw her head back, feeling the blood pulse down from her throat to where they were joined. She jerked reflexively, so strong came her release.

Drake pulled back once more and thrust inside her, and then in steady, pulsating bursts, he spilled into her. He shuddered a long groaning release. Sara fell against his chest, breathing hard, her hair stuck to her damp cheeks.

Gently, he pulled the strands away from her face and smoothed it over a shoulder. He caressed the skin there in soft, lazy circles that no longer possessed the ability to drive her wild; she was spent. She listened to the thrumming rhythm of his heart beating beneath her cheek.

"Wow," Drake said and she grinned with pure female pride. She hummed an agreement. His voice rumbled like distant thunder in his chest. "Was that...different for you too?"

She nodded.

"I didn't know it would be so wonderful."

She lifted her head and the scent of their lovemaking wound around her. "You thought it would be awful?"

"No, no, not at all." He caught her teasing grin and smiled. "I knew it would be wonderful, but I'm still surprised," he paused, ran the back of his knuckles down her cheek. "I wasn't prepared for you."

She kissed him, lingering along his bottom lip as his semi-hardness moved inside her. He felt so damned good, when she eased back, she ground into him, though in truth, she was too exhausted to start again.

He seemed to read her mind. "Don't move. We can't do this again. We both need sleep."

She nodded, kissed him twice more, and rolled. The icy blast from the air conditioner froze her completely and she yanked the covers back. Drake joined her, and in seconds, they were cuddled beneath the covers, her head on his chest, one leg draped over both of his. His arm was heavy, a comforting weight as he exhaled and relaxed.

He switched off the light and kissed her hair. "Sara?"

"*Hmm*?" She didn't want to talk, didn't want to stain the moment with worries about what might or might not happen in the future between them. She didn't want to risk the pure beauty of the memory they'd made.

Just this night, let me have just these few moments of utter happiness and I'll never ask for anything ever again.

His heart pounded slower beneath her ear, chest hairs moving gently with her breath. That was all the pillow talk she wanted.

"Nothing," Drake said, his tone considering. The silence stretched for a long, unending moment. She tensed, prepared to deny further discussion. "We can talk about it in the morning. Good night, Sara."

"G'night, Drake," she whispered, relieved, and closed her eyes.

She didn't sleep for a good while, her thoughts circling the need to know if he loved her, cared about her, if he thought of her as more than just another woman to warm his bed. Although she was certain their relationship over the years meant he did care about her as one would for those in their family, she had no confidence that he felt a deeper, more intimate emotion.

With an effort, she forced herself to move away from those thoughts. It would break her heart, destroy her, if he didn't love her for the woman she was and had only acted on the attraction and closeness of their friendship. That reality was too harsh to face. She placed a hand on the rigid muscles across his stomach and concentrated on its gentle rise and fall. His breathing deepened and he slept.

As she grew drowsy, the one question she'd tried hard to avoid since Drake first touched her at the table followed her into sleep. It circled in her mind, eclipsing Drake.

Where was Bruce, and was he still alive?

CHAPTER TWELVE

Drake dressed silently. Sara lay tangled in the sheets, one calf dangling over the edge, her hair splayed across the mattress, her bare back a sinewy delight. He dreamed of spending the morning making love to her over breakfast, and again over lunch. But they had no more time together.

As he buckled his belt in place, he checked the extra ammunition, then shook out the socks he'd worn the day before. He'd forgotten to pack extra.

Sara snored, not loudly, just a delicate sound that reminded him of the tiger a Russian client had kept chained to the wall of his parlor. Sara had definitely been a wildcat in bed, much more than he'd ever imagined. He smiled, but quickly sobered. A storm brewed inside him, one that escaped definition, but darkened his thoughts nonetheless.

What would happen between them now? He balked at traveling that road of thought and he turned his attention once more back to his father, cursing his inability to focus. Bruce had been in the bastard's hands for over eighteen hours now, and if Drake had his way, he'd be freed in less than twenty-four.

Unless his traitorous brain kept returning to Sara. It seemed as if the possibility his father might be dead already was too horrific to contemplate and his mind used Sara as a ploy to remain sane.

Mind-numbing activity would help, he hoped. He finished packing their equipment and tucked the file safely in with their gear. He ordered pancakes, sausages, and coffee. When he hung up, he found Sara sitting on the edge of the bed, clutching the sheet to her breasts and peering at him from beneath a mound of hair. She brushed the golden drape out of her eyes and gave him a tentative smile.

He bent and kissed her lips. She leaned into him, clutching the strap of his shoulder holster and nuzzling him like a contented cat. How he wished they had more time, that his father was safe and sound, and this was a well deserved vacation from their worries. "Good morning, Stark."

"Morning." She stood, the sheet wrapped around her toga style.

She seemed smaller this morning, more petite and fragile. He didn't care for the gut-feeling she'd shatter in the face of the arduous challenges ahead. "How do you feel?"

"Fine." She lifted her discarded clothes from the floor and moved toward the bathroom. "I'll just be a second. Did I hear you order pancakes?"

She closed the door and he leaned against the jamb to answer through the wood. "Yes, is there anything else you wanted?"

"No," she called back, her voice muffled.

Drake pressed his hand against the door as an overwhelming need to see her safe and out of harms way consumed him. "Stark, I've been thinking..." He stopped when the door opened.

"Yes?" She stood at the sink, brush in hand, and spoke around the band between her teeth. He didn't reply, simply watched her as he tried to understand his own thoughts. She secured the end of her braid and asked, "You've been thinking?"

Words evaded him. She wore a white shirt and black pants, the same as he, and the military style was a blatant reminders of her abilities. Stark wasn't the type of woman who would be pushed to the sidelines to watch the game. She'd dive in and quarterback the team. "What do you think about providing back up?"

"You mean, as in I sit around watching from the car and waiting to see if you come back alive?" She shoved past him to her suitcase and dug out the barrette from Carlos. "No way."

"Thought so," he mumbled and sat in a chair near the table.

She clasped the barrette at the top of her braid and followed him to the sitting area. "You didn't really think I'd agree, did you?"

"No," he sighed, "I only hoped."

She crossed her arms over her chest. "What happened last night did not change who I am, Drake." Her face flushed lightly and she pivoted, turning her back on the rumpled blankets. "I'm still as capable as I was yesterday when I saved your ass."

"You? Saved me?" Drake shook his head and stood, suddenly angrier than he should be, and knowing it. "I don't think so. Who was it that kept us from becoming road kill when you lost control of the motorcycle?"

"I was shot in the chest, Drake, that doesn't count. I'm talking about how you ended up on the back of my bike to begin with. You're too close to this, you need me."

He growled at her and hunted for a good come back, but it eluded him. "It's better if you don't come with me."

"For whom? You, or me?" She planted her hands on her hips.

Not a good sign.

"For you, of course. This is gonna get really hairy, Sara, and I can't be watching out for you and–"

"Watching out for me?" Her face suffused with anger, eyes becoming twin chips of emerald ice. "Since when have I ever needed your protection? I can take care of myself."

Drake glared. He knew that reason wasn't good enough to keep her in the car. He couldn't come up with a logical argument to keep her in the car.

A knock came to the door and they both turned their heads, shouting in unison, "What?"

"Room service," a man replied.

Drake stalked to the door, grabbed the rolling tray, and slammed the door in the man's face. He had no patience at the moment for chatter or tips. He thrust the cart into the sitting area. "Eat. We leave in fifteen minutes."

She looked at the tray as if it were covered in road kill, then shrugged, rolled a pancake into her fist, and started munching. "Give me five."

Perched on the bed, she ate quickly as she put on her socks, followed by the boots she wore for every mission, when she wasn't playing seducer, that is. He remembered the smooth curve of her calves, the subtle muscles well-defined in her heels, and one thought led to the next until he pictured her spread over him in the afterglow of their of lovemaking. He scowled in frustration with his traitorous brain and tossed their equipment bag toward the door.

The complexity of the need, weighed against the reality of the woman. He pressed his lips together to avoid pissing her off anymore than she was.

Together they donned loose short-sleeved button-ups to hide their shoulder holsters. He buttoned two, then popped the last off as he lost the battle with his anger. He couldn't convince Sara to sit this one out and if something happened to her, he wouldn't be able to bear it.

"I'm ready," she said. "Start with the mines?"

He nodded without looking at her, afraid that he'd make an ass out of himself. What was he thinking? This was not how he wanted to spend the morning with her after what they'd shared in the night. He hadn't meant to pick a fight with her.

The anger, fear, desire, all of it confused the hell out of him and he decided to save the rage for Acosta. He'd make sure to take him down before the bastard could hurt Sara.

Feeling better with a plan, Drake hefted the black duffle containing their equipment and opened the door. As she went through, he couldn't help making one last useless effort. "You don't have to come with me, Stark. It's not that I think you can't handle yourself, I just want you safe."

She gave him a scathing look. "Don't waste your breath, Drake. I'm coming with you. How do you think I'd feel if you never came out of there? If I lost both you and the Colonel? I would lose my entire family."

Why did she always have a good point?

He followed her into the hall. "Remember, no unnecessary risks."

"Wouldn't dream of it," Stark snarled.

In the elevator, she slapped the lobby button and leaned against the wall, obviously still irritated.

"I'll drive." Drake couldn't imagine her behind the wheel when she was this angry. *Talk about a public menace.*

She snorted. "Do you want me to ask permission to use the bathroom too?"

"No," he said with a sigh, though the idea of her asking permission for anything was laughable. "Listen, I'm sorry, I didn't mean to insult you."

"Then don't do it again." She prowled the inside of the elevator, restless. Again he recalled the golden tiger.

Drake pressed a hand to the small of her back and she stiffened. Leaning close, he whispered, "I don't want anything to happen to you, Sara. I...I care about you."

The elevator doors opened. Her throat worked as she swallowed and turned her face toward the lobby. "I feel the same way, Drake. So don't you take any unnecessary risks either. I'm going to have my hands full dealing with Acosta and his men."

She hurried ahead of him and out into the late morning sunshine. Drake stepped outside and heat enveloped him, a gauzy dryness that offered only the discomfort of being too bright after the dim interior of the lobby.

Stark led the way, her blonde braid a rope of bright-white down the back of her shirt. He could see the shape of her holsters through the cotton. Not fully outfitted, they'd finish arming themselves once they located Acosta.

Drake tossed the bag into the back of the Land Rover and slid behind the wheel. Stark settled into the passenger seat and they were off. He maneuvered through congested traffic, laying on his horn as if he were a native. Driving in Mexico was like initiation through a stampede of wild buffalo.

When they hit the open road heading northeast, he pressed on the accelerator.

"Have you thought anymore about what Acosta's up to?" Stark asked, boots braced against the dash, her hands clasped between her knees.

"Not really." All morning he'd failed to get Sara off his mind. "But let's go over it now. The file's inside the bag in back, on top."

Stark kneeled on the seat and reached over to unzip the bag. Her backside, wonderfully round, was a distraction he wouldn't allow himself to appreciate and he kept his eyes on the road. She turned and settled back again, the folder in her hands.

"Okay," she said in a businesslike tone he was grateful for. "You mentioned the HERF weapons last night. Tell me exactly what that is."

"It's an experiment in non-lethal combat. The idea is to use an electro-magnetic pulse to shut down an enemy's communications, computers, anything electrical. I think the actual use of a HERF weapon, though, was designed to scramble the insides of a human–stunning him."

"Like my Tazer?"

"No, not really. It doesn't emit a shock, but uses RF waves. The result is about the same."

"What are these RF waves? Isn't that like a radio signal?"

"Yes. But think more like a microwave oven. It uses the same type of energy, only in a different capacity." A nagging idea formed in the back of his head. Sara turned pages of the file, remaining silent. RF signals, HERF weapons, satellite uplink codes. He frowned, barely seeing the road in front of him. The puzzle was nearly complete.

The answer flooded him with awful dread. Whole, complete, he saw the entire scheme–the one logical conclusion, and everything fell into place. "Oh, God, it's too crazy. Impossible. But I think he's planning on using the satellite uplinks, not to launch a nuclear missile, but to send out an RF frequency."

"What would that do?"

Drake didn't answer, trying to gather himself to explain in terms Stark, computer challenged as she was, would understand. He breathed deep, his mind racing ahead of him into the dark realm of the horrible effects a weapon of that magnitude could inflict. "Do you know what an EMP actually is?"

"Yes. When a nuclear bomb explodes, it emits an electro-magnetic pulse. It wipes out all electrical equipment in the surrounding area, right?"

"Yes." He breathed hard. "Remember the aerial coordinates?"

She nodded.

He slammed his palm against the steering wheel, outraged with himself. Stupidly, he'd wasted time focusing on how an airplane could go undetected long enough to perform a bomb drop. "Imagine a nuclear explosion twenty miles in the air over the center of the United States. The explosion would create a ripple effect, sort of like a big rock in a lake, only in the air. Much larger than if you threw a rock on the ground. Of course mountains and wind sheer would effect the force, but an aerial detonation could, in theory, cross the entire country."

"And wipe out every piece of electrical equipment in its

path." Her voice filled with terrible awe. "That would be...disastrous."

Drake nodded. "Hospitals would shut down, vehicles would die in the middle of freeways, all communications would cease. We would have no way to protect ourselves, or our people. We would be, literally, sitting ducks."

"That means we'd have no way to explain what had happened. No emergency broadcasts, no radios." Sara's voice drifted in horror. "People would be in the dark, they would panic, it would be a cross-country riot."

Stark had a white-knuckled grip on the file in her lap. "But I thought you said that he's not planning on detonating a nuclear bomb. How could he do this?"

"I'm not sure." He loosened his own grip on the steering wheel. "But Kray's information shows RF frequencies, he must have left that in there for us to find. The only thing I can imagine is that Acosta is developing something to deliver an EMP wave equivalent to a nuclear detonation. Some kind of HERF weapon, but on a monstrous scale."

"Or has developed." Stark closed the folder.

He prayed she wasn't right. He prayed they got to his father and stopped Acosta before the man could carry out his plans.

"The satellite uplink codes." Stark tilted her face to him. "He's planning on using those to deliver the EMP charge?"

Drake nodded. "It explains everything. The missing scientists, and the medallions from all over the world. Each country they originated from has their own satellites in orbit. If he passes the EMP charge through all of them, he could take down the whole world."

"Not if we have anything to say about it."

Sara refused to be frightened by the implications of what Drake had put together. They would stop Acosta and get Bruce back; they didn't have any choice. Drake steered them over a large hill and the road dropped away to a basin.

"Stop!" When she'd been here last, this basin had appeared empty. Now, it teemed with activity.

He jerked the Land Rover onto the narrow strip of shoulder. The sheer drop was barely corralled by a low rusted guardrail. She opened the door, stepped out, and met Drake at the driver's side.

Drake stood beside her and stared at the battalion in the basin. Without speaking, he unloaded their gear from the back seat. They stripped off their outer shirts and tossed them into the Land Rover. Silently, they armed themselves.

Sara secured her hip holsters, checked the ammo in all four of her guns, slid rounds into chambers, and made sure the safeties were off. Drake did the same, the slick clacking of his weapons loud on the deserted road.

She accepted a headset and a pair of slim binoculars. Drake snugged a matching headset in place and draped another pair of binoculars around his neck. She assessed her gear, looked over his, and a sense of wonder struck her.

Together, armed and determined, the force of their combined abilities created an aura of extreme power. They'd worked together in the past, but after last night, the bond between them had strengthened, evolved, become a force unto itself and the change was palpable. As one they turned to the enemy territory below and raised their binoculars.

CHAPTER THIRTEEN

At first, Sara only saw men roaming over brown and green scrub brush. Then, she spied tire tracks and followed them. "There." She glanced up to point for Drake, who looked and turned the binoculars in the direction she'd indicated. "See them?"

He nodded. "They've got a full unit of trucks on standby."

She continued scanning the grounds. Men wore Mexican Police uniforms, but they had to be either phony, or if legitimate, rogue cops. The Mexican government would never sanction Acosta's work. The threat to them was just as real as it was to the U.S.

Brown and black uniforms were everywhere. Dozens of men roamed the area in trucks, 4-wheel drives, and on foot. The mine entrance must be the gate to their base camp.

How the hell would they get inside?

"I brought C-4," Drake murmured and dropped the binoculars.

She grinned. The man had to be a latent psychic, he read her mind so often. "Great, I'll go down and–"

"No." Drake went around to the driver's side. "I saw an access road toward the west. I'll go around and set up the C-4 to create a diversion. Wait here until I get back and we'll go in together."

"Why can't I go with you?" She searched him for more of the let's-keep-Sara-safe macho crap he'd pulled on her that morning. His face revealed nothing more than determination to do this his way. She'd grant him this one, if only to stay on mission and not argue with him. He was lucky she had such an even temper.

Drake pointed to a small, sheltering group of trees. "While I'm gone, scout out that area. See the tracks?"

She looked through the binoculars again. "Yes."

"Take a closer look, find out what they're hiding in there and meet me here when I get back." He opened the door but paused before getting in. "I promise, we'll go in together."

"All right, but if you don't come back, I'm not going to wait for you. I'll move in on my own."

"Fair enough." He started once more to get in, then stopped and came back to her. He kissed her hard on the mouth. "Be careful. I *will* come back for you."

"I will. You be careful, too."

He got in the car, closed the drivers door, and turned his headset on. She flipped her headset on, too, as he pulled away. Road dust plumed behind the Land Rover as he u-turned and headed southeast.

"You there?" Drake came through clear.

"I'm reading you." Sara didn't use his name. The minimal risk that their transmissions might be picked up by Acosta's men, made it safer not to acknowledge who they were. This way, the chatter could be mistaken for simple CB exchanges.

"Stay alert," Drake said.

"Will do. Out."

The engine of the Land Rover rumbled through the earpiece and reassured her. As long as she had the comfort of knowing he was close, it didn't matter if she couldn't see him.

A steep, twenty-yard grade led to the floor of the basin. Though the distance wasn't great, if she slipped, the loose gravel would propel her painfully to the bottom. She watched her step, mindful of the slippery, rolling rocks. Inching down took time, but Drake also needed time to get around the basin, plant the charges, and return.

Once she reached level ground, she ducked low, moving swiftly between stunted foliage toward the stand of trees. At an outcropping, she paused and lifted the binoculars.

The trees weren't as thick down low and bright sunshine filtered between the sturdy trunks. The center of the stand had been cleared, a wide center too, from the look of it. Perhaps half as big as a football field. Concrete glared white in the bright sunshine. Two trucks stood side by side on the otherwise empty slab. The size gave her the impression the area was meant for something much larger.

Her earpiece crackled with static and she caught men speaking in Spanish. The words came in sporadic bursts and she caught only two in five, translating them effortlessly.

No time...land here...shut down.

Weird. She risked the possibility they might hear and spoke to Drake. "Did you catch that?"

"Yes." He didn't add more and neither did she.

Easing forward, she slipped from one bit of cover to the next. From her count, only four men guarded the trucks, the rest milled closer to the mine entrance.

She paused behind a gnarled tree as more trucks joined the other two. Two men to each of the four new trucks, making their number twelve. Not good.

She stopped and scoured the terrain for other clues. The rumble of the Land Rover's engine died in her headset and she pressed the right side to her ear for better sound. A car door thunked closed. Drake had reached his destination.

The men smoked as they ambled back and forth between vehicles. Scenery flew through the binoculars as she swiveled for another look at the mine entrance. All the trucks sat parked in front of the mine now.

What, is it lunch time?

She scanned the opposite side of the basin for Drake and caught a glimmer of the Land Rover. She found Drake. He prowled toward an outpost. Falling apart, door half off its hinges, there didn't appear to be anyone actually using the shack. She breathed a little easier. It was a good target for the explosion. The guards would center their search around the blast zone, far from the entrance.

"Come in," Drake whispered.

"I'm here."

Then nothing.

The headset went dead.

A thick vibration emitted from the earth. Stones tumbled from the side of the cliff. Her stomach flipped. She stumbled backward and landed on her backside. *Jesus.* Did the C-4 explode before he could take cover?

"Drake!" she shouted into the headset and fumbled the binoculars to her face. The outpost stood intact. It hadn't blown up. An adrenalin rush churned her already queasy insides. She hadn't heard an explosion.

What the hell was that?

The binoculars picked out the men at the mine entrance and the dim sound of cheering carried on the wind as they applauded. The men in the stand of trees stepped on their cigarette butts and climbed into the trucks. Back at the Land Rover, Drake raced toward the vehicle. Relieved, she tried to raise him on the headset again, but with no success.

No time...land here...shut down.

Had she just experienced an EMP first hand? She glanced to her watch. The LED display was blank. An unmistakable sound, one inner-city dwellers knew well, one she'd learned to recognize as a kid, filled her with dread and she turned toward the noise.

From over the top of the trees, a helicopter loomed like a shark emerging from the water to attack. It's rotary blades blurred in the air above. The chopper banked north, along the perimeter of the basin, its shadow following on the ground.

The chopper, a U.S. Military Iroquois, had been sprayed black, but the paint couldn't hide the make and model.

Someone who should be on her side had betrayed their country to let Acosta have this gem. It pissed her off.

The pilot turned east, on a path straight for her. He was doing a fly-by on the outposts. Although she had cover from ground-level eyes, she had no protection from above. A dull throb emitted from her jaw where her teeth were clenched together and she took a deep breath, releasing the pressure. She couldn't allow rage to dictate her next move.

Sara uttered a long string of curses. Should she keep still, or run back to the road and hope Drake arrived before the helicopter? She ripped the dead headset from her hair and left it hanging around her neck. The binoculars showed the pilot and his passenger clearly. They returned her stare.

"Shit, shit, shit."

She sprinted for the cliff. The mechanical bark of high-powered guns chattered from behind. Clouds of dust plumed ahead of her. She swore and resisted the instinct to shelter her head with her hands, which would slow her pace and inhibit her vision. The din of the helicopter grew, an enraged beast gaining speed.

"Dammit!"

She grasped handfuls of dirt and raced up the incline, but it was already too late. Any second now she'd be mowed down, shot in the back, and there wasn't a damned thing she could do.

Hell with that. She flipped to her back and dug her heels into the dirt to brace herself. She drew both Rugers from the shoulder holsters and started firing.

Drake slammed his hand against the steering wheel. The EMP charge had caught him off guard. Acosta's capabilities were no longer in question, only the scope of his destruction.

Thankfully, he'd turned off the ignition of the Land Rover to save it from the effects of the EMP. The meaning behind the words he'd overheard on the headset became clear. The trucks had returned to shut down for the test.

But one word remained a mystery, *land*. As he began the ascent to where he'd left Sara, it immediately made sense. A helicopter hovered in the air, it's rotary blades turning a scant yard away from the guardrail.

The pilot struggled to hold the Iroquois chopper steady and flinched as bullets ricocheted off the reinforced metal skeleton and bulletproof glass. The man in the passenger seat leaned inward, using the steel floor as cover while rounds sprayed from his automatic.

Drake spat a curse and slammed the accelerator down. His anger over the chopper's origins was nothing compared to the rush of terror that squeezed his chest. They could only be firing at Sara. He would not allow her to be taken from him. Everything he'd feared was unfolding before his eyes.

How had Acosta gotten a damned United States helicopter to begin with? Who the hell had given it to him? If Sara was...injured–his mind balked at the worst-case scenario–he wouldn't rest until he discovered the name of the man responsible for betraying his country.

He stared at the chopper and scrambled for a solution, some way to disable the helicopter. Shooting it wouldn't do much damned good, not while he had to keep the speeding car on the road. The wind from the rotors churned a haze of dust on the road. Each millisecond that passed heightened his anxiety.

As he drew closer, the curtain of dust pulsed sporadically, allowing him a glimpse of the men inside. The pilot and the passenger, who tried his best to shoot Sara, didn't see him. The nose of the Land Rover drew level with the copter. They were oblivious to his presence, too focused on shooting and not getting shot themselves.

In a flash of inspiration he formed a plan. The outcome could be painful, if not fatal.

* * *

Sara gained precious seconds before the Rugers clicked empty. She holstered them and rolled, buying herself another second to pull the back-ups from the holsters on her thighs. The roar of the helicopter changed, the sound of the engine going from the muted rumble of a diesel to the high whining scream of tortured insects. Metal tore from metal with a tinny scream.

Had she hit the fuselage after all? When she turned, the helicopter didn't look any different. Gravel rained down and she twisted as ribbons of guardrail fell around her. The undercarriage of the Land Rover flew over her head, airborne. She saw the exhaust system, the dirt clogged in the wheel rims, the still spinning tires.

Her heart went cold, dead in her chest.

The vehicle collided into the chopper with an ear splitting, chest-felt *whump*. Sara covered her head and spun to the right. Twisted bits of metal flew through the air at such speeds they buried themselves in the loose turf. Hot wind washed over her and she continued to roll. Shards of glass, a long length of rotary blade, and other, more natural matter that she didn't want to see, dropped around her.

Black smoke followed the wash of hot air and when she looked, the ground was littered with indiscernible burning hunks of steel. Her eyes stung, her throat closed, and she coughed. "Drake..."

She yanked the collar of her t-shirt up and over the bottom half of her face as she raced to the top. Fear for Drake urged her to incredible speed. She landed on the top, feeling as if she'd only spared one breath to reach the road.

Her eyes swiveled, her terror making them feel large. Tire tracks ran crazily off the road and through the gap of guardrail.

Drake would have jumped. He would have jumped. He's here.

She pulled the shirt away from her mouth. "Drake?" She stomped in a circle and cupped her hands around her mouth.

"Drake?"

Oh God! Please answer me. "Drake!"

Tears clouded her vision. What if he hadn't jumped? What if he'd gotten stuck in the car? There wasn't anyway Drake could have survived that impact. He would have answered her by now, if he could.

He'd given his life to save hers. "No! No!"

Sara swallowed smoke and coughed again, choking on what felt like her own heart, it was swelled so large with grief. Drake. His handsome, crooked grin, the charming tilt of his head when he whispered in her ear, his strong body next to hers–all of him gone. Tears wet her face and she couldn't catch her breath for the pressure on her chest.

In the distance, trucks raced toward the crash site, but right then, she didn't give a damn.

Drake was gone. She'd lost him. Bruce was beyond her reach without him. She couldn't do this alone, couldn't take down Acosta by herself.

She buried her face in the palm of her hands and crouched low, her legs folding.

"God!" She screamed into her hands.

Why did everyone she loved have to die? She couldn't take it anymore. She didn't want to run from Acosta's men swarming the crash site below. Let them have her, let them kill her and put her out of her misery. There was no reason to keep on living in a world where good men died and bad men won.

Drake was gone, her father was gone, and Bruce would surely not survive this ordeal without help. Kray sat on his hands like a fool. If they'd had backup, none of this would ever have happened. She hated the General, wished he was near at hand so she could kick his ass to hell and back. He was the reason Bruce wouldn't make it through this, he was the reason Drake had died saving her life.

She gasped for air, hiccupping back the tears and glared at the men approaching the smoldering steel. They would win and her life didn't matter.

"No...no."

She wouldn't let Drake's sacrifice be for nothing. Sara wiped her face dry, held her head higher and resisted the overwhelming need to crumble. The men would find her and take her to Acosta. She had the chip in her barrette, and that was still leverage enough to get to Bruce. She would save Drake's father to honor the man she loved.

How stupid she'd been to withhold her love from Drake. She never told him how much she loved him. Now he was dead, and she couldn't tell him. Tears began to flow again and she rubbed them harshly from her cheeks.

God how she wanted to cave, to collapse into a blubbery mess on the road. Maybe she didn't care any longer if she survived this, but she would live long enough to save Bruce. She would do that for Drake.

She stood mutely and closed her eyes. Her mind spun as she prayed to heaven she could wake up in bed and Drake would still be alive, while simultaneously she searched for the strength to finish the mission alone.

Oh God, please help me.

The shouts of men below, the distinct clamor of many trucks answered her plea. She bowed her head. There was no heaven to help her.

"Sara?"

She whipped around, her heart thudding painfully fast in her chest. Across the road, Drake, his face battered, clutching one arm that was red with blood from shoulder to elbow, struggled to step over the far section of guardrail.

Frozen in joyous shock, unable to truly believe her eyes, she stood dumbstruck. Then he made it over the guardrail and the moment broke. She ran to him, crossed the road in four steps, and threw her arms around his neck, kissing him everywhere her mouth could reach and swallowing more sobs.

Oh God, he's alive!

He couldn't be, and yet he was. She cried, bawled against his neck. He kissed her hair, kissed her cheek, and held her tightly.

She pulled back to look in his face, her hands running over the hard plane of his cheekbones, the warm flesh of his neck, as if to prove to herself he wasn't a ghost. His eyes were bloodshot, his gaze loving. She kissed him on the mouth and breathed against his lips the words she never thought she'd get to say, "Drake, I love you."

"Oh, Jesus, Sara," he whispered against her cheek, eyes closed. "I've loved you for so long."

Sara cried anew, but the sense that time was running out, had already run out, urged her into action. She glanced to his shredded jeans. They told how he'd jumped from the Land Rover at top speed and slid down the far side of the rocky incline, opposite the crash site. She'd missed him by thinking he'd landed on the road. How painful the climb back up must have been for him. "Can you walk?"

Drake nodded. "Unfortunately, though, I think we'll have to run, and I'm not up to outracing a truck right now."

Sara caught the gritty sound of pain in his voice, the way his body trembled slightly beneath her hands and nodded. "We've got the chip. We'll pull a Trojan horse on them."

Drake nodded and exhaled largely. She wished there was time to see to his injuries, but the trucks had already started up the incline.

Together, holding hands, they walked slowly down the road toward the enemy and though Sara felt as if she'd exchanged one nightmare for another, she was no longer afraid.

CHAPTER FOURTEEN

Had he been alone, Drake would have drawn his guns on the men approaching and dashed for cover. But with Sara at his side, he wouldn't risk her getting hit. The wounds on his arm burned as he clasped his hands behind his head. This capture was just a means to an end. They wouldn't give up now.

"Que hace usted aqui? Quien es usted?" A stout man with a heavy mustache and black eyes, obviously the highest in rank, poked Drake with the muzzle of his WASR-10's cheap substandard semi-automatic. *"Quien es usted?"*

Drake didn't tell him his name, nor did Sara. Armed men surrounded them, each eyeing his and Sara's weapons.

Mustache poked Drake again. *"Se habla Espanol*? No? Who are you? What you doing here?"

Sara gave him a subtle nod and Drake spoke, "We're looking for Acosta. I have something he wants."

The guards joked how Sara was exactly what they wanted. Although they didn't realize their captives were fluent in Spanish, their chuckles were lecherous in any language. Drake scowled at an obnoxiously ugly man who trained his weapon on Sara and his eyes on her chest.

"We were tol' to 'spect you, *Senor,*" Mustache said. "Give me what you have."

Told to expect them? Drake shook his head.

Mustache glanced to the other five with raised eyebrows, then turned a malicious grin on Drake. "You not understand,

Senor, I tol' you, give me what you have and I take it to Acosta."

"No."

Mustache slammed the butt of his semi-automatic into Drake's ribs. Pain radiated from his side to each of his injuries as if a web of throbbing crimson connected each scrape, bruise, and cut. He doubled over.

Hands flying in animated gesturing, Sara diverted the aim of the guard's weapons to herself. "You idiots. Acosta will want him able to talk. Touch him again and I promise I'll see every one of you made sorry you even looked at him funny."

Mustache eyed her, his smile gone. "What is it you have?"

"We have the computer chip from the last medallion." At his surprise, Sara nodded emphatically. "Take us to him before one of your men sneezes and shoots us."

Mustache followed her line of sight and noticed his men's weapons were aimed at Drake and Sara's head. Drake straightened, a hand pressed against his side. Mustache waved the men to lower their guns and they did, though slowly. He leveled a calculating look on Drake. "We cannot take you armed."

Drake nodded. He'd expected as much and reluctantly tossed his guns to the ground. Sara dropped her weapons with an equal look of regret. A younger, slimmer guard rushed forward to collect them.

"Vests, too." Mustache nodded at the Kevlar.

She shot Drake an alarmed look, then unclasped the straps holding her vest in place. He struggled to get out of his, hissing when he twisted his arm too sharply. Sara stepped forward to help and his vest joined hers. Slim retrieved those as well.

"We check you now." Mustache waved the soldier closest to Sara forward.

Drake was in no way prepared for his hot rage as the

guard ran his hands over Sara's body. He held it in check until the stupid man's hands blatantly passed over her breasts.

He kicked the guard's legs out from beneath him. Head held high, he braced himself for their retaliation. They surprised him by laughing at their fallen comrade.

Mustache nudged the prone guard with his toe, and said, "*Levante, usted engana!*" To Sara, he smiled crookedly and said, "I am sorry. He is ah...how you say? A Don Juan. A ladies' man."

Drake draped his good arm around Sara's shoulders, hauling her up against his side. He gave each of the remaining guards a glare. Although Drake didn't have a weapon to back up his threat, they each averted their eyes.

"We waste time." Mustache gestured to the jeeps parked a good fifty feet down the road.

Drake needed Sara's support, to his disgust. His leg throbbed steadily and he might have fractured something in his elbow, the fingers of that hand throbbed whenever he curled them. He thanked heaven it wasn't his right hand, or he'd have been in serious trouble. The more he moved, the less stiff he felt. Sara helped him down the slope and into the back of the Jeep.

Don Juan and Slim, who carried their weapons, hopped in and sat across from them, their semi-automatics at the ready. Mustache settled in the passenger seat and another guard slid behind the wheel. The last two guards were left to walk back on their own.

Sara leaned into him as they sped away from the road. He couldn't believe she was there, unharmed, beside him. Every injury he'd sustained to take the chopper down had been worth it. He turned his attention back to the terrain. Leaning down, he whispered in her ear. "There was nothing here the last time?"

She shook her head. "No. I was about two miles north and had to pass this place on the way there and back again. I would have seen something as massive as this."

"So they're mobilizing."

The sun beat down, his mouth felt dry and he wished for a drink of water. The scent of smoke lingered in Sara's hair. He glared at the guards across from them. Though they kept their fingers on their respective triggers, the weapons were aimed at the floor. Which was smart as the jeep jostled violently over rutted ground.

"Drake." Sara spoke against his ear. "Before...when our headsets went dead, that was from an EMP charge, wasn't it?"

He nodded. Things were far worse than they'd originally thought.

"How come the Jeep runs?" she asked, still whispering.

"Remember what we overheard on the headset?" He waited for her nod and when she gave it, he continued, "They were shutting off all electrical equipment. If a device isn't on, it can withstand the effects."

Sara nodded her understanding and settled a little closer to his side. Dirt flew up from the back wheels of the Jeep and his eyes burned with grit.

The odor of freshly pumped gasoline and the noxious aroma of the unwashed guards suddenly overwhelmed him. He turned his head, pressed his face toward the cleaner air, and prayed his nausea didn't indicate he'd suffered a deeper trauma.

God, he'd been so damned frightened. He breathed deep and grasped for control of his mind and body. They weren't out of the woods yet.

Acosta must truly need the chip hiding in Sara's barrette, or these goons would have simply shot them in the back of the head, execution style, and left them for the coyotes. The jeep rumbled to a halt in front of the mine entrance.

It was show time and he wasn't armed for this matinee.

They exited the jeep. A streak of hot agony erupted in his arm as Don Juan ground his palm into the wounds, shoving him toward the entrance. Drake twisted away and hissed as he overbalanced and all his weight came down on the injured leg.

"You all right?" Sara gripped him beneath the arms.

"I will be if they don't shove me again." He spat and glared at Don Juan. The man had a massive overbite that accentuated the receding line of his chin. He was one butt-ugly ladies' man. "Watch it, Igor."

He looked puzzled for a moment, called Drake a *bendajo* and shoved him again. Drake, prepared this time, managed to keep his balance. If he were at full capacity, and alone, there was no way these jerks would have the upper hand. As it was, how could he protect Sara now?

Mustache led them inside the black mouth of the mine. As they stepped from sunlight to shadow, Drake hoped the underground labyrinth would not become their grave.

Sara balked when the long circuitous route ended at a set of double cells, the bars of steel and the bunks inside obviously new, but well-used, installments. She didn't want to be locked away, she wanted to confront Acosta and see this day end. Waiting was worse than whatever fate had in store for her.

The guards weren't gentle. They steered her inside with the barrels of their weapons, poking and shoving until she thought she'd scream the next time a black muzzle came near her. Drake entered the next cell and the doors clanged shut, echoing throughout the stone corridors.

"Sit." Mustache gestured to the low cots. "I tell Acosta and come for you." He dragged his automatic over the bars. The menacing clack set her teeth on edge. "Jose," he pointed to Don Juan, then to Slim, "and Marcos will watch you. No funny stuff."

Jose and Marcos stayed outside the doorway and turned their backs to the room. They began an exchange in Spanish that detailed Jose's most recent adventure at a strip club. Sara listened with only half an ear as she grasped the metal bars and tugged. They were firm, set into the ground and ceiling with cement.

"Make's you wonder what Acosta's doing that he needed these cells." Drake stood just opposite her, his wrists resting on the horizontal bar crossing the vertical ones between their cells.

"Yeah, not exactly operation world peace, is it?" Sara surveyed the dismal space. A disgusting bucket sat in one corner, a small and barren cot took up one wall. "Won't find much here. Why don't you search your side for something useful."

She began with the cot, moving it to check the rough stone floor beneath. There wasn't any clue to who may have occupied the cell before her. Nothing of Bruce, no message, nothing at all.

Behind her, Drake grunted in pain and she turned, about to ask if he was all right again, but the question died on her lips. Of course he wasn't all right. He'd nearly killed himself to save her.

She returned to her search and hoped for a stray item, maybe a button or a tassel from one of Bruce's shoes, but aside from the worn cot and reeking bucket, no evidence suggested anyone else had visited the underground holding tank.

"Look, Sara." Drake pointed to a portion of wall which had been hidden by his cot. She peered past him. In the dim light she could barely make out the numbers and symbols.

L(d^2 I(t) / dt^2) + R (dI(t) / dt) + I

She couldn't decipher the rest. "What's that?"

"It looks like a partial code for the circuits of a HERF weapon. This means that at least one of the scientists who disappeared was held here. They're not all Acosta's puppets."

"Which means he's harvesting anyone from the scientific community he thinks will help him, not luring them here or using only those who support his cause." Acosta had no ethics, no morals–no respect. "He's not going to deal fairly with us."

Drake nodded, a bleak considering look settling on his features. "You're right. If we give him the chip, he'll simply kill us, and my father."

Sara reached through the bars and he came to her. The physical contact reminded her once again that he lived. What if it was only a temporary stay of execution? She swallowed past the lump of emotion in her throat and looked into his eyes. "When the helicopter exploded, when I saw the Land Rover going over, I thought you'd been...that you were..."

He shushed her with a light kiss and rubbed her face with his thumb. The caress chilled her flesh and she realized he'd wiped a tear from her face. "I know, I had the same thoughts about you. But we weren't seriously hurt, and it *will* be all right."

She so desperately wanted to believe him. "I would feel better if we knew your father was okay."

"Me too." He kissed her again and rested his forehead against hers.

She drank in his calming presence, relishing the bond between them. To hell with fate, to hell with waiting for Acosta to make the first move. They had to take charge of their own destiny. She straightened. "What have we got to work with?"

He blinked, as if awoken from his own reverie and glanced around. "We can use the metal handles on the buckets. They should pop off easily. The guards probably weren't thinking about protecting themselves from scientists who spend their lives behind a desk, or they would have taken them off. The cots won't be much use though. Not as shields or as weapons."

"I have my barrette," Sara said, considering how they could use the explosive device and manage to take down two armed men. Regardless of how dumb they appeared armed men faced with a confrontation would shoot.

"I've got an idea." Drake kissed her quickly and stepped away from the bars. "Take that bomb off your head."

She grinned and took it out.

"Put the chip in a safe place..." He chuckled as she popped the chip out and stuffed it down her cleavage. "Guess that's a good place."

"Only friendly territory in there." She patted her bra.

He took the barrette. Sara didn't ask him what his plan was, didn't second-guess his intentions. She simply gave him the one true weapon she possessed.

I trust him.

Instinctively she wanted to draw away, to protect herself behind the wall she'd erected in foster care. But that wall no longer had a solid foundation. In the middle of this situation, she was overcome by the frightening joy of finally having the courage to trust with her whole heart, to jump off the tallest cliff and fly. She gave him a brilliant smile.

"What?" he asked, grinning in response.

"I love you, Drake."

"I love you too." He kissed her much too quickly and went to the corner. Face dark with disgust, he yanked the wire handle free of the bucket. "Do the same."

She mimicked his actions all the way down to the grimace.

"You got something to wrap your hands in?" He dropped the empty shoulder holsters to the floor and removed his shirt, wincing as it passed over his injured arm. His bare chest rippled with muscles, the six-pack across his stomach dangerous to her presence of mind. "Sara? You got something for your hands?"

"No." Sara jerked her gaze away. "There's nothing here. Except for my shirt." She lifted the hem to pull it over her head. There wasn't any room for modesty in crucial situations.

"Don't," Drake said when she had the shirt halfway up.

She paused, elbows caught in the fabric, her bra and midriff exposed. She lowered her arms. He yanked on his shirt, tearing it into four strips. "Here, use this. Without a shirt, you would make a nice distraction, but I think we can get by without it."

She shrugged and took the strips. "Thanks."

Drake wound them around his hands, tucking the ends in place. She did the same with both of her hands. Now, when she grabbed the twisted metal ends, the sharp points didn't jab into her palms and the fabric afforded a better grip.

She glanced at his hands, at his arm. "Are you going to be able to manage it?"

He nodded quickly. "Don't worry about me. Take your cot to the far corner. Hold it upright in front of you while I set the charge."

She did. In seconds Drake wired the connections and fitted the barrette into the keyhole of his cell door. She watched from the gap between the metal frame and the fabric of the cot as he took up a similar position in the corner of his cell.

The familiar cold drape of concentration dropped over her mind. Her body hummed, alert and edgy, prepared to face the guards as she waited for the bomb to blow.

The explosion was monstrous in the enclosure. The door clattered to the floor, rocking to and fro like a dropped coin. The sound should have been loud, but it played out in silence as her ears rang from the explosion.

Jose and Marcos raced into the room, their weapons drawn. Jose fumbled with her lock and got it open. The lack of sound gave them an almost comical appearance. Modern-day Keystone cops. At Drake's cue, she rushed forward, the cot in front of her, and threw it at Jose. She had a score to settle with him.

Both men, distracted by the flying cots, made the mistake of taking their attention off Drake and Sara. They wasted energy batting uselessly at the flimsy beds. Sara didn't wait. From the corner of her eye, she saw Drake spring into action.

She twisted behind Jose and wrapped the bucket wire around his neck. Her muscles burned from the intense pressure needed to keep the wire locked around the man's throat. Jose's weapon fell to the ground with a clatter as he clawed at the wire digging into his Adams apple.

Sara jerked on him, allowing her rage to give her added strength. She thought of Drake, nearly killing himself to save her, and she jerked again until the man arched backward, rising on his toes. She thought of Bruce held captive as she followed him down. Jose stopped struggling. From the corner of her eye she saw Marcos fall and Drake lean over to pick up the guard's weapon.

Jose's hands dropped to his sides. Sara let go and he toppled forward, his head *thunking* dully on the stone floor. The wire fell from her fingers and she kicked it away. She bent, picked up the automatic WASR-10 with distaste, and met Drake outside the cell.

"Ready?" he asked.

She nodded. They didn't have much time. Others had likely heard the explosion. They needed to disappear deeper into the mine and find the core of the complex. As much as she disliked using a semi-automatic, she preferred it to bucket wire.

In the hall, she checked the weapon to make certain the safety was off. Jose had felt her wrath, but it was nothing compared to what Acosta would face if he'd harmed Bruce in any way. She was ready.

CHAPTER FIFTEEN

Drake held up a hand to keep Sara back. Dirt walls had given way to concrete and steel and lights hung at regular intervals. He peered into a brightly lit room. Three guards sat at a card table eating spicy looking rice from bowls. They laughed amidst what looked like the bulk of Acosta's arsenal. Guns littered the tops of crates and weapons of every size and make lined metal, freestanding shelves. A library of weapons lay before him. Drake planned on checking out his favorite.

He whispered to Sara. "There are three. Don't use the guns if you can avoid it."

She nodded and pulled the band off the end of her braid. She ran her fingers through the tresses, spreading them over her arms. With the automatic slung across her back, the strap barely detectable behind the drape of her hair, she appeared as non-threatening as a virgin bride. Drake swallowed the need to drag her back out of harm's way. Sara knew what she was doing. She had trusted him, now he would do the same.

Sara gave him a wink and walked boldly into the room with a smile on her lips. Drake crouched low and set his sights on the first man to notice her. If he made one wrong move, he'd have an extra hole in his head.

"*Que pasa?*" Sara asked and placed a hand on her hip. She flirted well, the men, who at first sight of her jumped in alarm, all relaxed and sprouted idiotic grins.

Drake didn't allow their vulgar comments to rile him, but crept up slowly, using Sara to shield him from view. She leaned a hip into the man sitting with his back to Drake to provide better cover for his movements. As on the road, she waved her hands in the air, punctuating her Spanish.

He lifted the semi-automatic and pressed the muzzle against the neck of the man in the chair beside Sara. The guard stiffened, but his comrades remained intent on the flirting blonde and didn't notice. Not until Sara bent and swung her weapon around did they comprehend the threat.

"Don't move." Drake stood, allowing them to see the WASR-10.

Sara sidestepped until positioned between the two. "I suggest you sit."

They didn't move, and she repeated her order in Spanish. Drake told them to put their hands in the air. The three men understood that and did, though the biggest across the table sized him up, gauging if he should fight. Drake shook his head slowly. *Don't even try.*

The man reddened in defeat. Drake caught Sara's eye. In unison, they brought the butt of their weapons down on the two biggest men. The vibration in his injured arm turned his fingers into clenching blocks of ice, but adrenalin dimmed the pain.

As the unconscious guards slumped forward, the third rocked backward in his chair and reached for the 9mm behind him on a crate. Sara knocked the legs of the chair out from beneath him. He hit his head on the crate, sprawled on the floor and Drake used the butt of his gun to knock him senseless. Again, that ugly shiver, as if he'd skewered his funny bone, bloomed in his elbow.

That's gonna really hurt later.

Drake stared at the men littering the floor as the pain

receded. It had all happened so fast, he guessed–less than twenty seconds.

Sara lifted the burly man's head out of his bowl and set it to the side. "I'll tie them up. See if you can't find a Ruger for me." She started rummaging for rope in the crates.

Drake searched through the treasure trove of arms. Unfortunately, most of them were Uzi's and AK-47's. He and Sara preferred handguns, which were easier to carry and didn't jam as much. He continued digging through the crates, prying lids off awkwardly to save his injured arm. Jackpot. He found a crate of Sauers and grabbed four, two a piece.

In the bottom he found clips. He filled his pockets as Sara finished tying the men and joined him. She left the semi-automatic on a shelf and armed herself with the Sauers.

"We've got to be getting close. Hear that?" Sara checked the Sauer for rounds and rammed the clip back inside.

Drake listened as he screwed on a silencer, wishing he'd found more than one. He detected a low hum he'd not consciously noticed before. *She's got good ears.* "I hear it. Let's go."

Drake grabbed her hand and loped out of the chamber. His leg was better, not quite so stiff, but if he didn't place his foot just right, his knee threatened to buckle.

So far, they'd been lucky. Each time they'd encountered a guard, they'd taken cover and remained out of sight, moving again when it was clear. But as they wound further into the web of the mine, hiding places became harder to find. He panted, the sound loud in his head. Exhausted, brain numb with pain, he ran on the potent fumes of his rage and fear.

The closer they came to the heart of the underground compound, the more resistance they'd encounter. It was only a matter of time before they were spotted–or before Mustache found the cells occupied by the men left to guard them.

Sara peered backward occasionally, the pressure on their joined hands changing as she paused. She kept him safe from behind, while he protected her from the front. He was glad she hadn't agreed to stay in the Land Rover and out of harm's way. He could never have taken Acosta on his own. Without her, he would have failed.

The strange echoing warble of music reverberated in chasms and corridors. He frowned, surprised. The last thing he'd expected to hear over the growing hum was music. The operatic piece came from straight ahead.

A brown and black uniformed guard emerged from around the bend. Drake rushed forward, releasing Sara's hand as he punched the man in the windpipe to keep him from crying out. But the guard wasn't alone. His friend hardly had time to be surprised before Sara delivered a boot into the hollow beneath his ribs. Gasping for air, the two men curled on the floor.

The guard Sara had taken down reached for his weapon and Drake kicked it from his hand. Together, he and Sara knocked the men unconscious. They didn't have time to tie the men up, however, and stepped over their prone bodies.

The corridor ended on a suspiciously unguarded chamber. Drake didn't trust the empty cavern and pressed his back to the stone wall as he searched the dark ceiling.

There, in two corners, the red light of a camera glowed. He used the silenced Sauer to shoot both cameras. They paused for a heartbeat, waiting for an alarm to sound.

No whistles or ringing bells, no contingent of Acosta's men rushed into the room. With most surveillance equipment of this sort, no one monitored the feed on a regular basis, or if they did, they'd fallen asleep. They'd grown comfortable in their underground nest. But he and Sara would stir things up, hopefully without getting stung.

Sara cautiously followed him as they wound along the wall toward the large double doors at the opposite end. The opera music, he recognized *La Dolce Vita,* rang clear.

He reached for the door as a wiry, dangerous looking man with a single eyebrow walked through. He froze as he spied them, the white bandage across the bridge of his nose pristine against his swarthy face.

Drake jerked and pressed the silenced muzzle to the wiry man's temple. "Where's Acosta?"

Deliberately, the man pressed his mouth closed. His brackish brown eyes narrowed on Sara, then widened with unmistakable recognition. The man stiffened and Drake understood she must be responsible for the man's broken nose.

Sara stepped closer, a Sauer in each hand. "What's it gonna be this time? An arm? A leg? You choose, I aim to please." She pointed one gun toward each limb in question wearing a devilish grin, cold malice in her eyes.

"I'm not sayin' a damn thing."

"We already know about you–the Dulce Patriots–and what Acosta's up to," Sara replied. "We only need you to tell us where Acosta is holding Colonel Knight. Tell me and you'll walk out of here. Keep silent, and you'll have to crawl."

Drake pressed his gun harder on Wiry's temple. The man stiffened, but gave no other outward sign of fear.

"If you know so much, find him yourself."

Sara's aim didn't waver as she moved forward. The man squirmed in Drake's grasp.

"I suggest you do what the lady asks," Drake warned.

Wiry tried to twist his head away, but Drake followed him. "Fine." The man cursed. "You'll die anyway. He's in there."

He gestured with a jerk of his chin to the doors, but Drake didn't release him. "My father?"

"He's in there with him." Wiry sneered.

"Thanks." Drake smashed the base of the man's skull with the Sauer and he fell to his knees, but not unconsciousness. As Drake moved in to deliver another heavy blow, Wiry swung out and grabbed Drake's legs.

He fell to the ground in a teeth-jarring heap. He was reminded forcefully of every injury he'd suffered. His leg howled in agony and a trail of vibrating pain rose up and down his injured arm.

Sara slammed her foot against the man's head and Wiry dropped like a lead weight. She held out a hand to help Drake up and as he grasped it, he realized Wiry played possum.

"Sara!" Drake called too late.

She'd braced herself backward to help Drake stand, and when Wiry shoved her forward in a lop-sided tackle, there wasn't time to shift her balance and she fell on top of Drake. In an instant her face contorted in pain as the man yanked her on her feet with a fistful of hair.

Drake lurched up, fighting pain. No one touched Sara and got away with it. He wanted to shoot the bastard. Afraid he'd hit Sara if Wiry tried to use her as a shield, he decided to take him apart with his bare hands. Drake advanced, murder in mind.

Wiry whipped Sara against the wall before she could do more than grab at his hands. Her head smacked into the stone with a dull *thunk*. She fell in a heap, her face covered by a blanket of hair. Drake growled low in his throat.

Wiry met him in the center of the room and swung at the same moment he did. Drake's lip split against Wiry's knuckles as his fist mashed Wiry's mouth against his teeth. Knocked backward, they again rushed toward each other. Wiry growled low in his throat as he grasped Drake around the ribs and plowed him backward into the wall.

Pinned, Drake twisted the man around for a chokehold,

but Wiry wasn't a novice and managed to get in two hard jabs to Drake's already bruised ribs. He grunted in pain and doubled to protect his mid-section. A fist breezed by his chin as he lurched sideways to avoid the uppercut.

Wiry, caught off-balance by the force of the unconnected blow, stumbled. It was all the opening Drake needed. He punched the man square in his broken nose and the man whined with pain.

Drake didn't stop. He punched him in the cheek, and again in the jaw, driving the man backward and across the room. He pivoted and roundhouse kicked the man in the ear. Finally, Wiry fell, this time sincerely unconscious.

Drake breathed heavily and wiped blood from his pulsing, engorged bottom lip. He blinked hard, the blood rushing too fast to his head, pounding through him on a wave of pain.

He shook off the blackness and went to Sara's side, going down on one knee, joints popping and crackling. She moaned. His hand shook as he pulled hair aside to see her face.

She rolled to a sitting position, rubbing the back of her head. Her glance went from him, to Wiry and back again. She smiled ruefully. "I think I know how those guards are going to feel when they wake up."

"Are you okay?" He gently parted her hair and searched for signs of trauma. No blood, just an angry reddish knot above one ear. Relief trembled in every muscle.

"Yeah, I'm fine."

He helped her to her feet, holding his wounded arm tight to his side. "Are you sure you're okay?"

She rolled her shoulders, shook her head tentatively, then nodded. Her eyes were clear, but he sensed the hidden pain in her slow movements. She retrieved the Sauer from the floor and snapped the slide back with a wince. "Let's get Bruce."

"And finish this once and for all." *Before I can no longer walk on my own.*

One more obstacle, one more battle before the war, and he'd have nothing left. New anger accompanied his frustration and Drake turned to the wooden doors. The opera had ended, and so had his patience.

Sara stood beside Drake and at his nod, flung open her side of the double doors as he did his. The room beyond was sparse and narrow, resembling a wide hallway. They moved together, stepping lightly and silently, guns ready. Ahead, a bright rectangle of light covered the floor, indicating an opening into another chamber.

Eyes wide, heart racing, head still ringing dully from meeting the wall, Sara inched toward the next room. Drake stiffened behind her and she slowed, listening. Over the large humming noise came the sound of men talking.

They paused at the opening and leaned to peer into the room. Computers lined the walls, rich carpets draped the floor, and new, yet well lived in, furniture gave the dank, cavernous room a European flavor. In the middle of it all was Bruce.

He sat with his back to them in an armless chair, his hands cuffed behind his back. Rolled maps and electronic equipment cluttered the table before him. He held his head high and from her position, she thought he looked all right, no evidence of foul treatment.

Drake's inhaled breath was enough to tell her he'd spotted his father. Acosta appeared to be absent. Three elderly men, likely a group of the missing scientists, manned the computers as silently and obediently as drones. Sara wondered how close they were to fulfilling their plan, and if the chip remained a good enough bargaining tool. If it wasn't, they had little hope of rescuing Bruce and escaping with their lives.

She eased around the corner, the Sauer heavy in her hand. Drake, his weapon aimed toward the ceiling, stepped into the room beside her. No guards stopped them. The humming rose in volume until it was an entity that lived and breathed.

The sound pulsed along her nerve endings and she had to consciously keep from clenching her jaw. She and Drake moved stealthily toward Bruce, but it felt like a set up. As if Bruce were the honey pot and they were the bears lured into the den. She didn't like it and pressed her free hand to Drake's chest, holding him back as she frowned at the room.

Were there hidden dangers here? Or was it as non-threatening as it appeared?

"I see you've found us. I knew you would." A tall man, with dark hair graying at the temples stepped from the shadows on their right.

Sara spun around, and gasped–not at the man, but at the monster behind him. The room beyond, nearly hidden from view by an outcropping of rock wall, boasted the mechanism from which the humming emanated.

Forty feet tall and just as wide, the machine was much larger than anything she expected. The natural cavern housing it glowed from the light of dozens of computer boards installed around the base. The sheer size of the cylinder made Acosta appear small in comparison.

He stepped forward and pressed the muzzle of a. 45 to Bruce's head before she or Drake could react. Sara cursed. The shock of the gigantic machine made her pause when she should have acted. Now, her hands were tied. She couldn't risk shooting Bruce who sat between her and Acosta.

The barrel of Acosta's .45 looked entirely too large against Bruce's head. "I don't think we need anything as mundane as introductions."

"Release my father," Drake barked, aiming his Sauer at the madman. His voice rasped on an exhausted wave of desperation. Sara's heart ached to hear it.

Acosta chuckled and waved a hand at Drake as if he was a bothersome child. "I doubt you're ready to bury your father. You won't shoot."

"Watch me." Drake renewed his aim and inched closer. Sara added her gun to his, standing sideways so both weapons could occupy the same sight line, right between Acosta's eyes. *We work as one.*

"I wouldn't advise it." Acosta ran a hand, caressingly, down the back of Bruce's head. "It's amazing how very fragile the human skull is. You would think God would have given us something stronger than mere bone to protect the most delicate and important part of the human body."

She narrowed her eyes and turned the Sauer sideways in reply to his threat. "That doesn't mean we won't kill you where you stand."

"Sara Stark, I presume." He smiled at her, as if this was his party and he, their gracious host. "I've heard such interesting things about you. But let me first caution you both, if you fire your weapons, it will stop nothing. They," he gestured toward the men at the computers, "will continue without me in order to receive compensation for their efforts. You should consider what it will mean to not only bury your mother, Mr. Knight, but your father as well. Why don't you put those weapons away and we can have our little chat."

Sara looked at Drake who had gone pale at the mention of his mother. What should they do? His attention, fixated solely on Acosta, offered her no indication of what he wanted.

"Do as he says," Bruce said from the chair. He sounded winded and worried. "There's a big enough EMP generator in the other room to wipe all of us out if it's hit by a stray bullet. It's unstable. They nearly lost it this morning during a test. You have no choice."

Sara lowered her gun slightly and inched forward, a plan taking form in the back of her head. She stopped an arm's length from Bruce. Acosta eyed her, but seemed more concerned with Drake. "How are you, Colonel?"

He shook his head. "Doesn't matter. I'm fine. But you'll have to lower your weapons."

Drake grunted, showing his disapproval. "Dad..."

"Just do it son, it'll be all right."

Handcuffed to the chair, in the clutches of the enemy, Bruce managed to sound commanding. Sara did as he had asked, feeling naked without the protection. Drake followed, though much slower. His bare, bloody, and dirty chest seemed too big a target.

"Unfortunately, I don't feel as if I can continue until you've removed the rest of your weapons." Acosta pushed the muzzle of the .45 against Bruce's head until he was bent at an odd angle. "I would hate to prove just how necessary it is for you to comply at this moment. Slide your weapons across the floor to me."

She measured him, watching his eyes. He meant it. He would shoot. The thought of a bullet passing through Bruce's head sickened her and she did as he asked. Drake's weapons followed hers silently in a spinning dance across the carpet.

Disarmed, again.

"Ahh, now that's better." Acosta stretched a leg out and kicked the guns behind him. He allowed Bruce to straighten, but didn't remove the gun. "Now we can talk."

Drake, hands fisted at his side, glared. "We dropped our weapons, now drop yours."

"This?" Acosta stared with feigned surprise at the gun in his hand. "It's nothing, just a little something to help jar the Colonel's memory. But now that you're here, and from what I understand, carrying the information I want, I guess we won't need this, will we?"

"What do you want, Acosta?" Sara stalled, shaping the

plan, honing it, checking it for flaws.

"I would have thought you would know, Sara. You've got as much to hate this man for as I do." Acosta grinned.

"I have nothing in common with you." Jarred by the despicable insinuation, she gave him a scathing look.

"No?" Acosta didn't appear perturbed by her brusque tone. "Because of him, you lost your entire family, just as I did. Yet you remained loyal to the one person you should hate. Think of it Sara. You were abandoned, sent into foster care, victimized by the system. He left you there for four years. You think I don't know? I know, Sara, and I'm offering you the chance to gain justice against those who harmed you most.

"You see, I'm not so different than you. When this pitiful excuse for a man invaded my homeland." Acosta stopped, and Sara was dismayed by the crazed rage in his eyes. It was as she'd thought–he would never deal fairly with them. "When my daughter was...murdered, when my wife was killed, I knew that if I didn't do something to right this injustice, your government would continue its course of unjustified destruction."

"So you killed my father!" Sara shouted, startled by the unexpected strength of her own deep anger. How dare he compare himself to her? Drake's hand settled in silent restraint on her shoulder. He'd snuck closer during Acosta's tirade. Bruce stared silently at the table, his shoulders hunched with guilt.

Three heartbeats passed while Acosta considered her. He shrugged, as if concluding she was entitled to an outburst. "He was only in the wrong place at the wrong time. But, now you are in the right place at the right time and can finally find justice against the man who stole your father from you."

"Not a chance, Acosta," Sara bit the words out, struggling to keep her cool and think clearly. *The plan, the plan, the plan...*"Nothing changes the past. Not even this scheme of yours."

"My scheme?" Acosta said, his face innocent. "It is not just mine. There are many more involved here. I'm more like the...maestro."

"I don't give a damn what you are," Drake said. "You're going down, Acosta."

"So rude, Mr. Knight!" Acosta acted shocked, covering his mouth for a moment in a gesture that was almost feminine. "I do believe you've got better manners than that. I also believe you're smart enough to understand the benefit of what I'm doing."

"Benefit?" Sara snorted. "What benefit has ever come from attacking innocent people? You believe the U.S. is responsible for what happened to your family, but if you destroy hundreds of families in revenge, that makes you a thousand times more evil than you ever thought we were."

Acosta's face darkened dramatically, his eyes glittering with malevolence. "They called it Operation Just Cause! What cause would ever justify the death of my innocent daughter! Martina was my life and now she's ashes, crushed under the boot of your government!"

The .45 tapped the side of Bruce's head as he gestured wildly with his other hand. Bruce cringed. The blatant twisted madness on Acosta's face made her fear the gun might fire, blowing blood and bits of Bruce's skull all over her. She had no compassion for this soulless madman.

"Sara..." Bruce spoke her name in a cautionary whisper. He turned and she saw the right side of his face. It was blackened, the eye swollen closed.

The evidence of what he'd suffered since capture cleared her head and that cold curtain of calm dropped back over her mind. The plan completed itself. She positioned herself closer to the table.

"What makes you believe that *you* have just cause, Acosta? By your own logic you could grant the same name to this operation of yours. How do the deaths of other daughters honor the memory of yours? Your wife, would she be pleased to know you left countless children without mothers? Release the Colonel, there's still time to do what's right."

The room fell silent. The white-coated men at the computers had all turned to gape at the drama playing out before them. Sara registered them peripherally, unsure if they were a threat or not, and watched Acosta for a sign she'd gotten through.

He closed his eyes and as she prepared to move, Drake stepped forward. Acosta opened his eyes, his stare halting them both. For one wild second, Sara remembered the kid's game, *Mother may I*?

Nothing had changed in the depths of his gaze. This was no game, there was no talking him down. She waited, ready to spring.

"I don't think you fully understand what we can achieve here." A strange rictus of a smile spread over his features. "Imagine a world, Sara, where people have to speak to each other face to face. Where military commanders are forced to fight beside their men because they cannot communicate from thousands of miles away.

"Imagine a world in which people remain in their homelands, instead of crossing oceans to wage war and steal the resources that rightfully belong to others. Our high technology has left us weak, left the heart of our nations heartless.

"Why would you fight so hard to protect the very people and systems that have hurt you Sara, that have wronged you and destroyed everything you love?"

For an instant, she heard the echo of a scarred conscience telling her that no one cared, that the screwed-up system was an entity to be hated, that her lousy government had allowed her to rot in juvie and the laughable place they called foster care. The daughter of a hero, cast off like so much refuse from the White House table.

The voice faltered and died as she glanced to Drake and down to Bruce. "You're wrong, Acosta. You can't attack the system from the outside and save the very people you claim you want to protect. Too many innocent lives will be lost in the process."

"Innocent? Who is innocent?" Acosta stared off into the distance. "My children were innocent, and yet they were killed. You were innocent, and yet they didn't care for you. What are a few lives to the cleansing of the world?"

His voice grew strong. "When the uplink is complete and the EMP wave goes out over the world, everything will change. Did you know each large city has only a two-day supply of food? Men and women will be forced to work the land as God meant them to. We'll return to a healthier lifestyle, one which will not destroy the earth. The system as we know it will cease to exist. I'm giving mankind a gift!"

Sara sent Drake a look, trying to convey she meant to act soon and he should be ready. Now was the time, while Acosta was distracted by explaining the glory of his sick plan.

"We," Drake bit out, "will not let you to do this!"

Acosta grimaced in distaste. "You are too late. My men will have you in custody soon."

"Your men," Drake said in a low growl, "are lying face down in the dirt. Release my father or you'll join them."

Bruce's battered face turned to them, his eyes communicating caution.

Acosta shook his head impatiently and returned the pistol to Bruce's temple. "It does not matter. Give me the chip," he pushed again, bending Bruce's head backward, "or it will be your father who lies face down in the dirt."

"Not going to happen, Acosta. Give it up." Sara shifted, her hip touching the table. She calculated the angle and distance between her and Acosta.

"Sara, don't give it to him," Bruce called sternly.

Drake took another step. "Release him now, Acosta, while you still breathe."

Acosta's glare glittered beneath the sodium lights high on the ceiling. "The chip, or your father."

Calm, she thought, she had to remain calm. She recalled the American flag draped over her father's coffin. She recalled the stark bleakness of being set anchorless in a sea of hurt and loneliness at the tender age of eight. And here was the man responsible for it all. He would not take a second father.

Bruce pleaded to her, "Do not give him the chip." He raised his chin. "I will die for my country."

"No, you won't." Sara's voice cracked on the words.

"Sara," Drake warned. "Don't do it."

"I will not allow your father to die, too."

Acosta's leer stretched wider. "You are smart to comply."

She dug the chip out from her bra. Acosta might receive the data in return for Bruce's life, but her plan would stop him from using it. She held it up between index and thumb. "If you want this, step back from the Colonel."

Acosta didn't move at first, he continued to stare at Drake.

"Step back, Drake," she whispered.

"No." The word came out strangled, more a denial of what was happening than a refusal. He caught her eye and she tried to assure him. He stepped back.

Acosta immediately removed the .45.

"Give me the key for the cuffs." Sara held the chip up. "Or I'll crush this under my boot."

"This is my last concession." He tossed the key to the floor beside Bruce's chair. "Now, the chip."

"Don't do it, Sara." Bruce struggled against the cuffs, rocking in the chair. Drake bent to pick up the key.

She remained silent, watching, waiting.

"The chip." Acosta held out his hand.

"Sara, no!" Bruce was frantic. Drake slipped the key into the cuffs and unlocked them.

Sara placed the chip in Acosta's hand, forcing herself not to move too soon. Bruce rubbed his wrists and casting his one, incredulous open eye between Acosta and her.

She shivered when Acosta's flesh met hers, as if she'd just been exposed to a hellish disease through the minimal touch. Whatever Acosta thought he could accomplish next, he would be sorely surprised. Sara swallowed the urge to spit in his smug, grinning, face.

CHAPTER SIXTEEN

Drake thrummed with the need to act. His father stood, hunched slightly as if in pain. He wanted to check and make sure the scum hadn't hurt him, but couldn't take his eyes off Acosta. He asked his father, "Are you all right?"

Bruce nodded.

"Thank you." Acosta tucked the .45 in his belt, held the chip to the light. He pivoted and gestured to one of the scientists. "Yusoff, begin the uplink right away."

A scraggly bearded man, gaunt and exhausted looking, stepped forward and accepted the chip as if it were a precious gem. As Acosta turned back, Sara, in a swift move Drake hardly saw, clicked the blade out from the toe of her boot, and extended her leg until the razor sharp edge rested against Acosta's throat. One hand planted on the table, the other curled into a fist, her agility was breathtaking.

Acosta merely smiled. "I'm afraid you're already too late. Our scientists will not abort unless I give the order."

The blade scored his neck, a trickle of blood welled over the tip. Sara grit her teeth. "Then give the order."

Drake quivered, ready to back her up. Acosta's hands inched closer to the gun in his belt. Drake glanced to the floor where the Sauer's lay. If he could manage to dive for one, turn, aim, and fire before Sara was injured, he'd put a stop to all this madness. The terrible odds he'd manage such a feat in his current condition killed him with frustration.

He was reduced to a warning. "Sara, watch his hands."

She nodded. "Put your hands in the air, Acosta, or I'll slice you through." When he didn't move to do as she'd ordered, she spoke to Bruce. "Take his gun, Colonel."

Bruce reached forward as Drake eased toward the weapons on the floor. Three more feet and his plan might actually work.

"You can't stop us now." Acosta laughed, a high crazy sound and snatched the gun before Bruce's fingers closed around the butt. He threw himself backward. Sara's boot-blade opened his flesh from ear to chin, missing the vein in his neck.

Surprised Acosta ignored both the painful wound and Sara, but instead leveled his sights on the Colonel, Drake shouted a wild yell of warning. Unarmed and directly in front of Acosta, his father dove for cover, but was too late.

Drake, already flying toward the weapons on the floor, landed and fisted his hand around a Sauer. A shot boomed behind him and echoed in the chamber. The scientists all turned, their faces displaying like images of shock.

He stared, unbelieving, the Sauer forgotten. His father lay sideways, blood seeping from a hole high in his chest. The floor swayed beneath him, the world tilting in his devastation. "No!"

Gripping cold steel, Drake aimed the gun at Acosta, only to find the madman hadn't stopped with his father.

Sara, oh God! Sara!

Her white, stricken face gazed at him over the forearm wrapped around her throat, Acosta's gun poised to shoot her beneath the chin.

"Fire your weapon, Mr. Knight, and her pretty face becomes ground beef." Acosta snarled, all his gentlemanly demeanor gone.

"Damn you," Drake roared as he knelt beside his father. The blood was dark, his father's face ashen. He glared at Acosta. "Damn you to hell!"

Acosta started backward. "This is not the end, my friend. We'll see how skilled you are in a world where you cannot use technology to hunt me."

Drake wanted to scream with frustration. He lifted the Sauer uselessly, the barrel shaking as he prayed for one good shot, but none presented itself. He lowered the gun in defeat.

"Stop them, Drake," Sara said, her voice choking.

They disappeared into the blackness beyond the exit. Drake thought his chest would crack in half from grief. Torn, he couldn't go after her, his father needed him. He dropped the Sauer and lifted his father's head.

"Dad," he gasped the word. "Can you breathe?"

His father nodded slightly, but Drake heard the bubbling in his chest. "Give me a phone, son, something. I can call Kray."

Drake nodded, but didn't move away. He frantically tore at his father's shirt, exposing the gaping red eye of the entry wound. There wasn't much time. He yanked at the torn shirt until it came free, leaving his father in nothing but a bloody undershirt. He balled the fabric into a compress and held it against the wound. "Here, hold this, keep pressure on it."

Bruce clasped the wadded fabric and Drake faced the scientists who all typed madly. He lifted the Sauer once more. "Stop the uplink. Right now."

They didn't turn, they didn't stop, and a monitor set above the bank of computers flickered into life. It showed a mountainous expanse that Drake assumed to be Pico de Orizaba. A steel door lifted and a huge satellite dish emerged from its underground hiding place. "I said stop!"

Again, they didn't respond. He checked his father and saw

he breathed easier. How dare the scientists ignore him while his father lay dying, he got to his feet. There was no time for games.

With a calculated swing, he snapped the butt of the Sauer against the nearest man's head and the scientist fell without a sound. Drake placed the barrel of the Sauer in Yusoff's ear, wedging it in as much as he could. "Stop this now, or I'll kill you and do it myself."

Yusoff turned, his comrade beside him crouched low in his chair, his hands over his head in fear. "You cannot." His Russian accent was thick. "Once begun, there is no way back."

"There's always an abort system." Drake pressed the muzzle of the Sauer into the space between the man's eyebrows. "My father is dying. Stop the uplink now and give me a phone to call for help, or you'll be the first to die."

He shook, he wanted to pull the trigger. Never before in his life had he been so driven to kill another human being. The feeling was large, untamed.

Yusoff gestured to the cowering scientist. "Give him the satellite phone."

The frightened man scurried out and brought a bulky phone to Bruce. Yusoff spoke low, his tone sympathetic, "The pulse will make rescue impossible. I am sorry."

"Sorry?" Drake shouted. "If you are so sorry, you son-of-a-bitch, then stop this now! I won't ask again."

Yusoff swallowed hard, his eyes flicking left and right. "I am sorry. I can not stop."

Ready to kill the man where he sat, he started to pull the trigger. Yusoff's eyes grew to twin moons. Drake hesitated. He couldn't do it. As much as he despised the scientist for his complicity in Acosta's scheme, he could not gun down a man who was unarmed. He couldn't kill in cold blood. With a growl he knocked the scientist away. Yusoff gave a startled cry as he fell to the floor.

Behind him, Bruce gasped into the phone. Aware the other scientist must be close to his unarmed, vulnerable father, he spun around. "Move away from him!"

The scientist stepped back, hands in the air. "*Pas de problème, Monsieur*."

French, Drake thought crazily. "Leave. Run!" He fired in the air. "*S'en aller!*"

Yusoff didn't wait to be told. The men turned and fled. Bruce finished speaking and dropped the phone, his breath harsher. Drake went to him, knelt, and lifted the phone. The ugly hum of a dial tone mingled with the ever-present throb of the EMP generator and he tossed it away.

"Dad," he whispered and gave his father a gentle shake. Bruce opened his eyes. "Did you get through?"

Bruce nodded. "Help's...coming..."

He closed his eyes, his mouth going slack.

"No!" Drake leaned low, holding his cheek close to his father's face. Hot, warm breath touched his skin. His father still breathed, he'd merely passed out.

The EMP generator whined in a higher pitch, the massive weapon charging. Drake straightened and wiped the damp from his eyes, his heart pounding loud in his ears. He couldn't think about his father, about Sara, he had to stop the uplink.

With a massive effort, Drake regained his feet. He sat at Yusoff's computer. His exhausted body hummed with the generator. Fingers aching as they worked the keyboard, he read command lines, searching for the abort code. Help might come in time to save his father, but if he didn't stop the EMP from shutting down the country, there wouldn't be a hospital to take him to.

Acosta pushed Sara ahead of him. She stumbled, a tangle

of horrors filled her head. Bruce shot, Drake's stricken face, and the knowledge that while she was being forced through a new path of natural corridors, the uplink was engaged. She'd lost.

"You are a very brave young woman." Acosta guided her left and right with the muzzle of the .45 pressed into the small of her back. "It's a shame you'll have to die. I've watched you for some time. I had hoped you would be an ally in this endeavor."

"Never." Sara hated him behind her. She wanted him out front, where she could watch for a chance to fight back. She plodded through the shadowy passages, lit sporadically by hanging bulbs from the ceiling. The odor of water became stronger, the unmistakable rush of an underground stream louder.

"Are you certain?" Acosta asked, his tone perplexed. "You understand you would not be the first woman I've killed."

"No? Do you make a habit of it then?" Nervous anxiety and frustration rippled beneath the surface of her flesh. She wished she could turn and face him head on.

Acosta chuckled, then grunted, as if the movement hurt. *I hope it did.* "No, not a habit, but I've learned to do what's necessary. You'll soon see."

Sara kept her eyes open for a trap. Somewhere, up ahead, was the place he planned to kill her.

The path widened, the walls creeping outward until she could see the hanging stalactites and actually see the churning water far below. A narrow rope bridge, very old and tattered but still intact, crossed the river and led to another lighted path on the opposite side of the deep gorge.

Acosta stopped her with a hand on her shoulder. He pressured her into turning right where the body of a woman, her legs twisted beneath her, a bullet hole in the center of her forehead, lay in the dirt. The body gave off a gaseous stench. The cool interior of the cave had slowed the decaying process, but not halted it. Sara guessed less than a week had passed since Acosta had killed her.

"See," Acosta removed the gun from her back and used the barrel to point at the corpse, "Professor Salinger could not be convinced to save her life."

Professor Salinger? *Barbara Salinger*? Sara's stomach flipped. The woman she admired was dead, and again, Acosta was responsible. Never mind they'd never met, the woman was legendary for her knowledge, her expertise, and her generous nature. It couldn't be. But as she looked again, she recognized the strong, queenly features.

Rage, such as she'd never felt before, erupted with volcanic force. She loosed a guttural warrior's cry, pivoted, and grasped Acosta's hand holding the .45 with both of hers. She flipped him over her shoulder.

The gun fired, the bullet hit the fleshy part of her thigh, the pain immediate and dark red. With another cry of rage, she swiped Acosta's hand with the blade of her boot and he drooped the gun. She kicked it over the ledge and into the rushing water.

Acosta rolled and got to his feet. "That wasn't wise, Sara."

Her name sounded strange in his mouth–too familiar, too *close.* No, she was not Sara, not now. She was the woman who'd make him pay. "My name is Stark, you bastard."

She snapped her leg forward and flayed Acosta's cheek with the blade in her boot, ignoring the pain of all her weight on the injured thigh.

He hollered, his hands going to the torn flesh on his face. With a look of utter hatred, he launched himself at her. Sara waited, ready and eager.

His hands grasped her throat and they fell backward. Sara

tripped over one of the professor's upright boots and they slammed into the wall. Acosta squeezed, but she grinned, her hatred so complete the pain only added to her fury.

She kneed him sharply in the groin and his grip loosened a fraction. Bringing both hands up between his arms, she struck the insides of his elbows and he let go of her neck.

Acosta swung a large fist at her face, but she ducked, countering with her own uppercut. His head snapped back and blood trickled from the corner of his mouth. He stumbled backward, shook his head, and raced forward again–the lower half of his face, half his neck, soaked with glistening blood.

Again, she kicked, slicing the opposite cheek open and he fell sideways. On his knees, he threw himself forward and tackled her legs. She landed on her back and he clawed his way on top of her, ignoring her punches, her kicks, and the stream of obscenities she flung at him.

He grasped at her wrists, but she'd expected the move and brought her hands together to form a club. She swung and connected with his jaw. He flopped over and she rolled away.

She got one leg under her when Acosta grasped the back of her pants and yanked. Back on the ground, the dirt ground into her arms and head.

Acosta punched her before she could recover from the fall and her cheek exploded with pain that buzzed into her teeth. Her thigh throbbed in unison and she realized her pant leg was soaked.

"There," Acosta breathed heavily, his face a mass of torn and bloody skin. "Now you die." His fists closed around her neck once more.

She would not die this way, not at his hands. Heated anger vibrated the muscles of her arms and legs. Planting her feet beneath her, she shoved off the ground and forced him away. She bombarded him with deliberate and satisfying blows to the head and gut. Acosta stumbled toward the bridge.

Sara faltered as her wounded thigh went numb and again his grip closed off her windpipe. She clenched her hands around his throat and the fight became a battle to see who would lose consciousness first–either from loss of blood or oxygen.

They stood, elbows locked, feet digging into the hard-packed dirt. He stumbled again, moving onto the bridge until the black drop to the river stretched away on either side of them.

Her hands slid in hot, slick blood. She twisted before she lost her hold and broke free of his equally loosening grasp. With the all her strength, she shoved him backward until his back bent over the hand rope stretched above the wooden planks.

She gasped damp air, the sound of the river rushing into her ears. Acosta gurgled, his hands locking on her wrists. He kicked the bullet wound on her thigh. She cried out and rocked back against the hand rope opposite him. The board beneath her feet splintered and she clutched at the dusty, ancient rope.

Acosta kicked her in the chest. The board beneath her foot cracked in two, the ends tumbling away into the swift current below. Her death grip on the rope kept the rest of her from following her leg through the gap.

Acosta panted. "Goodbye, Sara."

He lunged and at the same moment, she dove right. His forward motion carried him onto the rope, then over it. Crouched low, she closed her eyes and waited for the splash. Instead, the bridge tilted violently downward. Acosta hung by one hand to the same frail hand rope she did.

The bridge swayed with the sudden dangling weight of the man scrambling to get back onto the wooden planks. Sara watched in horror as the hand-ropes unraveled and broke midway, dividing the bridge in two. They flew through the air, the wind cold on her skin. Their half of the bridge slammed against the cliff wall. She winced as her hands burned hotly down the rope.

Acosta dangled three feet beneath her, cursing and struggling to hang on. She hooked a foot into a plank of wood and fought her numb thigh for leverage. Acosta started to climb, bracing his feet against the stone.

His hand clutched the ankle of her wounded leg and Sara shifted her weight, her plan to shake him off dissolving in a burst of pain. He pulled, intent on flinging her into the roaring river below. She growled with frustration. Her hands were on fire. If she didn't dislodge him soon, she'd plunge to her death.

Again he yanked, and she screamed. His grip tightened and she sensed him collecting the last of his strength for a massive assault.

When he pulled again, she left the planks completely and swiped the boot blade through the rope above his hands. Acosta switched all his weight to her bad leg. Her palms shredded as she slid further down. Her vision dimmed, she blinked, afraid she'd pass out from the bone-throbbing pain.

She glanced down, tears of weariness splashing a path down her hot cheeks. His leering, bloody face turned up to her. Their eyes met.

"Can you fly, Stark?" he asked, his voice hollow. His hands groped for a better grip on her ankle.

New fury dried her tears. *Could she fly?* Bastard. "Can you?"

She swung Acosta backward, arching herself in a kaleidoscope of red, orange, and black agony. She slammed him forward, twisting as she did so. He hit the cliff wall and her foot swiveled in his hands, the blade on her boot slicing into his wrist. He let go, a look of shock on his face as she twisted once more and cut into the wrist of his other hand.

He fell, his scream a siren of refusal. She turned her gaze away. After a suspended, eternal moment, he hit the river with a muted, distant splash.

She clung to the rope, breathing hard. Relieved to be alive, she didn't feel a damn bit guilty for killing the sadist. He would have killed her, had killed already; she refused to give him a token of her pity.

The wreckage of her leg thwarted her efforts as she worked her way up the rope. The boot blade couldn't penetrate the sheer rock face and the wooden planks, though forming a nice ladder to climb, proved too old and brittle to trust. One misstep, one unexpected lunge downward would be all it took for her lose her grip. She fought the urge to scramble haphazardly to safety.

Her arms protested, the muscles shaking. More threads disintegrated the higher she climbed. Only seconds remained before it gave way completely. Sweat ran into her eyes and she crushed her lids closed to protect them.

Trembling, she grasped the top ledge with the numb fingers of one hand. The rope gave out, broke, fell like an albino snake into the river. With a startled cry, she slapped her other hand onto the ledge. Her cheek pressed against the cool stone, she yearned for Drake, for his touch, for his comfort, and to get her the hell out of there.

Drake stabbed the keyboard in mounting alarm. A timer in the corner of the screen spiraled down at an alarming rate. The incessant whine of the EMP generator ransacked his nerves. The abort code was almost uncovered, but there wasn't enough time.

He'd run a log scan covering the last twenty-four hours. If a mistake was made, every entry could be checked for the error and when it occurred. Their test earlier, the one he and Sara had experienced on the surface, was in the log.

At the end of the log, he found the series he needed; the key to stopping the charge from reaching the satellite and being pulsed across the entire world.

But, the damned computer kept rejecting the numbers and symbols he frantically typed in. He didn't understand why it wouldn't accept them and with mere seconds left, he had no time to figure it out.

His heart raced, his throat closed as his mouth went dry. Eyes burning in his skull, he concentrated on the monitor. He scrolled back through the code, searching for where he'd gone wrong.

He found it. Hope rippled through him as he opened the correct path to the abort procedure. He'd been one extension away.

Let it work, let it work, let it work...

His fingers fumbled on the keyboard and he cursed as he backspaced to reenter the right keys. The command corrected, he slammed the enter button hard enough to turn his fingertip white.

5.2 sec...

He gripped the edge of the table.

4.3 sec...

A glance to the screen mounted on the wall showed the satellite continuing on its slow spin north.

3.1 sec...

God! Would it stop? He checked the code. It was the right one. He rose, frantic, and rushed for the Sauer's on the floor. One gripped in each hand, he stopped at the entrance to the cavern and braced himself. He fired indiscriminately at the silver generator and the computer panels. The guns jumped in his hands, the reports an echo of his pounding pulse. Bullets zinged, sparks flew. He glanced to the computer monitor.

0.2 sec...

Abruptly, the swarming hum of the generator cycled down

and the words "Sequence Aborted" flashed across the screen.

Drake exhaled hugely and rested his forehead against the Sauer's in his fists, eyes closed. His stomach trembled, the fast fluttering of a frightened bird. He couldn't pause to recover and shook himself.

At his father's side, he said, "Dad."

Drake pressed a hand to the cold flesh of his father's face and his panic subsided. Bruce breathed, but barely. Drake checked the thready pulse. "I'm going to get you help. I'll be right back."

Drake paused, hoping his father would open his eyes, tell him to go, that he'd be fine and wait for him to get back. But Bruce didn't twitch, didn't move at all and dread filled Drake as he got to his feet

The EMP generator hissed. A great gasp of white steam ballooned from behind it. The steady electronic warble took on a menacing throb. An alarm rang and red lights pulsed.

Oh-oh.

He couldn't leave his father here. Drake flexed his injured arm, the elbow emitted it's own siren of pain. He searched for something, anything, to help get his father out. His elbow burned, large and fat on the back of his arm. No way could he carry him out.

The table, Drake thought, and flipped it over. The items on its top skittered across the floor–the sound lost in the blare of the alarms.

"C'mon, Dad." Drake dragged him onto the flat underside, resting the center of his back within the rectangular brace for the legs. Grasping the front table legs behind him, one in each hand, he pulled his father through the door, queasy from the ripping agony in his injured arm. Thankfully, the rock floor allowed the makeshift stretcher to glide swiftly behind him.

Fingers numb, he ran toward the arsenal room, swerving around felled guards. It felt as if a year had passed since they'd wound through this corridor, but in reality it couldn't have been more than thirty minutes.

Where was Sara? He glanced into chambers, searching–all the while dreading he'd run into a conscious guard. The corridors were eerily quiet.

Between the foghorn blasts, a shout echoed to his right and he stopped. The catacombs acted as a fun house hall of mirrors, reflecting sound in every direction and leaving the source a mystery. Drake held his breath, standing completely still in order to hear better.

Again, the shout came, definitely a woman, and he centered on the sound. He checked to make sure Bruce still breathed, and took off at a dead run.

He prayed it was Sara, that she had defeated Acosta and was safe. If not, if Acosta still lived, he wouldn't be breathing for very long. He wouldn't waste his father's precious time with Acosta, he'd simply eliminate the threat to his family for good.

CHAPTER SEVENTEEN

"Great," Sara whispered, the siren drowning her words, "back to hanging over a really big hole."

She resisted the urge to holler for help again. Who might hear her? Acosta's guards? For a dreadful moment she pictured Professor Salinger, her reanimated corpse slithering toward the gorge and grasping for her with bony fingers. She shoved the idea away before she could shudder herself off the edge.

She was slipping, and there wasn't anything she could do about it. Her heart pounded in unison to the wail of the pulsing alarm. She scrambled for a foothold. The wooden slats broke apart every time she placed weight on them.

The alarm finally ended. The earth vibrated beneath her hands. Not a good sign. She prayed it didn't mean Drake had failed. Exhausted beyond measure, she contemplated the best way to die if it came to that. The river might break her fall, but it was so far down below, she'd likely plummet straight to the bottom and break apart on the stones beneath the surface. If she didn't aim for the river, she'd bounce off the stone ledges below, a more painful way to go. Not much of a choice.

Curled in claws by the weight of her body, her fingers slipped. She renewed her determination to live. It couldn't end this way. Not this soon, not this way, not when a lifetime of Drake's love stretched before her.

With the last of her strength, she surged up, gaining palms

full of the ledge, but she was weak, and her thigh would not cooperate. She bit her lip to counteract the throb and slid backward again. Her throat closed on an unexpected sob.

"Damn it!" She closed her eyes and breathed harshly, her exhaled air bouncing off stone.

A hand curled around her wrist and she shrieked. She opened her eyes, half expecting to find a zombie Salinger grinning down at her. Instead, she saw her knight in shining...bruises.

"Drake!"

He hauled her up with grimace. On solid ground, she threw herself into his arms.

"Sara." Drake kissed her and pulled back. "You okay? Where's Acosta?"

"He fell." She swallowed, shocked and overwhelmed by love for her rescuer. "How's your father?"

"He lives, but we need to get out of here."

Her hand in his, she limped after him. Had he succeeded in shutting down the EMP generator? Could they even call for help? "Drake, the uplink? Can we get him help?"

"I stopped it. But the generator's unstable. Dad made the call, though, before...before he passed out."

Back in the corridor she got a good look at Bruce and made an urgent, aching prayer for him to live. He was ashen, barely breathing, the compress on his chest soaked red.

Drake grasped the legs of the table and started pulling. She nudged him out of the way and shared his burden. Together, each with a leg fisted in their hands, they continued at a breakneck pace through the mine.

Sara corrected him once when he went to the left instead of straight ahead, but otherwise he unerringly directed them out. As they neared the exit, the vibration beneath their feet grew to earthquake proportions and the leg slid from her hands. She stumbled sideways, her injured thigh refusing to support her.

Drake turned, concerned. She shook her head and grasped the leg once more, nodding him on toward sunlight filtering down the shaft. She didn't want to die here, not in this hole and not from any device made by Acosta.

The exit turned from a pinpoint of light to a large glowing signpost of freedom. She was about to smile in triumph when a mass of men filled the exit and darkened their ray of hope. Sara stumbled, certain they'd escaped the underbelly of the beast with their lives, only to be gobbled up at the maw.

"United States Marines!" A man shouted, the silhouette of his weapon clear as he swiveled the muzzle toward them. "Where is Colonel Knight?"

Relief swept through her at the Texas twang. American soldiers, men sent by Kray, and able to give Bruce medical help. She heard the distant rumble of a helicopter and tinny chatter, proof positive of the world's electrical well-being.

"He's here." Drake gestured frantically, releasing his grip on the table. Soldiers swarmed around the Colonel, shouting commands to get him to the waiting choppers.

She meant to step aside, but her ankle twisted beneath her as her thigh refused to move. Drake spun back in time to grab her elbow and keep her on her feet. "I'll be fine–stay with your father."

He paused, his eyes growing wide as he glanced at her leg. "You've been shot?"

She nodded. "But it's not bad. Go, now. I'll have a medic look at it."

Drake bent, kissed her hard. "I'll find you soon."

She nodded. Total fear for Bruce's safety filled Drake's face and broke her heart. She knew how it felt to lose a father, and to live twice through the grief of losing a parent was not something she would wish on anyone. Her love went with him even if she couldn't.

He explained to the Marines about the generator, the vibrations, and the threat of an explosion. She didn't question him, there wasn't time, but the idea of that massive machine blowing up was enough to keep her on her feet.

"Ma'am, can I help you out of here?" A young soldier asked. His American good looks swam in her vision. No longer fueled by adrenalin, she barely found the strength to nod.

Drake caught her gaze once, conveying a window to the emotional battle he waged inside himself. She wanted to go with him, to never leave his side, but he passed at a run, the soldiers carrying his father on a snap-together stretcher ahead of him.

The earth jumped, the ground swelled and a strange growl rushed from the depths behind her. Two soldiers grasped her under the arms and together, hustled her into the blinding brightness outside. The growing thunder followed.

A bang, like a gun fired inside a steel room, echoed upward. Dirt sifted into her hair and hot air slammed into her back. All three of them blew forward in a shower of dirt and stones.

Sara landed, huffing clouds of dirt as she panted. The blast itself continued to throb through the basin floor, and from her ground-level view, she saw small creatures zig and zag through tufts of foliage, startled into a mindless race for safety. Then she closed her eyes as sand sifted over her. The mine entrance collapsed, leaving only the thump of rotary blades to break the stillness.

The soldiers recovered first, helping her to sit.

"Ma'am?" the southerner asked, "Are you all right?"

She nodded, the motion sending a wave of seasickness through her. For the first time in her life, a black cloud of oblivion encased her and she fainted.

On board, Drake saw the explosion and glimpsed the swarm of Marines corralling Acosta's guards into covered trucks. He turned from the window and watched the medics work frantically to save his father's life. He squeezed his father's hand and waited for the squeeze to be returned. It wasn't. If his father survived, Drake would make sure he retired fully and immediately.

"It looks like he's hanging in there," one of the medics shouted over the drone of the chopper. His smile faded to a frown as he glanced at Drake's wounds. "Let's look at those abrasions."

"I'll be fine, just take care of my dad," Drake shouted back. He didn't like the gray patches around his father's eyes.

"We've done all we can for him here–they'll fix him up at the hospital. Besides, Jarvis has him covered."

Without waiting for the go ahead, the medic poured antiseptic over the wounds on Drake's arm and he hissed air between clenched teeth.

"How's this elbow?" the medic asked, holding the back of Drake's upper arm and rotating the forearm by the wrist.

Drake yanked away, the pain molten as nerve endings and muscles reacted sharply. "Don't do that."

"That might be fractured. Let me get you a sling." The medic rummaged through his kit and returned with an Ace bandage and a sling. "You'll need stitches on this cut," he prodded a scrape high on Drake's shoulder, "but the rest look like they'll heal fine on their own."

Drake stared blindly at the wall as the soldier worked on his arm. He thought of Sara and wondered if she were all right, if the wound on her thigh looked worse than it actually was. When this was all over, they'd both take a long vacation.

"It's lucky we were on standby." The medic said. "You have General Kray to thank for that."

Drake snarled. He had a lot of things say to Kray, and none of them were 'thank you'. "If he'd have sent you sooner, my father wouldn't have been shot to begin with."

The medic looked reproachful as he finished securing the bandage with the metal fastener. "I just follow orders, buddy. But if you want to blame the guy who saved your ass, go ahead."

The fuse in him reached its store of explosives and Drake blew his top. "Blame? You want to talk about blame? My father put his life, and my life, and Sara's life on the line to take down that son-of-a-bitch, all at the request of your General Kray. That bastard had the gall to send us in there alone while you and your men sat on your hands? Who do *you* think I should blame?"

The medic turned icy and began cleaning up the refuse littering the floor of the helicopter. "I follow orders. I don't know your situation."

"Just follow orders, huh?" Drake spat the words out and leaned his back against the cold metal shell of the helicopter's interior.

That's the problem with this country. Too many followed the orders of people who had no business being in charge, or who were motivated by greed and power. It made him think that perhaps Kray wasn't as noble as he'd thought.

Kray's influence, though diminished by his desk assignment, might have given Acosta the access and ability to allow his scheme to get as far as it had. Was that how Acosta had gotten the Iroquois helicopter? Was Sara right? There was little else he could conclude.

"We're about to land," Lieutenant Jarvis said. "The Colonel's doing well."

He leaned over his father. Bruce opened his eyes, though still glazed, they focused on his son. Drake was choked by his relief. "Dad, I'm here."

"Son..." Bruce exhaled the word.

"It's going to be all right. We're getting you to the hospital now." Drake squeezed his hand, and to his utter relief, his father squeezed back.

CHAPTER EIGHTEEN

Sara stretched, the bed beneath her an undeniable temptation for laziness. Truly awake for the first time in three days, she still wanted to sleep, to spend the rest of her life nestled into the pillows and blankets around her. She yawned as a fuzzy halo of pain medication softened the worst of her injuries and completely obliterated the rest.

She opened her eyes. The hospital room faced west and the sun turned the sky brilliant, casting an orange light over the white in the room. The last few times she recalled looking out the window, starlight had glimmered in a night sky.

Drake lay slumped in a chair, his darkened chin resting on one hand, eyes closed. One arm hung in a blue sling, the rigid outline of a cast visible beneath. She knew they'd spoken, but couldn't recall what was said, or for how long, just that he'd been there every time she awoke.

She hesitated, not wishing to disturb him for he seemed to need the sleep–if the darkened circles beneath his eyes were any indication. At the same time, she wanted to hear him, be near him, now that she was truly alert.

A nurse walked pass the open doorway and Sara flinched, as if Acosta's guards were waiting to attack while she remained bound by IV lines to the bags hanging beside the bed. She calmed herself with a breath and ran a hand over her face. Acosta had fallen to his death, his guards were disbanded, or in custody, depending on what the Marines had decided to do with them. The threat was over.

But what of Bruce? She chastised herself for the late thought. Drake couldn't catch up on his beauty rest when she so desperately needed to know if Bruce lived or not. She shook one of his arms urgently. "Drake?"

He spasmed, jerking upright in the chair. "Sara?"

She smiled. "Yes, it's me. How's your father?"

Drake sat forward, clasped her hand in both of his. "He's fine. They think he'll be ready to go home at the end of the week. The bullet missed his heart."

"That's wonderful." Relief dampened her eyes. "God, I was worried. It's great to know he's okay."

Drake rose and perched on the side of the bed, pressing her back into the pillows with a gentle hand on her shoulder. "How are you? Can I get you anything?"

She shook her head. Right now, with Drake there, and the Colonel on his way to a full recovery, she had everything she wanted. Well, except for a kiss. That would be nice.

As if he'd read her mind, Drake leaned closer and brushed her lips. He cupped her cheek and kissed her more fully, working his mouth gently over hers. She wound her hands around his neck, ignoring the IV and anything other than his wonderful heat.

A woman cleared her throat in the doorway. "Excuse me."

Drake pulled back reluctantly, his eyes twinkling with mischief. "Busted."

She chuckled and looked past him.

"Miss Stark." The young, brunette doctor came forward. "I'm Dr. Prieto, do you remember me?"

Sara frowned and a glimmer of the woman bending over her shimmered in her head. "Sort of."

"Sort of's better than nothing." She nodded and cast a grin in Drake's direction. "I can see you're feeling better."

"Much better," Drake said as Sara clasped his hand to keep him from moving completely off the bed. He settled on the very edge of the mattress and to her disbelief, looked slightly embarrassed.

Sara smiled at the doctor. "When can I leave?"

"You've been out mostly from exhaustion and the pain killers we had you on. But now that you're awake, I don't see any reason to keep you here. I'll have a nurse come in to take out your IV and get started on the discharge papers right away." Dr. Prieto scribbled notes on a clipboard. "You'll have to stay off that leg for a good week–we can't have you tearing those stitches. Don't submerge it in water–sponge bath's only."

Sara waggled her eyebrows at Drake. "No problem."

Drake chuckled. "I'm yours to command."

Dr. Prieto flipped the pages on the clipboard closed and shoved her pen into a pocket. "All right, you two. I don't want Sara here to overdo it. If you're going to do anything...physical, make sure she's careful about that leg."

"Will do, boss." Drake saluted the doc.

The doctor smiled and patted Sara's foot through the blanket. "You take it easy. I'm glad to see you've recovered so fast. Mr. Knight, you take care of her. I don't want her back in my ER with anymore bullet wounds, you hear?"

He nodded, but the smile had disappeared from his eyes. "Thanks, doc."

"Yes, thank you." Sara raised herself higher on the bed.

"My pleasure." She turned away, but paused at the door. "I mean it, Mr. Knight, she needs her rest."

"Gotcha," Drake said, and this time, he sounded less amused, and more determined.

A dismal sensation knotted in her belly. A concerned

Drake was one thing, a determined nursemaid with his ego was another. "You're not gonna fret over me every second of the day, are you?"

Drake shook his head. "Not if you don't make me. Follow her orders and we'll be good. If you want, we'll move you to a room in the house and Fritz and I can take turns taking care of you."

"No, that's all right." Sara thought of her cottage, of the gym and all her belongings. If she were to fully recover, and quickly, then she'd need the chance to build her muscles up, along with her strength. "I'll be fine in my cottage. Besides, you'll have your hands full with Bruce. He's not going to take lying down very well."

Drake gave her a suspicious stare that made her want to avert her gaze. "I wasn't going to bring this up until much later, not until after I'd had a chance to discuss it with my father, but I think it's important to discuss it now."

"What?" On alert, nerves boosted her energy until she was ready to take out the damned IV lines and get dressed on her own.

"With Dad recuperating, and since we've discussed me taking over Knight, Inc., I've decided there's no need to wait any longer. I want to step up and take over now."

"And this means what?" Sara clenched the sheet with both hands.

Drake went to the window, hands clasped behind his back. He didn't turn as he delivered the news. "I've decided that I don't want my future wife working in the field. I can't have her risking her life every time she leaves on a job. So, I'm going to ask you to retire."

Sara gawked at his back. She snapped her jaw shut as soon as the reality of his declaration set in. Retire? Because he feared for her safety? His wife?

"What?" She swung her legs over the bed, cursed the IV line, and muttered another expletive as the stitches in her thigh burned. "What? Wait. One thing at a time."

Sara stood, grasping the IV pole and rolling it with her as she came to a stop at the end of the bed. She closed her eyes to think, one hand holding onto the rolling tray table, the other on the rolling IV pole–she grimaced at the irony–everything she clung to had a way of spinning out of control.

"Let me get this straight." She opened her eyes and heaved a breath. He faced her, his stare more stubborn than noble. "Are you proposing marriage?"

As soon as the words left her mouth, her heart began to flutter. A dream she'd not dared to visualize, had not really understood she even wanted, hung on his answer.

He nodded.

She wanted to be elated, but instead, found herself caught between a rock and the hard-ass in front of her. "And if I agree to marry you, I have to forfeit everything I've worked my entire life to achieve?"

"No," Drake said, much to quickly. "You'll continue to work for Knight, Inc., just not in the field."

"In other words, I have to forfeit everything I've worked for." Sara straightened her shoulders. Who did he think he was? "Well, then, I refuse your offer of marriage. If you won't let me work at Knight, Inc., there's this very nice gentleman in Barbados with a similar operation..."

Drake grabbed her shoulders, the sling sliding from his cast as a stunned paleness dropped over his features. "No."

"No?" She wanted to laugh, perhaps would have if he didn't look so serious. "What, no?"

"No, you can't go to Barbados," Drake said firmly. She felt his need to shake her in the way he grasped her arms–though not painful, his grip was strong.

"Why can't I?" she asked again. Maybe, by questioning him, he would see how illogical his thinking truly was.

"Because I said so. Because I need you here." His grip loosened, though he didn't remove his hands, as if afraid at any moment she would rush out the doors and board the nearest plane headed south.

She quirked an eyebrow. "Are you asking me to stay on as a field agent then?"

"No." Drake shook his head. "That's impossible."

"Why?"

"Because you might be injured, or...killed."

"I've survived the worst assignment you or I have ever seen. Do you really think I'll ever be in this much danger chasing down statues and lost coins?" She wanted him to see the folly in his own thinking, wanted him to come to the right conclusions on his own. She didn't want to fight with him.

The thought surprised her. A week ago, she'd have been ready to flip him over her shoulder until he agreed with her. *Chalk it up to a bum leg and a black and blue body.*

"That's not the point, Sara. I can't marry a woman who might not live through the next week." Drake released her and stepped back.

"You know how much this job means to me. It's my whole life. It's all I've ever known. If you feel this way, why would you consider marrying me at all?" Sara held her breath.

He stared at the bed, at the IV pole, glanced to the door, and finally whispered his answer, "Because I love you."

She went to him then, turning him to face her with a gentle caress. "I love you too, but not as something you're not, for just who you are. I wouldn't ever demand you change anything, because I fell in love with the man before me, not something else you might become, or someone else I might try to change you into. I love you as you are."

He touched her hair, her cheek. "But I can't, Sara. I can't live through the fear of never knowing if you'll come home or not. If you love me, you'll do this. You'll be my wife and give up field assignments."

She stepped back, the force of his words fracturing her heart until it felt as bruised and beaten as the rest of her.

"Sorry to interrupt." A nurse walked briskly into the room and went straight to Sara without pausing for permission to enter. "You should still be in bed, Miss Stark. At least until I get that IV out." She patted the bed.

Sara waited a moment, eyes locked on Drake's and hoped he would take back his ultimatum.

"I'll check on Dad," he said, moving toward the door. "I'll be back soon."

She nodded, struggling against the burn of tears. This was her own doing. She knew the outcome wasn't certain when she'd allowed herself to make love to Drake. But against her better judgement, she had hoped.

"Okay," the nurse said briskly. "If you'll just sit down, I'll get started."

Sara blindly found the edge of the bed and sat. The tape came off with a far away sensation, she dimly felt the pinch of the IV leaving the back of her hand, but her heart continued to bleed. The nurse left and although finally free of the IV, Drake's ultimatum made her feel more constricted than ever.

"Oh, Drake," she murmured to the empty room and closed her eyes.

Drake sat mutely with his father. The old man looked good, color had finally found his face. He toyed with the evening meal. They'd already discussed the contents of the letter Carlos had given them and the terms of Bruce's retirement. With nothing much more to say, they simply enjoyed the quiet. At least, Bruce did. The mounted television was turned to CNN. The sound off, the scrolling text in the closed caption box riveted Bruce's attention.

Drake cursed Sara for her stubbornness. Most women would jump at the chance to quit working and be free to shop, dine out, and travel as they wished. He hadn't forced her out of the business either. If she wanted, she could be his executive secretary.

He snorted at the image of Sara sitting at a desk all day. The folly of his own wishful thinking wasn't lost on him. He didn't think she could type, let alone field calls. She'd likely run off half their clientele with her impatient nature.

"What's got you looking like the goose just cooked your gander?" Bruce pushed the food away and lay against the pillows, clearly exhausted by the effort.

"Sara," Drake muttered without thought.

Bruce raised his eyebrows. "What's *Stark* done now?"

Drake turned from the television, suddenly realizing his father did not know about their new...relationship, though he wasn't certain he could call it that. "She refused to become my wife."

Bruce coughed and sat straighter. "She refused?"

"Yes, Dad." Drake sighed heavily.

"You asked her to marry you?" Bruce's voice squeaked.

Drake frowned. "Yes. I asked her."

"And she refused?"

Did he have to rub it in? "Yes. I asked her to marry me and she refused."

"When did you...I mean...how did you and she...come to this?" A nervous tremor ran through his words. His father seemed almost beside himself with agitation.

Drake didn't know what to make of his odd reaction. "Is

there a problem?"

Bruce controlled himself and waved a hand. "No, no problem. You say she refused?"

Drake sighed and stood, running his hand through his hair. His father sounded almost pleased she wouldn't marry him. "For the last time, yes. She refused me. What's going on?"

"Nothing," Bruce said quickly–a little too quickly in Drake's opinion. "Maybe she's got the right idea, son. I didn't even know you two were a couple–it's probably better to wait."

"I didn't plan on getting married tomorrow," Drake mumbled. He'd hoped his father would help him talk some sense into her. "I only wanted her to retire from the field, stay in the office."

Bruce chuckled. "Can you see her sitting behind a desk?"

Drake smiled and shook his head.

"You're young yet, Drake. Give it some time. Your mother...well, we dated for quite a while before we tied the knot." Bruce stared at his tray.

Drake understood. His father never spoke about his mother, the subject always devastated him, even after all these years. He worried for his son, that Drake might love Sara like that and know the pain of his loss.

They both turned as the door opened.

A nurse pushed Sara in a wheelchair. Dressed in unfamiliar clothes, likely from the hospital wardrobe, the confidence in her posture and the glitter in her eyes showed she was ready to finish the argument.

"Sara." Bruce smiled as the nurse retreated. "We were just discussing you. Come in."

"Discussing me?" She raised her eyebrows at Drake and shoved on the wheels of the chair, coasting to Bruce's bed.

Drake shrugged. "Don't worry, he's on your side."

She smiled at Bruce and Drake growled, looking away and catching sight of the television. General Kray stood behind a cluster of microphones. Drake nodded to the television. "Turn it up, it's Kray."

Sound immediately filled the room and a rush of electric tension gathered like a cloud over them. From the screen, an excited, yet tired looking Kray spoke.

"...audit committee is already being gathered to investigate Senator Halley's activities over the last year. If it's determined there has been a significant breach of confidentiality concerning highly classified information, Halley will be prosecuted to the fullest extent of the law." Kray paused, his eyes staring into the news camera as questions bombarded him. He shook his head and held up a hand. "We cannot divulge the exact nature of the information he's alleged to have shared with unauthorized persons."

Bruce sucked in a breath of air. The live feed switched to an efficient looking newscaster with a digital world globe swirling behind her. "Senator Halley's electronic security bill, scheduled for vote later this month, has been postponed pending the outcome of the investigation. The Senate Select committee will hear testimony after the first of the year. In other news, Miss America has been banned from–"

The sound clicked off and silence fell between them as Drake waited for his father to speak.

"That son-of-a-bitch," Bruce whispered as the bed whirred to a sitting position.

"What's happening?" Sara asked Bruce and cast a quick, searching look at Drake.

Bruce slapped the arm of the bed. "That bastard is behind all this. It makes sense now. When they first brought me to that damned mine, there was a lot of talk about Acosta making a fortune with his plan, they specifically said he would have enough money backing him *to take over America*. I never put two and two together until now."

Drake groaned. It wasn't Kray after all.

Sara looked at him. "It was Halley?"

"Yes," Bruce answered. "He's been trying to install his own version of TEMPEST in all civilian infrastructures–which would protect them from an EMP attack. If Acosta had been successful–the entire world would be clamoring to get their electronics protected–those companies could raise the cost to whatever they wished. He and Acosta would have indeed ruled the world. Halley's background, his connections, would make him a shoo-in for the presidency. Acosta would have ridden his coattails."

The full impact hit Drake with a sense of forehead-slapping stupidity. "If Acosta had succeeded, all the electronic evidence concerning Halley's affair would have been lost too. Plus, if further electronic evidence existed between Halley and Acosta, that would have been wiped out as well. The senator had nothing to lose, and everything to gain."

Sara nodded at the television again. The image of Senator Halley being led away, his coat draped over handcuffed hands, filled the screen. "Looks like they got him."

Drake turned away from the set. "I'm glad it's over."

"Finally." Bruce let out a deep breath.

All except for one thing, Drake thought. He glanced at Sara. "Have you thought any more about what we discussed?"

She smiled, cocked her head to the side so the glorious drape of her unbound hair fell forward. Pushing it behind her ear, she replied, "Yes, I have. I also have a proposal of my own."

Drake raised a brow.

"I want to be your partner, running Knight, Inc., I mean." Sara glanced at Bruce who gave a nod of approval.

"No." Drake spoke harshly. It wasn't a bad idea that they

become partners, but he didn't want her on a mission again, and if she had equal power, he couldn't keep her home.

"I think it's a great idea, son, you should listen to her. She's got a good head on her shoulders." Bruce gave him a secretive kind of smile, more strange than pleasant. "As I said before, there's time. You don't have to be married right away."

Sara nodded. "Of course there'll never be another mission like this last one, so there's nothing to fear. We can carry on like we did before, except I'll be able to run things with just as much authority while *you're* in the field."

Drake latched onto a possible solution. If he could get her home, lavish her with affection, work some of his charm on her, he could manage to keep her in the offices far more frequently than if he fought her. He heaved a great, acquiescent breath. "All right. Partners it is."

The wattage of her smile drew him to her side. She tilted her face up for a kiss and he obliged. Bruce cleared his throat and broke the moment. When he looked at his father questioningly, he caught a fleeting look of deep concern before the Colonel masked the expression.

"I'd say that it's resolved now." Bruce smiled.

Drake nodded as Sara shook her head. "One last thing."

"What's that?" Drake asked, feeling the sudden need to get her home, get her alone and show her just how tenderly he could nurse her back to health.

"I was thinking." She paused, her hand grasping his. "We could make a little wager."

Drake rolled his eyes, but grinned despite himself. "What's the wager?"

"If, under our partnership, Knight, Inc. continues to grow, say over the next year. We get married *and* I continue to work."

"If something happens? If you're nearly killed again?"

Drake stiffened at the mere thought of her in danger.

"Then I'll retire with Bruce once we're married."

Drake studied her, saw the sincerity, and nodded. "It's a deal." He sealed it with a kiss that deepened and continued longer than he intended, but once he'd begun, he couldn't make himself stop. He cupped her face, loving the feel of her heat, her hand on his arm, at the back of his neck...

Bruce groaned. "Can't you two just shake hands?"

MEET THE AUTHOR:

Born blonde and Polish, J.R. Turner writes action adventure thrillers and romances. She resides in Wisconsin with her husband Eddie, a red-headed Texan, and her three children, Dustin, Molly and Matthew. Raised by an eclectic assortment of artists and musicians, her upbringing helped shape and hone her imagination and dedication to the romantic arts. Between her commitments to family and writing, she actively pursues three things–white chocolate, dark chocolate, and more chocolate.

Also available from Echelon Press Publishing

Three Strikes You're Dead (Golden Age Mystery)
Robert Goldsborough

In the mob-ridden Chicago of 1938, a reform candidate for mayor is gunned down, and Steve Malek, a police reporter for *The Tribune*, senses the story of a lifetime. Incurring his editors' anger, he ranges far beyond his beat, plunging headlong into a maverick investigation of the murder.

$12.99 ISBN 1-59080-420-0

Fear of the Unknown (Horror Anthology)
Poppy Z. Brite, Jack Ketchum, Owl Goingback, *et al*

A chill wind blows through the thirteen stories in this new collection. It rustles dead cornfields and diseased grapevines, travels through dark train tunnels and small railside towns, brushes across the killing floor of an abandoned LA shop and tugs at the garments of the bouncer at Death's own nightclub. Proceeds benefit Bone Cancer International, Inc.

$12.99 ISBN 1-59080-386-8

Pedestals (Suspense)
Jane Shoup

The last year has been a nightmare for Jack Wilmont. So when a serial killer–after a year of nothing–strikes on the first day of Jack's personal leave, he knows the nightmare is only beginning. Jack agrees to look at the evidence, but his one good deed leads him into the case of a missing nine-year-old girl abducted from her home.

$14.99 ISBN 1-59080-426-0

Redemption (Western)
Morgan J. Blake

Kinson women aren't known for sitting idly by while others decide their fates. This keeps Wylie Kinson going when his mother and sister are kidnapped in an Apache raid. But Wylie's hopes are dashed when he stands over his mother's mutilated body. Worse, he suspects the Apaches aren't responsible. If not Apaches, who would do such unspeakable acts? Vowing revenge, Wylie unravels the treacherous trail.

$15.49 ISBN 1-59080-380-9